camera phone

by the same author

Swallowing Film: Short Film Fiction

Black Cat, Green Field

Teaching Creative Writing

Signs of Life: Cinema and Medicine (with A. Moor)

Small Maps of the World

Moon Dance

camera phone

brooke biaz

Parlor Press
West Lafayette, Indiana
www.parlorpress.com

Parlor Press LLC, West Lafayette, Indiana 47906

Characters, Names, Places, Recipes and Cocktails contained in this book are not meant to be actual Persons or Things and should not be considered, approached, or treated, as such.

Printed in the United States of America
S A N: 2 5 4 - 8 8 7 9

Library of Congress Cataloging-in-Publication Data

Biaz, Brooke.
  Camera phone / Brooke Biaz.
    p. cm.
  ISBN 978-1-60235-162-2 (pbk. : acid-free paper) -- ISBN 978-1-60235-163-9 (adobe ebook)
  I. Title.
  PR9619.3.H324C36 2010
  823'.914--dc22

                                    2009049118

Printed on acid-free paper.
Cover image:
Cover design by David Blakesley

Parlor Press, LLC is an independent publisher of scholarly and trade titles in print and multimedia formats. This book is available in paperback and eBook formats from Parlor Press at www.parlorpress.com or at brick-and-mortar and online bookstores everywhere. For submission information or to find out about Parlor Press publications, write to Parlor Press, 816 Robinson St., West Lafayette, Indiana, 47906, or e-mail editor@parlorpress.com.

contents

camera phone

part I

There were years when I went to the cinema almost every day and maybe even twice a day . . . It was a time when cinema became the world to me. A different world from the one around me, but my feeling was that only what I saw on the screen possessed the properties required of a world, the fullness, the necessity, the coherence, while away from the screen were only heterogeneous elements lumped together at random, the materials of life, mine, which seemed to me utterly formless.

Italo Calvino, The Road to San Giovanni

Capture the action. . . . Video clips are ideal for those unexpected great moments that happen when you're out there, enjoying life.

Sony Ericsson, The K770i Cyber-shot™ phone

3

one

Being There
1979, 130m
Comedy, PG-13
Lorimar (U.S.)

I

Man, there is Karen. Close-up. Tight as you like. Humping her
fist like a seahorse riding a warm current. Up and down she goes,
her head thrown back in and out of frame. This is high-key, off-
balanced, improv and it's Expressionist, I guess. *Cinema vérité.* My
camera phone loves her. It absolutely does. It's like watching Rog-
ers with Astaire, Kahn with Hank, Lassie with Joey. She sweeps
away a cobweb which has floated down from the basketball hoop
above the doorjamb. To which I say: "Nice. Real nice. Go on."
I bounce over the duvet to catch her eyes which, momentarily
but significantly, pause on me. She is Kim Basinger in *Nadine,*
only smarter, of course. For a moment I have what is certainly
eye-contact, an address to my phone, but in Karen's body not in
any words. Then she's away again, doing her thing. Moonlight
through the window, which is a bay but not a casement, moves
in and out like a tide. Sallow and dusty, it moves softly in. What
a romance! I'm planning all match cuts here. From me at the
window shooting into the dark. To me in the kitchen, using a
low-angle which elevates things considerably. To me, a breathless
Cameron Crowe, Joe Dante, Gus Van Sant, Atom Egyoyan, John
Woo, bounding from bed to bathroom to bay window to bed. I

shoot all night in our flat above the Halfmarket while my camera phone seduces her in ways she has never heard of. She thanks me for coming up with the idea of making a film of her life.

This is not, well, the whole story. But the pleasure, nevertheless, is going to be all mine.

2

Below, the morning beach traffic mewls a steady aching spewm. It's sickening, hard-hearted and as pumpingly urgent as a drum . . . but it does not distract me from Karen who wakes shortly in the bed beside me, rolls over aglow with something that I can only describe as escape and points, with her pale and somewhat anorexic fingers ringed in Balinese silver she bought on vacation in . . . well guess?, Bali; and, here and there with Amerindian turquoise, toward my phone.

From my cane chair, I stand up to pan the room, which is shabby but large and solidly built. Langford Terrace, our building, a good-sized share on the Halfmarket, is Victorian in hardware but built as if it was put together by who? . . . Romans. All bathrooms and hand basins on the landings. Weird arched ceilings and these crazy cornices carved with roses and vines and so forth. Like in *Caligula*. Like in *Spartacus*. Like the great set design in *Spartacus* with these cracked domed roofs and marble doorsteps and the stores down below, right along the front. I love this building.

Karen dresses for work in an A-line skirt with back zip fastening, a short sleeve turtle neck sweater in purple, a pair of ankle boots with inside zip and strap detail, while I shoot her, dreaming of how my life fits me. How firmly and simply it fits. Like a glove, a form-fit platform boot. *Whatever!*

She says to the mirror that I have fixed with double-sided tape to the wall beside the toilet: "I'm in love"—subjective camera: Karen in the mirror watching Karen watching Karen in love, just a hint of me to the right side like a busboy waiting for some crummy tip—"with my life."

Downstairs the mail arrives. I slip down to find it in the stair-well like Kleenex boxes discarded by who? Halfmarket whores possibly (probably), but none of this mail is ours. There is some for Alice who is studying social work, Cole who is in Archae-ology, Piper who skis, Susan who slings sandwiches at El Mon-key on Tuesdays and Thursdays and also is doing some sort of degree in History, for Kevin and Grace (straight above us), So-phie who drives a beach cab part time and doesn't attend South-port, Vern who apparently is a tutor but I don't know what in, Monika from Pencils and Colleen Donnelly who first met Karen when they both took Nightline Counselor training, Helen who's working this week in a stock broking firm on placement from her degree program, Fynella who is a new house officer in general surgery, Tony who is a flight attendant for Midland and can get cheap flights but not overseas actually, Kyle, who just moved in with Fynella, is a minor animation student, and works in the cafe, Candia, across the mall.

Is that groovy or what?

They do not, however, come to collect. Not in my phone film. They stay in their flats, on their own phones, eating Rice Krispies, Corn Pops, Hi-Fiber and watching Anne and John, Penny and Paul, Brian and Denise, Terrytoons, Street Sharks, Bear in the Big Blue House, Kickstart, or sleeping it off. My film shows none of this but that's not the point. It's suggested. It's there like an undercurrent of absolute mediocrity which in my film is what I'm trying to avoid.

I precede Karen downstairs, bracing my right arm with my left like I'm wearing a Steadicam, and film her from the shoulder emerging from the entrance with her head thrown back in the sunlight and her Side-Street tortoise-shell Ray Bans down on the end of her subtly angular nose. I'm actually using a Nokia G567, the 16x zoom GPS model (VMPS120). Hey, but so what, Rodri-gez shot *El Mariachi* on beta tape with a wireless mic and one jib-armed dolly. And look what he got!

Karen lets her cranberry colored backpack slip down on her left arm and thumbs me from the right as she passes, grinning like Elsa Cardenas in *Fun in Acapulco,* though what I'm actually after, as I've explained to her, is kind of a homage (pronounced *hoe-marge,* naturally) to Schlesinger. Essentially *Midnight Cowboy,* with Karen playing Sylvia Miles to my Jon Voigt.

For fun, we call Helena McCabe from a payphone on the corner near Langford. The payphone is rancid and stuck with cab cards. I make a note to call Eve who has (quote) "the body of Uma Thurman." Brilliant. Karen explains the situation. If there's one thing about Karen it's that I can count on her to explain things better than I do. It is, notably I think, something to do with her substantial right brain ascendancy. She's also an Aries.

She says, brightly: "Hey Ms McCabe, it won't take too long."

I jump in with a simple and obvious explanation.

"Tell her," I say, "that we need back story."

Back story has a pretty annoying spiritual air to it actually and I repeat it with a touch of urgency to try and flush the thing right away. "Back story, tell her. . . You do know what I'm talking about?"

I hear down the line Helena jabbering about something to do with her plans, her job, her life, her, her, *her* until then, as I suspected, agreeing to meet us at Candia.

3

Incidentally:

> The telephone is connected with two branches of science—acoustics and electricity. The veriest tyro in the former branch of science knows that sound is caused by the impinging of sound waves upon the ear, and that the kind of sound if dependent upon the velocity and length of the waves. Thus the ear-splitting shriek of the advancing railway whistle is caused by the sound waves being driven one upon the other and so shortened— for the shrill tone is caused by short waves of great velocity, whilst the deep base tones are caused by much longer waves of less velocity.

(Library Shelf: B02318: *The Engineer,* No.1, July 1877)

Go figure!

4

Now here's the back story I was talking about, but I'm not going to waste too much time on it because I, for one, am not convinced by flashbacks. Just a quick cut then, and save the ripple dissolve for Preminger.

For one thing, Helena McCabe (Irish parents, 25), who's on the way now, is cutting through traffic at the corner of Pitt and George in her Morgan (that's a Plus Eight, if anyone's interested. Though—Poke alert!—I'm not), works in an office, the office of Lystead and Wishhart, L&W, and has done since she left Roeford before even starting a degree here at USP, rented a place right out near the marina, overlooking the Aquarium, Aqua Park and Oceanarium, and started her stumble up the corporate ladder. L&W, that's Insurance, Life Policies, Pensions, Death, Destruction, Dental Plans, all the big words. She wears her hair in a short bob, because it's that thin hair that some people have, wispy kind of, and if those who are watching her pass with the top down and those optional dual airbags neat as flowers in the bud of her dash (to quote some modern *looove* poetry) mention that there's no reason to have her hair that way, that in this day and age she could have any damn hair she wants and, likewise, with a little Night Secret lose those frown lines already appearing around her otherwise shining eyes, she'll merely point out that in her profession a retro attitude pays its way. Today she wears a Happy Joe watch, in the rear tray there's two pieces by Maslankowski and one by Pauline Parson (don't know?) that she's picked at a house clearing that she found out about through L&W, but she isn't choosey (she's left at home in the glass mirror display unit a cheesy pewterware dragon on a motorcycle by Myth and Magic), and the one real memory I keep of her is that one of her tripping down the black marble stairs into the dim-lit foyer of Langford Terrace like some kind of baby giraffe while her boyfriend, Calum, who now lives in Lucaya running Guanahani's, or so he says, and claims to have been the inspiration behind their papaya ginger pork, just taps away at his discman and swears he should never have missed *Edge of Darkness* to pay a visit to a place like this.

As to the business with Lystead and Wishhart—let me try and get this straight because, even though it frankly bores me brainless, there's no avoiding it and, by tomorrow every little suburban outcrop from Southport to Roeford will know that the University audit office is finding "inconsistencies" (read: "one of the bank accounts is missing") in one of our quaint College arts festivals' accounts, a subject on which the University of Southport Arts Festival Committee will issue a statement denying there's any problem ("whatsoever." Yeah, right.) followed by several long blasts out its collective artistic poke probably, and two senior charity managers at Arts for College Old Folks or The Arts 'n' Farts Foundation or whatever, who are probably, as far as I know, screwing each other like what?, minks I guess, really old minks, will eventually resign, and disappear in the direction of the Palais Schwarzenegger Hotel, Vienna, probably . . .

"They do a real nice green apple chutney, Harold."

"Oh yes, Maude, so I see."

The trouble with back story is that it is so incredibly trite, so totally stalled, so plain monkey-headed dull, that nobody in their right minds wants to watch. Back story's like some mopey foster kid turning up in a house of real cute brothers and sisters, and if it wasn't for the connection with the Festival of the Waters Film Festival I wouldn't mention it at all. The best thing to do is just to get on with your film—that is, with the forward movement of your film. But the connection's here:

The University of Southport "Festival of the Waters Film Festival" started way back. I guess in, what, 1967, or '69 maybe? Either way, it started when two guys from USP decided to screen at the Roxy, during the Waters Art Festival, some 8mm shorts they'd made on the beach that summer. The screening was a hit, and soon other USPites and film-makers from the beach and the Valley were wanting to screen their own films, both professional, by that stage, and amateur. By the 1970s (bored yet?) the festival had become a noticeable Southport event. They launched a regular awards program, screened *Mondo Trasho* one year and, in the third year ('74, I believe), actually had both George Romero and Karen Black as guest presenters. Later that year the festival was taken over by the Arts Festival Committee as a formal USP annual event. Local council support was "thus forthcoming" (to quote the flyer); followed by such corporate sponsorship from the likes of: KB Beer, Mixx Surfwear, Monstrol Pharmaceuticals, Loon Bach clothing, the Mitsui Motor Company and, recently, One-Tech Supa-Phone Shops. Growth continued through the '80s and 90s to now "combining the best local talent with a varied program of major independent productions, new talent showcases" and the occasional first release studio slot. Everything is screened at The Roxy cinema.

End of History 101.

Down at Lystead and Wishhart, the office is buzzing as they're starting to comb through Christ knows how many University accounts (all very Miss Marple), looking for monies in, monies out, trying to pick up where the cash went so the College doesn't have to lose their government contract for overseeing this kind of big public arts spending, acting like nothing is happening, while the two senior charity managers (unknowing) are going on attending board meetings at Hycraft Concrete, the Montreal View Gallery, Donatii Constructions, the Festival of the Waters Film Festival, and the Board of Governors of the University of Southport. Before they leave, that is, for Greece to view the Mycenaean palace architecture in ancient Pylos.

The way I figure it, it's always possible to reject the performative ineptitude of some crimes and still gaze on their beauty—to quote Truffaut who does it, after all, in *La Mariée était en noir*. And really, having said all that, who gives a shit? He also says: "All you need to make a movie is a girl and a gun." Or was that Godard who said that? Anyway, it's relevant.

"Candia O Candia," Karen sings.

I go in first and phone film her from behind the Kencaf machine, entering through the cafe doors whose glass is partly covered by such things as STUDENT UNION APRIL 3: GOMEZ, TICKETS HERE and THE GAY CHRISTIAN ALLIANCE WANTS YOU and FENDER BASS FOR SALE, CHEAP. She does not know why she sings and is embarrassed to have done it. She laughs and apologizes. Karen's laugh enters my soundtrack like . . . the scent of cinnamon, a pinch of vanilla, some sweet cake shop. She reveals that she may have done it because she is happy at having been accepted to do a master's degree in English Literature, and has taken a job in Supa-Video on the Halfmarket, overlooking the beach.

The mall is already cranking up and glaring and the traffic follows a curve, like some kind of giant knee raised abruptly into downtown, and pedestrians, mostly office bods and shop assistants from places like Linens n Things and Best Buy, Target and Big Shoes, alight from the buses which, at this hour, having access to the entire street, growl and smoke and give off heat which hangs in the air.

As Karen sits down next to me, I say, pulling back to keep her in full frame: "So here-- voice over-- we have Karen Munson who is writing a thesis on Joan of Arc. . . sorry, I mean representations of Jeanne d'Arc."

She takes a lip liner from her pocket and gets ready to do her lips. "Well thank you, Mr. Droste," she says, to my phone, "and I believe your own work is coming along a peach on Love and Death in the films of Roman Polanski? Or is it Dreams and Nightmares in the Hollywood Blockbuster? Better still: What Ever Happened to Farley Granger?"

"The latter," I say, thinking Karen may not know that Farley Granger is still alive and appeared in *The Whoopee Boys* in 1986, and also thinking that Karen is obviously planning to let her hair grow out so that she looks like Ingrid Bergman.

She orders the Viennese coffee, medium ground. I order a brulot of the medium ground Costa Rican, along with some Honey Madeleines.

Candia is quite full for breakfast. I figure it's because this week is Freshmen Week and also because there's that upcoming local event called the USP Arts Festival for which step vans and floats and electricity company trucks are passing in the direction of the beach, and which would be pure poke if not for the Festival of the Waters Film Festival, which is attached to it. I decide also, in the same moment that I decide a medium long shot will give a sense of depth to what is feeling at this moment like a very narrow and hard place to tone, that I might write something on the films of Sam Raimi, being as Wes Craven has been all done to death and nobody really seriously believes he will ever do anything better than *The Hills Have Eyes*. I might also join the Student Film Society, though I hear they're all into Gandhi and what Antonioni likes best and spend most of their time talking about what Harry Dean Stanton did to Nastassja Kinski in *Paris, Texas*. . . . like it's not obvious!

The food arrives. My Madeleines look like something from a tomb, the clear amber they find in Egypt, I mean.

Karen says: "Considerable!"

She points at the wall opposite and says: "That's In the Car by Roy Lichtenstein." But she doesn't stop there, pointing one by one. "Person Throwing a Stone at a Bird by Miro. Something by Hockney. Uh. Uh. That's . . ."

"Sigourney Weaver," I say, "In *Gorillas in the Mist*." admiring the cinematography of John Seale and Alan Root for which neither of them, I might add, was nominated for an Oscar. "You're very arteestic these days, Karen," I say ironically, but she doesn't bite.

We unwrap the cutlery which is wrapped in red paper napkins, though neither of us is planning on using it; but before I've even started my brulot, Helena walks in.

"Film what, did you say?" she asks Karen, kissing her on a cheek in a manner I can't help noticing. Karen is her best friend and once when they were temping (she told me in confidence, but what the Hell) Karen slept with her when they shared a flat on The Corso and Helena was dabbling in film, acting, running and so forth and Karen was a USP freshman . . . though Karen may have been totally lying and just trying to get a reaction from me. Then it didn't happen at all. It's difficult to tell.

Karen looks up in my direction. I phone shoot them both in American shot, shaking their heads and grinning like juveniles, and then I call out from behind the Kencaf: "Hi, Helena."

"What's got into you, Ciaran?"

I don't bite at this and just go on filming until the waitress, who reminds me of Drew Barrymore, comes over to take Helena's order.

"You won't believe this," says Helena, "but what I really want is the moussaka, but I know it's like impossible. So I guess I'll just have the *au lait*—a Kenyan—and, by the way, is it okay to use the . . . ?"

Drew Barrymore points her out through the bead curtain (Candia is, to my mind, a cross between '70s retro and a place done over with nice white enamel touch of Zanussi) and Helena, first lighting an MB Light Tar, then leaving it smoking in foil ashtray on the table, sidles out.

For some reason Karen has her face dipped into her Viennese, which she has half drunk, staring at me, and I think it's just lucky that Candia serves decent sized coffees or she wouldn't be able to do whatever she thinks she's doing. I try to ignore her and, looking out into the mall where maybe a hundred people are now sliding past in the direction of The Eastside and Grantham which have not yet opened but which have turned on their music which sends into the mall Sex and Candy by Marcia Playground and also The Daddy of The All by The Space Monkeys which really surprises me, I describe to her for no good reason the differences between J. Lee Thompson's *Cape Fear* made in 1962 and starring

Robert Mitchum and Mark Scorsese's *Cape Fear*, made in 1991 and starring Robert de Niro. This is basically the difference between Polly Bergen and Jessica Lang and just how good Juliette Lewis really was. Personally, I think Gregory Peck had no range.

"So Ciaran," says Helena, returning, "what's your film going to be about anyway?"

I think that maybe I would like to phone film her in a thunderstorm on the beach with the sea the color of gunmetal like something out of *Apocalypse Now*, but put this aside and answer (lying a little):

"Actually Helena, it's about Karen."

Karen smiles, finishing her coffee, and Helena, who tips two packets of NutraSweet into her *au lait* which has arrived, pulls her white gloss lips into a shape which resembles one moon smothering another:

"Koo-key!" she says, lighting another cigarette, inhaling. "You're one weird guy Ciaran."

5

I think this is totally relevant:

> *Photography implies that we know about the world if we accept it as the camera records it. But this is the opposite of understanding, which starts from not accepting the world as it looks. All possibility of understanding is rooted in the ability to say no.*

Also this, more accurately:

> *Whereas the reading time of a book is up to the reader, the viewing time of a film is set by the filmmaker and the images are perceived as fast or as slowly as editing permits.*

(Library Shelf: T055589, Susan Sontag,
On Photography, Farrar, Straus & Giroux 1977, 23, 81)

So fab!

6

In the video shop where Karen works there are four other assistants. Neve Campbell, Liv Tyler, David (Duchovny, possibly) and Denise Richards. The place is owned by Nic Cage. I mean, seriously.

Now I know this sounds crazy but you can make of it what you will. I figure everyone has a role model and, to be honest, they could do worse. Also, I just want to set the record straight that I don't have a thing about Gwyneth Paltrow. Not even when she was going out with Brad Pitt and starred in *Mrs. Parker and The Vicious Circle,* which was filmed in three weeks using three Bolex's, I'm told, did I have a thing about Gwyneth Paltrow. The fact is, I can take or leave Gwyneth Paltrow and felt exactly that way when she was interviewed by *Film Mania*—or was it *Cine-Ma?*—and said, and I quote, "I need to express every emotion that I have, the second that I'm having it, which is bad." Actually, I think she should have kept her hair long, too. But, of course, they can do something about that with hair extensions and thinking that she had better hair in *Sliding Doors* than any other film is no indication that I have a thing about Gwyneth Paltrow. It's just that very few women look like her. Hell, Karen is trying her best to look like a younger Ingrid Bergman, and she does (enough anyway)!

I crouch in Modern Film Classics while Karen, coming in from the backroom, and from the left, ten minutes after opening, makes some comment about some writer or another looking like Rene Russo. To which I call out: "O, right, who exactly?"

I phone shoot her in medium shot with a wall of films by Scorsese behind her.

I believe the world's most perfect car is a white 1968 Corvette Stingray convertible. That also is a classic. A Scorsese classic is like that. Definable—to the knowledgeable—by its parts. The '68 'vette has a large block V8 developing a maximum power of 339 bhp at 4800 rpm. The nose style is straight, zippered, like an Empire fighter from *Star Wars IV.* The motor is blueprinted and the wheels, naturally, are deep dish alloy. There's a gauge for oil pressure, battery, and a tachometer which redlines at 6000. The instruments are heavily cowled (meaning, they are set back in circular slots). The upholstery is cowhide, in white. I would fit, personally, a twelve disc CD auto-changer or more probably use the MP3 from my phone and plug that into an amp, probably a Class D Monoblock Premium Digital Amplifiers Series Amplifier, though I'm also partial to Kenwood. But that's another story, and as long as it has dynamic base control and a joystick remote changer then that's fine by me.

Things seem to go well this morning. Supa-Video is down below the street and, at first, there's no one much coming in, just a woman of about one hundred and twenty who seems to be looking for a doco on natural dietary fiber and then changes her mind and stands with her wheely bag in front of a dump bin full of 3 for the price of 1's. I try to defocus dissolve her but for a long time no one else enters and the shelves impose too much contrast of a kind I'm not happy with and I decide on editing the sequence so that when three GI Janes walk in down the stairs I'm ready for some light relief and give them considerable gravity as they move between the bright of the street and the dark of the shop.

"Cast your eyes," whispers Karen to David Duchovny, with whom she is now loading shelves from a box marked RETURNS, because she can see that the Janes are not from any known university but from the community college, Machin College (named, apparently, after some local poke who discovered, sometime around the last pass of Haleys, the reason why Saturn has its rings and Mars its Martians). They wear zip pocket skirts, strap vests, black, fetish shop pvc, KA boots.

"What are these three looking for," says Karen to David, "the life and times of the New York Dolls?"

Duchovny, in close-up, begins to sing in a voice which is a mere whisper but certainly masculine and the words that come out are the lyrics to Alison by Elvis Costello. Duchovny was born, as this confirms, in 1960. "This world is killing you. Al-li-son" and all the while he keeps his eyes looking straight at Karen, with a intensity which can't have just come out of nowhere."—your aim is true."

Meaning that Karen must know what's true. Karen kind of chirps, and dives into the box so quickly that she drops two of the DVDs on the carpet and there burst open, then has to spend a minute picking them up (which I film in ECU to capture her eyes which are relentlessly flickering, as if she's lost a diamond earring she's bought but hasn't yet paid for, and I hope the red tinge of the blush that spreads up her neck from that hollow in her breast bone actually comes out). Until, finally, the Janes make their move downstairs where no doubt they locate Soft Core and Indie Classics and spend some time discussing how good Divine was in *Shampoo* (not the Travolta version, right?).

Duchovny says, with his hands in his pockets and his head craned back so he can look out the windows, which shows the lower part of the street: "It's like looking into another world from down here."

Oh, reeally! . . . Dare I say: Poke alert!

"This," I say to myself, "I just got to get." So I come over closer, behind Documentary and Foreign. But Duchovny, who actually knows exactly what I'm looking for here, stares up at me as if I'm trying to assassinate The President.

"Don't get any closer with that thing, it's libel to go off," he says dumbly. I imagine him shot in Panavision with the colors all saturated and the balance wacked. Deep purples. Hard reds. Bug greens. Frozen blues. All primary colors.

"Yep," says Duchovny, staring up into the street again, "it really is like we're integral to the street down here."

Jesus!

"Excuse me," I whisper desperately, "but this is not a genre film."

Holding the box, with which I somehow get stuck, I sit my phone on the top of the display for Polanski's *The Ninth Gate,* but without a clamp (which worries me, but what choice do I have?).

Then I move along next to the two of them while knowing what I'm probably getting, entirely for Karen's benefit, is completely offset framing and no headroom; but I'm thinking of Hitchcock's fixed camera in *Rope*. I'm thinking that Hitchcock did it in Rope, and so maybe something will come of it. Maybe something good will come of it.

Karen is passing along the shelves of Rom-Coms, Thrillers, Sci-Fi, slotting in this DVD and that one, BLU-RAY, old skool, each one, alphabetically!

She says: "I feel like I'm replacing the thoughts of the people in the street."

I refuse outright to react to this.

Slotting into place a copy of Scholondorff's *The Handmaid's Tale,* she says: "When Margaret Atwood did this it was a great piece of feminist literature, but this. . . ."

"This is crazy," I'm telling myself. "My film's going to be a comedy if I'm not careful."

"It's like axing the last fingers off the statue of the Venus de Milo," Karen says, picking up a copy of *The Naked Lunch.*

It's occurring to me—because all of a sudden I realize that my film's being directed by me and I shouldn't be expecting anyone else to know how it should be composed and, certainly, it's up to me because I'm directing it and I'm also technically directing it. I'm set designing it, I'm engineering it, I'm mixing it, I'm propping it, I'm lighting it, I'm booming it, I'm vision controlling it and I'm FX-designing it—it's occurring to me that what I have actually been doing is shooting myself.

"Well. Well. Well," I say, standing there replaying what I've done.

And there I am. A cameo. I'm to the left of frame with the light from the street catching my face equally on the left side. I'm wearing a Futori denim floral shirt, a pair of Evisu jeans and a neck tie from Angels. My hair is cropped now and looks black though really it's dark dark brown like the hair on that pastel-loving guy (Christopher Marciello) in the Explorer Sandal ad. In the center is Karen and she looks, to be honest, absolutely brilliant. She's wearing a pink Etam satin slip dress and a pair of black flat-fronted trousers from The Dispensary. Her hair is pinned in three places so it hangs over her right eye, but is bunched up over her left ear. She has on buff colored lipstick which makes her lips look like pure skin, like her lips just pick up where the rest of her leaves off.

Karen calls: "So, Ciaran, how is it looking?"

"Awful," I lie. "It's looking awful. Too much red."

"Oh, God," I think, "I can't stand this." Every shot visually brilliant. Pans. Zooms. Dollies in and out. Trucks. Arcs. Elevates. All having to be in the right place now. Everything properly paced. Height. Body position. Every frame matching every frame. Seamless continuity. All the possibilities covered. And *verite*. Very very *verite*. Overmodulated sound. Cutting on my movement. Just lingering now and then on one thing or another. The sequence disordered but every message clear. Karen. Duchovny. Campbell. Tyler and Paltrow. And now Nicolas Cage, who is coming into the shop wearing three days of facial growth, a black suit, a bad shirt (bamboo pattern, Fijian), and a look like he's going to eat the gherkin right out of your bun, leading in Holly Hunter, who is not his wife, and followed by, and this I do not believe, Woody Harrelson. I mean, that is Woody Harrelson isn't it? I see Detective Rick Santoro, Jack Singer, H.I.McDonnough, Smokey: the whole Cage oeuvre playing out right in front of me. I could get it wrong any second. And then what? My film will be nothing more than daytime TV. It will be no better than *Quantum Leap*. No better than *The Six Million Dollar Man*. My film will be nothing then.

"When's lunch?" says Karen, abruptly.

Duchovny smoothly checks his Heuger. "Now," he says. "Now . . . if you want."

7

Cooking a meal on a small student budget doesn't have to be a problem. Under any Financial Aid options, it is still entirely possible to construct something interesting, tasty, and also nutritious. Take for example this recipe, among others:

Andean Mountain Bread

(10 Servings) To be served with meals or combined with ale to give that keeping the cold out winter boost. The cardamom seeds are optional but are authentic, and the whole thing should be served on a rough cloth if possible. A sweater can work, if it comes down to it.

400 ounces cornflour, plus extra for dusting
1 tablespoon of salt
2 tablespoons of cardamom seeds
1 tablespoon pumpkin seeds
1 tablespoon caraway seeds

Cooking Time: 25–35 minutes

1. Combine the flour, salt and seeds in a bowl. Add, at steady slow pace, 15 fl oz of tap water, mixing all the while until the texture is soft but firm. Knead for 30 minutes. Form a smooth ball. Put it under cloth for 30 minutes
2. Split dough into 10 equal balls. Smooth and flatten into pancake style. Cover with cloth.
3. Bring griddle pan to warm on a medium heat. Put two breads at a time in a griddle pan. Pat down with palm of hand. Do not allow seeds to burn. Turn each over and over until brown (2 minutes). Remove from the heat and place on woven mat. Keep covered with cloth.
4. When all are cooked serve immediately, while still warm.

(Library Shelf: Z03478: Nitinia Lugushi, *Warm Tastes from Down South*, Condominium Books, 2006)

8

I can't believe they made me cut that right where they did. I can *not* believe I'm not now shooting five guys around a brass coffee table, upstairs, using a cuke, while Bridget Neilson is in the corner dressed in white fox, a shit load of Amatyl caps which have been hidden in dug out copies of Patricia Craig's *International Cookery Bible,* now opened on the table; but instead I'm sitting here in El Monkey, overlooking the beach, ordering the Inam Bayildi, a banana cake and coke while Harrelson and Cage are three tables away with Holly Hunter and someone new, whom I'm positive is Milos Forman, and they're talking about spending a cool $60,000,000 on a new film of *Starsky and Hutch* while I look Colleen Rumsey right in the center of the lens. Colleen who is also doing an MA in English literature, the subject of which escapes or, frankly, doesn't interest me, and who is asking Karen if she can come with us this afternoon when we register with our supervisors. And Karen says, before going over to the counter to get a Lucosade:

"Cool!"

Alone, I try to smile at Colleen who is probably, I decide, dating a McDonalds' trainee manager. Captain Big Mac or someone. She wears Sportif sunglasses but I can see her eyes behind them racing each other from side to side. A McDonalds' trainee manager who also goes fly fishing at weekends, has a father named Errol and drives a silver blue '82 Town Car, a 3.8 V6 auto quite incidentally. I send her in and out of focus and I'm thinking I might use Body Bumpin' Yippie-Y-Yo by Public Announcement as a background here. I'm thinking I might cover whatever it is she is now saying that I am not listening to with a full three minutes of Body Bumpin' Yippie-Y-Yo. She orders the Reuben Sandwich.

"So Ciaran," she says, "you know Christopher Isherwood was an honorary graduate of Southport?"

"And?" I say.

She raises her eyebrows which are not plucked but spring up like moustaches above her thoroughly forgettable glasses. She seems to think I don't understand what she said: "Isherwood. Christopher Isherwood, the writer, is an honorary graduate of this university. Didn't he write the screenplay for *The Loved One?*"

Because I have no intention of answering she goes on: "You know. *The Loved One.* Evelyn Waugh?"

"Yes," I say, defeated. "Yes."

"I suppose you're a member of the USP Film Society?"

I dig my fork into my Inam Bayildi, pull out a small round union and slice its heart open. "Those planks?"

I can see her eyes behind her sunglasses have fixed on me.

"They're into Gandhi," I say, stating the obvious.

"So?"

This, obviously, is pointless.

"So what are you into exactly . . . Freddy Krueger or something?"

For some reason, now taking up my phone, I zoom in on the Mexican Beans with Chorizo and Chilies sitting on the table next door. I'm picking up in tight shot the pinto beans which are oily and black and then the *guajillos* which are red and thin. I'm finding the macro setting is very useful. I'm wondering how low the battery is by now but the warning symbol isn't showing in the window so it's probably fine. I'm picking up the chorizo sausage, thickly sliced, the onions, the garnish of coriander.

"My supervisor's going to be Heather Rebane," says Colleen, like a voice-off. "Rebane."

"Listen . . ." I say, but now I notice Karen is coming back.

Colleen continues, whispering: "How is that Karen ended up with Krotow? I mean, I know he does body theory or . . . medieval bodies. But he is not a woman."

Colleen is our terrace's resident "theorist," our Sigmund Freud, our who? Mary Ann Down, Doon, Doane, our Kris . . . Kristina Kristoffa, our . . . lady of the . . . Oracle.

Only now Karen is stopping because Milos Forman has spotted her and, lifting the index finger on his right hand, which I notice is short and thick, he is actually calling her over to his table.

Colleen continues: "R.E.B.A.N.E. . Rebane, the installationist. The . . . art animator, you know?"

"Listen," I say, composing myself and raising my voice so that Karen can certainly hear it where she's sitting. "I'm making a film here. Okay? I'm making a fucking film here. Do you understand that?"

Karen turns and mouths across the cafe: "We should go."

I swear Forman smiles at me. He whispers in Karen's ear and then he smiles at me. If anyone knows, he knows. Milos Forman knows.

9

At the university Karen will not tell me what Milos Forman said. She will not even admit it was him. All she says is:

"Get off my case, Ciaran."

"Well, like, ex*cuse* me!"

I would persist, except I figure she's far too strung out about two things. Firstly, her meeting Professor Julian Krotow, who's most famous works, *Bodies of Sacrifice: The Anatomy of Medieval Matrydom* and *Entertainment in the Era of Jeanne D'Arc,* were Book Club bestsellers. Secondly, my decision to go against her advice and agree to have as my film project supervisor: Dr Steven Milroy.

Steve Milroy whose book *The Film Revolution: Independent Cinema and the Hollywood Machine* was featured in last month's *Clips* as "a book to warm the hearts of all true cinema lovers" and, when it comes out in paperback (date so far unknown), will be on the top of my private shopping list.

More importantly, Steve Milroy who directed last year's Festival of the Waters Special Category winner *Judgment Days,* a film which struck me, actually, as not only reminiscent of John Mc-Naughton's early work, *Henry: Portrait of a Serial Killer,* before he went on to make the truly crap *Normal Life* then recovered with the ink-black comedy *Wild Things,* but is also excellent in its own right. Captures that same terrific pace that McNaughton got in *Serial Killer* and, even though the cast is unknown, has never probably been in a film before, wouldn't even know a geared head from a zoom motor, really does work.

24

Interestingly, it was in one of Milroy's early films that Helena McCabe once starred (a short, maybe fifteen, maybe twenty minutes, about a girl that gets lost in a harborside warehouse and the things that assail her in the dark, the way the imagination brings to life inanimate things, gives them the power to change lives, distress, live I guess). The lead in *Judgment Days*, however, was Leesa Kennedy, whose mother is the artist, Heather Rebane, dropped out of USP to helped run the Film Festival, shot in shadows mostly, kind of Gwyneth Paltrow, in cheesecloths and florals, is excellent. I'd love to cast her as Lavonia in a remake of *Beneath the Valley of the Ultra Vixens* or feature in a documentary about children with famous artistic parents—Sophia Coppola would be another obvious choice, of course.

Turns out to be entirely true that Milroy once worked as 2AD for Brian G Hutton (*Ryder, Night Watch* etc). Before that he did locations for Alexandre Rockwell (*Four Rooms* and so on). These things I checked with the press office at Universal who, though not prepared to give full details—in fact were pretty damn cagey about providing any information at all, even though I explained again and again who I was and what I wanted—confirmed that a Steve Milroy has definitely worked for Universal and, yes, he has been paid by them.

Why Karen thinks she can comment on any of this, actually, why she thinks she can insist that "you and Steve, Ciaran, is not a good idea" when she's chosen to abandon her undergraduate interest in film (majoring in performance, in fact) to concentrate at postgraduate level on literature is beyond me.

She says she knows Steve Milroy pretty well—which maybe she does. Says he's a '70s freak, likes blaxplo films, Tobe Hooper, rubbish about . . . rock-n-roll road trips. She says he was one of first people she met at Southport. That Helena introduced him to her. She says that, if she hadn't needed the money, she would never have met him at all, never have acted in one of his stupid films, though I've never seen this film, and she's never offered to show it to me . . . Certainly, though she says she loves film no less now than she did when we met, I think this new anti-film attitude of hers is an issue building up between us.

These things considered, I decide to wait until we're alone in our flat. Then I'll press her about Milos Forman.

Instead, I stand on the balcony of the Griffith Building, with the leaded glass windows of the professors' rooms behind me, and I phone film the whole undergraduate body swarming onto the front lawn like a sea. I film them like I'm Cecil B. DeMille. I sweep across them from what must be 100 feet in the air.

"Like a sea," I say to myself, and I think of that sequence in the Peter Weir drama for Silver Screen Partners IV/Touchstone, *Dead Poets Society,* when church bells ring, the sun shreds the sky in oranges and pinks, a flock of birds (which I notice are mostly plovers or something) rises in a parabolic arc from a lake which is back lit, and the boys come down the wooden school stairs while Mr. Pitts, first name Gerald, played by James Waterstone, comes up the stairs telling them to slow down. And the whole sequence (8 minutes 23 seconds) summarizes the film in . . . in 8 minutes and 23 seconds. Though Weir, to my mind, fails in a number of important areas. For instance: it is well known that masturbation is rife amongst boys of that age, and Weir knows of it. I would also have thought Dead Actors Society was a more appropriate title in that for the most part it's nothing to do with poetry and everything to do with acting.

I wait outside Dr Milroy's office and phone shoot Karen, two doors down, sitting on a steel chair outside Krotow's room, looking accusingly in my direction, willing me not to go into Milroy's room, but to follow her. The shot I use is a low, shallow focus, knee shot. The corridor recedes with her on the right so that the shot favors her side and runs out of frame. She is the first to go in, so I do decide to follow behind her, holding my phone at shoulder height, hoping to God the battery will last, and keeping the angle level to give the effect of an ever filling, unbalanced three-shot.

Krotow says: "What's this?" as we're entering; but Karen, who is so very nervous as to be showing an eye tooth on the left side which is clamping down firmly on her bottom lip, where it's leaving a red mark like a cold sore, is quick to reply:

"Professor Krotow . . ." she says.

Julian Krotow, who is obviously not just a Joan of Arc specialist but also a Blues Brothers fan; he is obviously a Blues and '60s freak, loves the The Doors for example according to the poster on the wall (Jim Morrison, left) and Jefferson Airplane (who knows? right), pulls his wiry terrier hair back into a knot. His face covered in what is a clipped white growth and his lips are fleshy like they belong to John Belushi. Like Belushi didn't die via speed ball, leaving Dan Aykroyd to screw up the sequel, also starring John Goodman, with Aretha Franklin returning from the original. And Krotow—who I don't know personally because my last university was Roeford and here in Southport I don't know anyone except Karen who is also a Roeford graduate—I close up on.

Though he isn't saying it in so many words, I personally can hear him say to my phone: "Don't take any notice of all these old books, I'd rather be listening to 'My Baby Must be something something' by, uh, Puff Adder.'"

I hear him say, I'm sure: "I'd rather be smoking something stronger than Marlboro Lights, off the record, and listening to . . ." who? ". . ."Rod Stewart!"

"Well, as long as it doesn't turn into a circus," he says aloud.

"No sir," I say, propping in the corner beside some sort of ancient lance and his red academic gown with white fur collar hung on a hat stand. "No. It's a film. Director's rules! Definitely."

He slumps down into his chair. It is strangely low backed and wooden. There is, I now notice, something said to be "A Fragment of the Thigh Bone of Jacopo di Ronc" in a silver framed glass case on his desk. There is a statuette on the window sill of a naked guy, draped partly in what looks like a toga and labeled Vesailus. There is a collection of brown plastic half cups from the Cafebar. There are exam papers in pink piles on the floor around the room. There's the smell of wet wool, an open packet of Anadine on the floor, a briefcase with its clasp twisted and a sticker worn across it with a picture of a screaming child, looking like Kenny in *South Park,* in a red crossed circle like something out of Ghost-busters. Being very anti-noise, anti-child or anti-child-abuse; I can't work out which.

"Geez," I say, involuntarily.

He adjusts his tie, which is blue paisley to his jacket's bleached grey, and asks Karen to explain what it is that she wants to do.

"To the camera," he says, "if you want." And I notice his lips when he smiles are cracked and pale and that his teeth are bone white behind them, but unevenly collapsed onto each other, and the highpoints of his cheeks, which are pinkish, are positively glowing.

Using the light from the window as backlight, which is fair-ly atmospheric, I catch the left side of Krotow, and Karen full frontal. I turn Krotow into a silhouette and Karen's nervousness, which has spread into her fingers which now barumbas across the synopsis she has brought with her, I tilt myself towards.

I keep saying to myself that basic rule: "Form follows func-tion. Form follows function . . ."

I film the two of them like it's *Basic Instinct* (in which the cin-ematography of Jan De Bont is truly a treat, I might add), while Karen reads from the synopsis she's prepared on two sheets of legal paper she typed up last night, by the bay window in the pale moon light (this, of course, only being suggested).

I think to myself: "There are things you can do in a situation like this to increase the tension. Scorsese says: 'Don't split the screen.' He says: 'Don't go flying with the Rolling Stones.' 'Don't crash cut. Never.'" But then again Scorsese also made *Kundun,* so what would he know?

Now I'm catching bits of conversation.

Karen is saying, somewhat tonguingly, I think: "What was that stuff again about Joan of Arc and the butterflies?" (some-thing like that).

To which Krotow comments: "Oh, Karen! Babe you are Madonna, you know. You are that famous singer whose name is Madonna."

Okay, so maybe I don't hear this at all; but the battery warning symbol is showing and I have other things to worry about. Namely: is the battery running out before I get back to our flat for a new one? Like: I am supposed to be a professional here and this shouldn't happen. Like: I bet this never happened to Rodriguez, ever. The light flickers red, indicating my time is nearly up.

I notice, suddenly in my panic, a Roxy Cinema flyer for the Festival of the Waters Film Festival, pinned up right on the wall behind Krotow.

9

Goethe once wrote (and Professor Alton of the USP Department of Languages, Cultures and Civilizations quoted it, photocopied)— that's Johann Wolfgang von Goethe (1749–1832), the famous poet, novelist, playwright, natural philosopher and diplomat, author of *The Sorrows of Young Werther*—Goethe once wrote:

> *What a man notices and feels about himself seems to me the least part of him. He is more inclined to see what he lacks than what he has, to remark what worries than what delights him and enlarges his mind. Soul and body forget about themselves when things are pleasant and happy, and they are only reminded of themselves again by something unpleasant. A man writing of himself and his past will therefore mostly note what is cramping and painful.*

(Library Shelf: Short Loan: Lecture Notes—A. P.
Alton "An Introduction to European Philosophy")

10

As we leave Krotow's office, me tracking back, Karen is happier than she's been all day. She says she doesn't want to wait around while I ruin my life. She says this quite brightly, I think. She says if I want to get hooked up with Milroy, and won't listen to her, then she just can't wait around to watch it happen. She says:

"You know, you're wrong about Julian Krotow. I happen to know he's treasurer of the Film Festival Committee. So he's hardly 'anti-film,' Ciaran, or whatever you say. If that's what you're thinking."

"Whatever," I say.

But then she says she wants to go to the library to meet Colleen and then to the Student Union where they'll plan Satanic rituals and choose the people they want to sacrifice.

Of course, I don't actually catch all of this, but my camera phone is capable of picking up undercurrents, sub-surface things that would otherwise go unnoticed, and I tell Karen I'll see her in the bar at two, and if she wants to bring Colleen then that's her business, but to my mind she is no more than an extra and should probably get on with her own life.

I stop at Steve Milroy's door (on which I note, a little ominously I admit, there is a poster of Gérard Depardieu), and I knock loudly.

When behind the door a voice seems to say "Hi! Hi!" I think I'll just forget the whole thing and go out onto the front lawn where a band is now playing "Solved" by Unbelievable Truth, though it's not Unbelievable Truth only a band that wants to sound like them. But, figuring this is just being spooked by Karen's increasingly anti-film, anti-life, anti-us attitude, I don't go.

Instead, I turn around so my phone is catching the corridor receding behind me and I go into the office. Backwards.

The effect (though I'll have to check this in the rushes) is that the whole film seems to be disappearing into a new scene, a new low key, without cutting at all. And I think:

"I should have thought of doing this earlier!"

The corridor becomes bright and hard. Keeping it in focus, I catch the edge of the door with my left shoe, and push. The door sweeps across the frame from right to left. And slaps closed. The venetians are half open. The shot looks dark over all, with a few highlight areas (see: Michael Ribager: *On Directing*).

"Dr Milroy?" I ask.

I'm continuing to phone film the back of the door, which is quite grainy actually, and on which there is a dimly lit cute calendar from Pete's Pets featuring a muppet (name unknown), a rainbow colored scarf that hangs down to the floor, a peeling sticker for Classic Coke, a poster of Jean Harlow.

I pan slowly to the right. A half turn. Then left. The bookshelves provide a rapid line of composition, leaving behind the door in the direction of the window and passing such absolute winners as *An Introduction to Communication* by Gerhl and Wesserman, past *Radical Underworld* by Iain McCalman, then his Festival of the Waters Special Film Award, shaped as it is like a bronze wave, then several novels by John Updike, *Modern Myth in the Films of Jesús Franco*. Light reading, right? until I'm meeting the glow through the venetians straight on, which is splitting the frame into seven identical widths, and I can make out Milroy.

There's an obvious flaw in all this which I cannot immediately pinpoint. I think perhaps I have done something wrong. The linearity of the thing. The way the action rises. The sense of thematic purpose. But for the moment there's Dr Steven Milroy: his head thrown right back as he lies collapsed in his chair, his head in a clear plastic bag, his neck in some kind noose hung from the curtain rail, and completely buck naked.

two

Beauty and the Beast
1991, 84m, Color
Animated/Musical/Romance, G/U
Walt Disney Productions/Silver Screen Partners IV (U.S.)

I

Phone facts, some interesting differences of opinion:

> *The rapid changes in cellular and wireless technology combined with the large number of phone available means it is more important than ever to review cell phone comparisons and ratings. The comparisons show differences in mobile phones, including information about different phones' features and capabilities. With so many new features available, it is easier to observer the differences between various models when they are placed side by side in a chart.*

(http://www.cellphonefacts.com/ Last accessed: 25th December 2008)

Alternatively:
*   An estimated 250 to 300 million cell phones are being used in the U.S.
*   The average American cell phone user owns three (3) or more expired cell phones.
*   The average US consumer only uses their current cell phone for 12 to 18 months.
*   Over 70% of Americans do not know that they can recycle their old cell phone.

- In a recent survey, only 2.3% of Americans recycled their old cell phones and 7% threw them in the garbage.
- Cell phones contain precious metals such as gold and silver.
- A total of 500 million cell phones weighing an estimated 250,000 tons are currently stockpiled and awaiting disposal.
- Cell phones contain numerous substances that need to be disposed of in a safe and efficient manner.

(http://www.earthday.gatech.edu/Cell%20
Phone%20FACTS.pdf, accessed: 1 January 2009)

2

I'm still thinking I can get to The Roxy before seven where they're showing *The Last House on the Left,* which is probably my favorite Wes Craven picture and, to my mind, far better, structurally, than *Deadly Blessing* and certainly better than *Scream* (because it's based, he says, on Bergman's *The Virgin Spring,* Ingemar Bergman, that is). I believe strongly in occasional stylization. How else can subjectivity be established?

At the Roxy the experience is strictly of the old school. One "screen." "Stalls." "*Dress* Circle." Screenings SE7EN 'til DAWN. But The Roxy! Hell, it's like Notre Dame. Like Notre Dame in Paris. Like?

I don't know. Like the Temple of Olympian Zeus in Agrigento, Sicily (?). In the foyer (which has on the wall near the ticket office a brass plaque stating OFFICIALLY OPENED BY MRS W. B. DAVSON, WIDOW OF THE LATE WILLIAM DAVSON, SCREEN ACTOR, WHOSE PERFORMANCES IN FILMS SUCH AS *MY LITTLE DARLING* DELIGHTED THE WORLD, JULY 7TH 1947, which glitters as I close up on it and should, if I reshoot, be lensed with a polarizing filter) there is a bar which is long and made of genuine mahogany, with a real marble spill and brass railing. There is a chandelier the size of a double bed, made of eighteen hundred Viennese crystal drops, that turns the ceiling, filmed with me on my back on the mosaic floor spelling out the words LEGENDS OF STARS, into a night sky in which several galaxies have collided. On the wall are life-size photographs of everyone who ever was (Garbo, Flynn, Grant, Powell & Pressburger, Pickford, Ophuls, Welles, Streep . . . and, inexplicably, Nick Nolte!). Going down the stairs to the restroom I feel like I'm stepping down deep inside The Earth. The plumbing is strictly pre-industrial, pre-sound. The light is florescent. There's cold creeping out of the sick green stucco. This is no place to take a crap. The hand-dryer sounds like a chain-saw. The atmosphere is pure noir. And the music, which is something by someone called Peaches and Herb, I believe,—"Shake Your Groove Thing" by Peaches and Herb—is literally being piped through the walls. The place looks over the beach and the movies run all night.

Meanwhile, into the bar comes Karen, flanked by Helena who has arrived straight from work and, dressed in mid calf height boots and animal print stretched jeans, walks like she's bungee jumping.

"Ciaran!" she cries out, literally. "Ciaran. I don't believe it. You are incredible! So tell me: what happened?"

"Come on," she says, lowering her voice and stretching right across the table towards me with her lips glittering in pearl and her earrings a full 1/2 carat each, "I mean, what fucking happened?"

"Calm down," I suggest.

She eats me with her eyes.

Naturally, I have no choice but to lie. I am obliged to do it (I am Kevin Costner in *No Way Out;* Marco Leonardi in *Like Chocolate for Water*), and joke to myself (though it is only half a joke) that because Helena is Miss Marpley in Accounts she will respect me for this.

I say to myself, referring to a part of the plot which amounts to nothing and is, in itself, absolutely uninteresting: "There wouldn't be some poke auditor about to go through the Festival of the Waters Film Festival accounts if office feeders like you, Helena dear, hadn't practiced a little truth ping-pong, a little financial hide-the-puppy, a little computer fraud. Now would there?"

Karen is asking: "So how did he do it, anyway?" But for the moment, though I'm aware of Karen hanging on my next word, but pretending not to, kind of weirdly doe-eyed up against my shoulder, I'm still concentrating on Helena. I'm thinking that without her clothes on she would look like a seagull. Her neck craning thick and white. Her chest out. I am sitting in El Monkey, the decor a jungle of potted palms and stuffed brown monkeys in cages and Vox posters and blackboard menus, the music of Portishead, and a gull is trying to make my two-shot into a big close-up, demanding: "Come on, Ciaran! Come on!"

"With a razor blade," I lie. "Very traditional."

"God!"

"That's crazy," says Helena who, of course, knows Milroy from her early, amateur film days.

"Sure," I say. "Sure it is." Even weirder, I think, because in actual fact he did it in exactly the same way that Michael Hutchence from that '80s rock band INXS did it. And because, of course, no one was quite sure if Hutchence had really meant to commit suicide or if he had, in fact, been engaging in some kind of bizarre sexual game, something borne in the angst that the corporate mentality of the '80s, the terrible dissolution of that period, produced in the young that grew up amongst it. Or whatever.

"But he's alive, is he?" asks Helena, lighting a cigarette, inhaling.

I start doing this great voice-over (in the tradition, actually, of Adrian Lyne's *Lolita*. "O gentlemen of the jury," that kind of thing), but Karen stops me, almost distraught:

"And then what? You went in, and then what?"

So now I'm explaining to her how it happened, though I'm lying of course. How I cutaway from the corridor into his office. How it is difficult to know whether the books, many of which have glossy covers, will reflect comet tails through every phone shot. How the background music is "Solved" by Unbelievable Truth, playing out on the front lawn. And his office walls, "Which are plastered," I lie, "with Def Squad posters, pictures of Bill Murray" mask the set, as does the stippled ceiling, and slowly, panning, the colors "like something out of Hairspray," hitting the first sun-lit aspects of his desk, until my lie somehow finds its way back to the truth and I'm describing the doctor with his head in a plastic bag and the way his face had turned a deep shade of red and his flickering bulging eyelids and the clutter on his desk, at which point I am tempted to freeze frame but instead I'm lowering my phone so it's recording just Dr Steven Milroy's mouth, his now gaping mouth, and the spot effect of sirens (off) tells everyone that the ambulance is arriving, the police also, one of whom turns out to be some character actor whose name escapes but looks a bit like Mel Gibson if not for having absolutely no chin, and the other is Jamie Lee Curtis, taking a statement as Steve Milroy, now revived (because he had clinically died), and conscious again, is crying something like "Tell Leesa . . . ," by which I figure he means Leesa Kennedy who lead for him in *Judgment Nights,* and works for the Film Festival.

"Oh, God, tell Leesa will you, please?" he's yelling as they wheel him out (they've bought a chair) and just at that moment there's this clatter and murmuring (off) and from along the corridor (pan slowly right), the whole freshman cohort is being shown into the building as part of their introductory library tour, it is Orientation Week after all, and they prop at the sight of him being wheeled out. The whole set falls silent. There's an old wall clock (you know the type) and it clocks out the seconds like a drum beat as Milroy is wheeled right down the corridor past them (me not letting him out of left frame for ten, twelve beats; the corridor checkered black and white, receding busily away), and I know exactly what the undergrads are thinking? They're thinking:

"Hey, I want to make movies. There is nothing else."

"And the thing is," I say, "later the police wanted to know if I had anything 'on tape.'" (?)

Helena is silent, inhaling, exhaling. Karen is clenching her fists over her eyes.

"Tape? 'Film?' I said. . . . Well, I'm not going to tell them, am I?"

"I don't believe this," says Karen, her face suddenly annoyingly hidden by the rim of her cup.

3

It doesn't stop there:

Baked Sultanas and Red Cabbage with Yogurt and Honey

(Serves 2) For this recipe you can use bulk sultana buys. If Red Cabbage is unavailable, ordinary cabbage will do. Plain yogurt is best; but sometimes this is expensive. So, flavored yoghurt is okay, as long as you use some of the less powerful flavors, such as applesauce, peach, guava, custard or caramel.

1.5oz caster sugar
2lb Yogurt
4lb ripe sultanas
4 tbsp wine (such as red wine)
1 Red Cabbage
1¾oz unsalted butter
freshly ground black pepper
6 tsp honey
4oz peanuts
crème fraîche, on top
Cooking time: 20–25 minutes

1. Place the caster sugar and yogurt in a saucepan and stir over the heat until the sugar has dissolved. Remove the pan from the heat.
2. Preheat a normal oven to 400F. Prick the sultanas all over using a fork and place them on a baking tray.
3. Swiftly heat the wine in a dish or, if necessary, in a kettle. Poor into a bowl and add the butter, six tablespoons of honey, and black pepper. Bring to the boil, in a microwave, and then add the sultanas and the honey.
4. Transfer to the oven for 15 minutes, basting the sultanas every 2 minutes with the liquid.
5. Meanwhile, take the cabbage, place it in a pan, sprinkle with peanuts. Bring to a boil. Then place on tray in the oven for 8 minutes, until golden-brown.
6. To serve, arrange cabbages on plates and drizzle the sultanas onto it. Serve with a crème fraîche.

4

I don't follow Karen. I don't understand what she's saying. This whole Milroy thing has thrown her into this mighty fine fit. Even though she does not know the full truth of what happened, because I figure that's something she doesn't need to know, won't benefit from, and I don't want to tell her. She's actually dissed Helena because of it; won't talk to her about it, stormed out of the Plexus, though it was her that had arranged to meet Helena there and her that had insisted on speaking to Helena alone, after I had revealed to them the full extent of his injuries, and her then who even refused to let Helena come home with us, though Helena stays with us regularly, when it's too late, or too . . . whatever, to go home to her place at the marina.

Now Karen's the most obvious person in Candia by far—even though the place is getting pretty packed now with a whole lot of us from Langford, with other students from Southport, with city workers from NEXT, COLLINS SHOES, EXCALIBAR, RUFUS FOR MEN, APPLEYARD KIDS CLOTHING, WOOL-WORTHS, WATERSTONES, GO SPORTZ, THE HEART FOUNDATION, VIRGIN MEGASTORE, THE HALIFAX, RIVER ISLAND CLOTHING, HMV, HABITAT, FOODLAND, RAGWEED, PEPE, PROVOCATEUR'S T-SHIRT, MOTHER-CARE, with the guy from DIABLO CLOTHING who gives discounts for holders of concessionary rail cards, with assorted space cadets from Machin College, with people I don't know but who are probably here in Southport for the forthcoming Arts Festival, maybe even for the Film Festival, though frankly they don't look like it, they're too "well, gee whizz," they're too "well, shucks, is that a special effect or what?," they're too . . . too un-film.

Still Karen goes on, her voice pretty much ruining anything I'd want to do with the ambient sound.

"You should have just left him there, Ciaran. It was none of your business."

"What"—I zoom in on her face in full blank stare, placing my phone at an oblique angle of, I guess, 30°—"is your problem?"

She tries to smoke and drink her Indonesian Java *au lait* at the same time and the ash of her cigarette falls on her new white Diesel top and she dumps the coffee cup on its saucer, spilling the Java, shouting "Shit!" at the top of her voice, wiping off the ash with one of the Candia napkins, which are thick and soft incidentally, while Monika (who works in Pencils, the Student Union stationary shop) tells her:

"It's okay. Karen, it's okay" sounding like someone right out of *Singles.*

So there's a big problem, apparently, with how I dealt with finding Steve Milroy, how I called Emergency, maybe even how I shot the whole thing in a steady doco flow so that not one minute of his rescue was missed, not one reaction left to the viewers' imagination (who knows, maybe even that). Frankly I can't get a handle on this being a problem, or why Karen won't shut up about it. Now she is getting other people involved.

"You really shouldn't go near that guy," says Alice (Social Work, third year).

"O?" Me shooting in high shot over Alice's neatly blue-tipped hair.

"No," says Cole (Archaeology, from France originally, parents some kind of mountaineers or engineers or something, doing a dissertation about runes, or ruins is it? Whatever).

"Why's that?" I say, circling the table as a guy from RUFUS FOR MEN checks out the menu nearby, plumbing for the Kamaboko which, had he asked, I would have recommended anyway.

"There's other people who do film," says Colleen. "What about Dr Hallam?"

"Poke," I say.

"Keith Negus?"

"Poke. Po-ka!"

"Hey, Bronwen Rainey is supposed to be brilliant. Didn't she direct that animated film about the . . . the mice? You know The . . ."

"The Mighty," I say. "And, poke. Pokella! Pokofsky! Poke!"

"Listen," says Kevin Lewin, who is studying American . . . Studies I think, going out with Grace (seated next to him), who knows Goody, the projectionist at The Roxy, who gets both of them in at all the Roxy's late nighters for nothing, and who is a limey light in both the USP Sail and USP Climbing clubs.

"There's issues here, Ciaran," he says, "which you don't seem to get."

He sweeps a look around the table and, by their pouting half-interest, I figure the whole of our building actually agrees with him. At which point, it all becomes perfectly, achingly, sickeningly clear to me: Kevin is far too distant shot from the far end of the booth like this.

I scramble up to my feet and lean on in. He almost jumps out of his seat.

"Look, you jerk, just leave it alone!" he screeches.

"O, this is great, Kev!" I say, tilting my phone to catch his left ear reddening, his giant John Candy head swaying back and forth. "Keep going!

"To *Hell* with this!" he screams and pushes himself up from the table.

"I'm out of here, Grace," he says, pushing along the booth past Alice and Colleen and Monika and Cole and Grace, who tells me she is absolutely not named after Grace Kelly, though I doubt very much that this is true. Kevin leaves the booth, heading home to Langford. Grace follows.

When they've gone and the place seems to be returning to normal I suggest that maybe we can order one of Candia's excellent all-you-can-eat *Llaningachos* and share it between us.

"I got this idea," I say, "where I shoot these ten friends, who all live together in a terrace by the beach, right, as they start a meal and their whole lives kind of spin out around the food so that for

every potato cake there's a story, you know?, for every baked egg
there's a little anecdote captured on film, for every spoon of orange salad there's . . ."

At this point Karen, who for no apparent reason has been gently spooning more and more sugar into her now cooling coffee,
simply loses it and, grabbing her string bag from the floor under
Monika, tears now forming like great glue balls in the corners of
her eyes, sprints for the door.

I follow her into the street and catch her on the corner of
the Halfmarket and Beach Street; propping there against a lit-
ter bin and the signpost pointing south to "The Southport Toy
Museum."

"You don't love me, Ciaran," she says.

"That's not true," I say, catching her three-quarter profile
against the mock graystone façade of RAGWEED. "I do, but . . .
I just don't get you anymore."

She goes to speak but doesn't. Begins wandering instead down
the sidewalk toward the escarpment, her head thrown back a little, swinging her string bag in slow Ferris wheel circles.

"Look," I say, catching her up, "what about we head out to
Ras's. He's just downloaded a full copy of *Bats* off this new site he
found and it's . . . flawless!"

"I don't think so."

"Okay," I say, "how about we don't. That's fine. How about
we just go home."

. . .

"Karen, I don't know what to say here. Help me out."

"Ciaran, you are not listening!"

"What?" I say. "What?"

"Would you just turn that thing off?"

I stand propped against a white convertible as a truck the size
of a house passes, and I catch the huge tail lights in a full elongat-
ing phone shot away to north and it just looks great as a slight
but maybe even slightly red dust whirls up behind it and the cars
parked on either side of the road rock a little and the load, what-

ever it is, train wheels or cogs or huge buttons or something, rattle, and clink against each other.

Then I turn around again, but Karen is gone.

5

Ras Bregendahl, my closest friend, who is famous for once running *Jacob's Ladder* from dusk till dawn every night for a whole week, worked as an assistant projectionist at The Roxy over summer (three evenings, SE7EN—MIDNITE). Ras is a biophysics MS (now in his second optional extension year), and an absolutely first rate Horror freak.

Catching the landline as I come in, I agree to meet him this evening at eight at Plexus, the student union bar, and I swear he says in a breathy voice: "Come alone."

"What?" I say. "What did you say?"

But he laughs and is gone.

Still, by five, Karen has not come back to the terrace and I'm forced to watch DVDs of Ricki Lake alone. Tonight a longstanding friend's partner reveals her intentions while Ricki acts as a mediator. I eat a Greek salad that we bought on special from New World because it was near its date, and also a tuna mini-pizza, a Granola Bar, and drink some Evian, then I set the DVR to record Jerry Springer and, with my phone now charged, head out of Langford onto the Halfmarket where the street lights are now lit and there is a mist rolling in from the sea. Now this, I think to myself, takes the cake.

Soon I'm traveling down The Promenade in the direction of Chester Circuit and shooting without a corrective screen, despite the lag effects. I suppose I could have shot this during the day with a night filter but I'm thinking "Honesty and integrity," I'm thinking "You can fool some of the people some of the time" Also: with coming of high speed film no one much does it anymore. I think it will pay off. Bladers pass me, heading along the beachfront wearing black lycra cycle shorts and red stretch sateen jeans, their bodies absolutely piped. The sea is black and sketched with neon

DIABLO CLOTHING, TATTOOOS, REXUS HOTEL and M
in several colors. Outside the Lobster Room, which is notoriously
gay and charges blood to get in, four lush undergrads wait for the
doors to open, wearing white stretch lace dresses and ankle boots
and watching kids skateboarding up the bandstand steps, doing
floaters and hi-backs. Across the road two old bottle hounds,
total wastes-of-space, are drinking white cider on the bench.

In a moment of inspiration, I phone zoom in on one of them
and he cries out:

"You from MTV?"

"That's right," I say. "Newsnight."

At which point he (yellow t-shirt, elasticized draw-string jog
pants) gets up and steps out into the road in my direction and is
nearly hit by a convertible (possibly a Mazda, an MX6 I mean),
whose driver (insurance professional: INCREMENTS) hits the
horns. But the hound's saying: "I used to be in show business. You
know? I used to be in films."

"Yeah?" I say. "Really?"

I've got him in the most incredible deep phone focus with the
whole promenade behind him flaring like an oil fire. He's nothing
more than a silhouette swaying left and right and blubbering:

"I was in *The Guns of Navarone.*"

"Really," I say, noticing now that the lush four, having been
alerted by the car incident, are now tuned in on this. I prop down
on one leg and put my elbow on my knee to keep my phone steady.
"Which one were you . . . Captain Mallory or Colonel Stavros?"

"Mallory," says the hound.

"Nope," I say, "couldn't be Mallory. That was Gregory Peck."

"Well," he says, looking for his bottle, "the other one then. .
. . Staverros."

"That was Anthony Quinn."

His face, which is asymmetrical, now falls to his neck.

"Maybe it was the sequel," I say. "Maybe it was the sequel you
were in . . . with Harrison Ford."

"What?" he says. "No. The what? Hey, I'm talking about the film *The Guns of Navarone*." He staggers over close, unbalancing my picture. "You're doing that wrong . . . Here! Here, give it to me!"

He's coming at me now with his arms out, grinning like a chimp, waving his hands about.

"Listen," I say, standing up and stepping back. "It'll be on the news."

"Alright?" I say, starting to walk away. "Ten o'clock. Okay?"

"You're doing that wrong," he screams.

6

Ras puts this month's *Black Heat* on the table between us and he reads aloud as follows:

"What is wrong with *The Institute Benjamenta: Or This is What Dream People Call Human Life* is what is wrong with all the Quay Brothers films. It's a question, you know, of making the morbid detritus of life into some kind of psychic substance and these days these two guys, terminally attached at the hip, seem to take this to mean an endless cycle of repetitive scissor shots. I didn't even like *Rehearsals for Extinct Anatomies* that much. If they'd just get back to existential dread they managed to dredge up in *Street of Crocodiles* we could all go back to not sleeping at night. As to The Institute I'd rate it a "don't even think you'll get a hand-job after this one." I suggest you rent *Body Chemistry 2* again instead."

"Justin Madden," says Ras. "I mean: how can you take that complete poke seriously?"

There's about half a crowd in Plexus, but there's at least several people I recognize, and I film Neve Campbell and Liv Tyler from Supa-Video tonguing their drinks in a booth to the right, and Gary Oldman, I think, no I'm sure, in the corner. But still no sign of Karen.

I mention this to Ras. And then I try to give him some idea of how my relationship with Karen is panning out since she left Roeford, moved in with me into the terrace, registered at USP, but now has turned her back on film in favor of "literature."

"I mean," I say, "what is she doing? I direct, she acts. It just doesn't make sense. I mean, when she finishes here, what? Look how Julia Stiles started, right? Mena Suvari? Patricia Arquette? In In . . . dee . . . pendents. Independent labels."

For reasons I guess I understand well enough, Ras looks awkward and pats his coat pocket, looking for a cigarette.

"She's got things on her mind," he says.

"Sure," I say, "medieval literature."

He hesitates to agree, but finally, in a hard, stiff nod of his head, he does—then, turning away, picks up his magazine again.

"I just get really pissed off when I read shit like this," says Ras, flicking through *Black Heat* with his head to one side, sucking from a bottle of Beechams, which is part vodka, part Frangelico and part pineapple and comes in at 33%.

"No talent," he says, looking up at me. "You know what I mean. Pokes like Madden have just got no talent."

I notice Ras is dressed in a black t-shirt and an embroidered carpet bag waistcoat. He wears his hair long, in a pony tail, and amazingly still carries a pager, rejecting all talk of a WAP, cellular or mobile system (it's apparently something called a Mynilta TX101 which has, he proudly, pokeshly, tells me, nine musical alerts). He's been at USP four years now and, although his MS degree was only supposed to last a year, he has extended twice and now has no more possible extensions and must finish before the summer.

Because Ras works at The Roxy a lot of people passing stop to talk. One guy, pure Neanderthal, possibly a gymnast or something, a weightlifter, is wondering why they never show *Prime Cut*. Why anyone would want a Michael Ritchie Film starring Sissy Spacek is beyond me, though Gene Hackman does his usual admirable Popeye Doyle and the thing is held together by a bunch of completely deviant hicks who inhabit a country fair in the Midwest. There's also a respectable wheat field chase scene; but isn't that just a little too *North By Northwest?* Hardly original is it?

"So," says Ras, "Milroy tried to top himself? A friend of mine—Gary You know? Works in the USP Staff Club?—says that he personally always thought the guy was a full blown soup kitchen. From my experience, I gotta agree with that. You know, he used to have these regular film parties at his place and . . ."

I prick up at the sound of this, but Ras won't go on.

"Fook-hit, I shouldn't talk!"

"I didn't hear about that," I say, interest severely piquing. "About those. His film parties. When was this?"

Ras, shaking his head in a weird kind of circular fashion, seems lost on this. "A month or two back . . . I don't know. A month ago maybe. He sure used to do some heavy gear. Hyoscine and thiorpropazate mostly, I think. Anyway, you should know that. He's one crazy pup."

I have known Ras since July when he was a USP peer guide on a postgraduate induction tour and we spent two hours together being bussed around the Harbor Zoo while a guy called Louth described his *alstroemeria aurantiaca,* or whatever, and the commitment that all the Southport teaching staff have to transferable learning skills. Dr Francis Louth, who apparently is a world specialist on amphibians, toads, newts, their slime and slimy habits, and just to prove this point was dressed in a toadish charcoal blazer and amphibious taupe twills.

"Anyway, forget that. You played *Outwars* yet?"

"No," I say, closing in on him, still wondering about these film parties that Milroy was supposed to have had.

"Frankly," Ras says, looking into my phone, "if he don't put my name in the credits I'll be telling everyone you're actually remaking *Klute.*"

"What, and you're Jane Fonda?"

I notice now that he's ridden his bike because his helmet is under my seat. Meanwhile, the place is filling up and the singular narrative (one section neatly slotting into the next like a fishing pole), which I hoped would hold my film together in a way that a film hangs around a certain set of recognizable motifs or images (such as the whores in *Interview With A Vampire* or the 1961 Ferrari in *Ferris Bueller's Day Off* and, in Karen's case, in my film about her which is suffering from her complete detachment from things lately, the battle between good and evil which could, in fact, go either way) is slipping away into something more like a concert film and, to be honest, I'm getting annoyed.

"Are you ready for this?" asks Ras.

But seriously, I really am getting annoyed. I can't help it: I'm thinking about Steve Milroy lying their naked with this head in a bag, the bag steamed up like some kind of Chinese take-out bag, his eyes rolled back in his head and the slim-line venetians closed, and I can smell his office (though it is probably really the smell of nachos which they do here, or the potato skins, veggie-burgers, seafood platters) and I want to shout out:

"Excuse me, my film is not a genre film!

"This is not some formulaic studio film that you can manipulate and ruin!"

On the other hand, it really is a unique achievement to have phone-filmed an attempted suicide (if that's what it was?), to have caught on film the moment at which one ordinary guy was, let's face it, out-of-here. I feel I know the guy a little better at least because of it. In that sense, I'm even more concerned about Karen's new, weird attitude. Not least, because I have a genuine moment of life and death in front of me and, because of her attitude making me wonder about my own life, my own steady, unrelenting march toward death, I play it again and again. At will.

"You know," I say, "I have an idea."

"Wait a minute," says Ras. "I was trying to tell you something. Guess what?"

Now at this point I can either say "What?" or ask him why he didn't mention that he'd come on his bike which means we won't be staying here tonight because when he bikes he always wants to ride somewhere, usually out to the western suburbs to the Lizard

Lounge which used to be, I'd guess, a pinball parlor in, maybe, the '70s, perhaps there was even eight-ball!, but now has racing simulations and infantry strategy games, graphic platformers, tank strategies and the newest arcade *Toonstruck*. But instead, because I'm annoyed that I'm going to have to cut most of this out and then there's the question of how to distil a dramatic premise from Karen's extremely notable big-fit absence, and because I have an idea which maybe will solve everything if Ras would just shut up, I don't say anything, just sit back in my chair and focus on the blackboard menu which features, this evening, a Special Fruit Fool.

"Okay, then," says Ras, "this is it. If I fail my degree, I'm going to Honduras."

Hell, I think, if I was just shooting this with an Aaton 8–35 or a Mitchell BNC I wouldn't have to worry about whether I'm going to suffer generational losses when transferring tape to tape, and possibly color shift in the direction of red and, if I'm out of luck, picture break up.

"So?" says Ras.

"What?" I say, though I heard the first time and I'm simply wondering how this fits with my plans, the film I'm making, where it came from, what it means and so forth.

"Why's that?" I say.

But Ras won't answer. He just repeats in a strangely rushed and high tone. "Honduras, yeah. It's one remote fook of a country, Ciaran, that's for sure."

I figure this idea has got to have come about from his study of plants in sub-tropical regions, or from his loving avocadoes, or from how many times in Candia he's ordered *esquites* or *ensalada de jimcama*, or from the fact he is the only person I know that knows anything about the work of Jaime Humberto Hermosillo (*Confidencias, Dona Herlinda and Her Two Son,s* etc) and over the years here at USP has championed his films.

"You don't know anything about Honduras," I blatantly lie.

Two lush girls from the Halfmarket, who I think actually want to move into Langford Terrace, and who work in NEXT, have noticed I'm shooting them and they pucker up like Monroe or Mamie Van Doren (or so they think) and I give them the thumbs up because if you're that stupid you need some attention. I zoom in on Gary Oldman, who's having a bad hair day, but what does he care, he's a hard man (as his performance in *Sid and Nancy* proves).

"Manzanillo," says Ras. "Chihauhua. Guadalajara."

"You've got to be joking!" I'm saying this while drinking a Lilli, which is part calvados, part cherry juice, part Angostura, and comes in at 37%.

"Why?" Ras seems, genuinely unknowing.

"Because," I say, "you'll lose your job. And what are you talking about anyway? When would you go, spring term? Honduras, in *spring*, for Christ's sake!"

"No," says Ras, looking dreamily into his drink, "I'm talking about now. I'm talking about tomorrow, next week. Before my ol' man turns up and . . . Just leaving, Ciaran. . . . you know. Everybody behind."

I close up on him as he's putting on his helmet. "Groovy," I say, him filling the frame, "you should have told me. You're actually Peter Fonda, right?"

7

Theodor Ludwig Wiesengrund Adorno says this:

> *Picture-book without pictures.*—*The objective tendency of the Enlightenment, to wipe out the power of images over man, is not matched by any subjective progress on the part of enlightened thinking towards freedom from images. While the assault on images irresistibly demolishes, after metaphysical Ideas, those concepts once understood as rational and genuinely attained by thought, the thinking unleashed by the Enlightenment and immunized against thinking is now becoming a second figurativeness, though without images or spontaneity. Amid the network of now wholly abstract relations of people to each other*

and to things, the power of abstraction is vanishing. The estrangement of schemata and classifications from the data subsumed beneath them, indeed the sheer quality of material processed, which has become quite incommensurable with the horizons of individual experience, ceaselessly enforces an archaic retranslation into sensuous signs. The little silhouettes of men or houses that pervade statistics like hieroglyphics may appear in each particular case accidental, mere auxiliary means. But it is not by chance they have such a resemblance to countless advertisements, newspaper stereotypes, toys. In them representation triumphs over what is represented.

(Library Shelf: P044448. Professor's Notes.
Z. L. LaTroal. "Politics of Popular Culture"
35:077 Adv. From Theodor Adorno, *Minima
Moralia,* Verso: New York, 1994, 140)

8

We're riding up into the hills with Southport beach behind us and the terraces giving way now to allotments, farm shops. What this would look like in widescreen you'd never believe, with the night so clear that, as we ride, it feels like it's taking my skin off. Like an ice loofah scrubbing away. We're travelling at what?, sixty miles an hour, which is not even half of what this thing can do. Ras is down low and his helmet, which he's proud to say is an Arai Quantum E, shoots black and red. I'm pulled up behind him with my hands round his waist and my phone, which I cannot operate, tucked into my jacket. I'm trying to imagine Honduras but I can't. Hondurans. *Lluvia de Peces* (Fish Rain). Cheap sandals. Shrimp sizzling right through summer. But all I can see, all that is suddenly visible to me, apart from the rush of scenery which blurs into blacks and browns unless I look upward to the sky which is lined and shot with low white cloud, is Karen.

Voice absent: Karen. Joan of Arc: Karen. Ingrid Bergman: Karen. Karen: SupaVideo: Karen. Close up: Karen. Karen. Karen.

I can't believe that in just a few weeks she has completely abandoned her love of film, replacing it with some unexplained new
belief in literature, when it was film, and film alone, that brought
us together. She and I studying American Cinema with Professor Pullman at Roeford and Karen acting in five undergraduate
productions in that term alone. And I could see from her total
devotion to performing for the camera that she loved cinema as
much as I did. When she topped Pullman's class that only confirmed what I already knew. We got together properly heading
to Southport on the train, for pre-registration, and I shot her in
full profile across the carriage, reading (come to think of it) *The
Great Gatsby* and she said that she loved Francis Ford Coppola's
work, and I pointed out that Coppola had directed *You're A Big Boy
Now* when he was just 26 years old, as part of his UCLA graduate
thesis, and we talked about how a movie camera can be an eye,
an insightful eye on our world, and about how much our graduate
studies would equip us for this very world, which was rolling out
so rapidly in front of us, even though the cost of graduate study,
she pointed out, was phenomenal.

I phone shot her there in that crowded carriage with the windows reflecting her back at me, the scenery passing blurred behind her, the passengers trying to stay in their fixed, unfocussed
lives and she, who seemed to easily drift off into trying to calcu-
late how she would survive at USP, the cost of a room in the college, the cost of meals, the cost of books, the cost, cost, cost of
education, she said, that in all this tremendous turmoil me with
my camera phone at least made her feel kind "special," her eyes
clouding over as she said this, Roeford now behind her, Southport
rolling bright and shiny out in front, and me loving her cheesy
overplaying of this, her almost cheese-shop Cameron Diaz playing of this scene as she described a job she'd lined up in Southport
already, with a guy who was both a film maker and a teacher.

Now this! Just to add insult to injury, Ras is talking about this
crazy Honduran thing of his. And nobody is fully explaining to
me how this could be happening, or where it fits with me or my

plans or the whole gamut of relationships which my existence entails and which make up my film. I want to know how Cole feels about all of this. About what Monika thinks. What David Duchovny thinks. And Nic Cage. And John Cusack, whose range and versatility show him to have insights beyond the ordinary. How Drew Barrymore would read it, being a child of the Hollywood system who has endured both hard times and ridicule.

The fact that Karen is still missing, has not been back to the terrace all day and, though I have called her phone who knows how many times, is still entirely uncontactable, only confirms that whatever is coming between us is growing larger by the minute. Like the black star in *The Fifth Element* or the rats in *The Watcher* or . . . maybe, I'm thinking, like the surging evil which fills, and then expands, in each and every frame of *End of Days*.

Before we left Plexus Ras mentioned his favorite Honduran film-maker, Paul Amador, and I had to admit I had never heard of him. Now I feel awful. My head is aching and I think the cherry juice in the Lilli may have been off or something. I do know as follows: Buñuel lived in Mexico City in the 50s and 60s and the films from his middle period were shot there, *including Los Olvidados*. Likewise Eisenstein filmed *Que viva Mexico!* in 1931 but that is thorough trot, having no story to speak of and no great characters, and I can't understand why anyone would go some place that was so visually claustrophobic. Meanwhile, Ras is giving the bike some.

The corners seem to be coming up now increasingly fast, one after the other. Increasingly fast. I hang on, right hand holding left, and I feel him moving in front of me, his waist rolling up and down in the circle of my arms and his shoulders, which are broader than mine, shifting up and down into right bend then left. And I go with him. Ras's parents live out at Stoneycroft, in a 19th century barn conversion on 3.5 acres, freestanding, own a Lexus, because they don't believe (I'm guessing) in being ostentatious about their wealth, and spend three weeks in summer in Kos, Greece, picking oleanders and drinking ouzo. His parents are paying for his science degree and he is guaranteeing them that he'll finish it—which strikes me as a dubious deal, given the remote subject of his degree (centipedes or centrifuges or something). But each, I say, to his own. He says that Karen is the best thing that could have happened to me and that I should go away with her for a while, shoot maybe a surf movie and get things into perspective, but I don't see how or why. So he just doesn't mention it any more, only mutters something about if his father turns up before he leaves for Honduras, or gets a first term grade on his MS project, then his whole life will disintegrate before him.

Now, with the houses gathering again, we're picking up the outer ring road. The bike's an Aprilla, foreign, new (2-stroke, reminds me of my pop cutting our front lawn in summer, kids in the street being Jedis: I imagine my strong but graceless ol' pa replacing the spark plugs. I see him sharpening those blades with a flat file on his bench which never is uncluttered but is always purposeful. I picture the tools he has pinned out on a white peg board which says, wordlessly, out from the shed: "Get a Life, dad!") and Ras can ride. Suddenly now there's a Burger King, a Happy Eater, an F&M Superstore. The road is turning into a highway and the lights have become yellow and there, finally, is the sign for the hospital.

When we pull up into the bike bay Ras, taking off his helmet, says (only half, I believe, to me): "I want to get a big bore piston kit. Then it'll go."

I use an objective establishing shot, wide hard angle, and then tilt (subjectively, into our realm) toward the hospital doors, to move us through the glass. Therefore, my phone is now our eyes and if I catch, to the farthest right, the blue of Ras's sweatshirt I'm giving the sense of us both moving together. The corridor is packed either side with shops and, just to really make my night, each one of them is headed by a gold promo strip, lit from behind, so it seems like I'm flying through the Milky Way. There's everything here from 7-Eleven that sells mostly soft toys, to a (quote) "unisex" hairdresser (Quuaint! Sounds like it's composed by Sonny and Cher), an insurance agent, a florist, of course, and an antique shop (no idea). We take a right at radiology and walk along through the Eye Center, past Dialysis and the Red Cross until we can either take the lift (a choice of seven) to Male II—XI or go straight ahead through Oncology and Immunology. Ras suggests, however, that we take a left and go instead through Accident and Emergency (A&E).

We seem to be off the main route now: the corridors becoming narrower. I can smell metholated spirits, chlorine, Dettol. Nurses in green, and with masks hung around their necks, are replacing nurses in white and there's none at all now in pink. There's a chorus line of cleaners with mops doing a dance number from *The Rocky Horror Picture Show* ("we take a jump to the left. Then a jump to the ri-i-i-i-ight"), led by Dr Frank N. Furter (aka Tim Curry) chewing an ExtraMint and speaking into his mobile. The corridors are lined both sides with stainless steel trolleys. Someone's preparing for launch. *Flesh Gordon. Lost in Space.*

Staying as steady as possible, I duck out from behind my phone to say: "I don't think this is the right way, Ras." But Ras, who is walking ahead now (great over the shoulder shot), only shrugs. His shoulders, narrow and bony, giving the impression of being two CGI arms, cranked up, made of stainless steel, just sharp and hard and pinned there on the pivot of his neck.

We pass Cardiography, all red lights and thick plastic curtains; CCT, REANIMATION (???). And then the corridor turns abruptly. At this point a whole shit load of zombies from Hell appear in front of us, their arms out in front, whistling the tune from the *Bridge Over the River Kwai.* When we turn to run the lights flicker and go out. Now, in inky darkness, the ever-present sound of a heartbeat, growing faster . . . okay, not actually, but suggestively. The first thing Ras does when the corridor ends is say:

"Hey Ciaran, I'm Jack Nicholson in *The Shining*" and he raises his hand over his head as if it's an axe and brings it down on my shoulder.

Wox! We're at the back of this building, overlooking the chimneys and boiler room, ambulance bay and some sort of office block that bears the coat of arms of the university (that is: Sigourney Weaver rampant on a crest of aliens). Ras is talking about the wonders of Science, the kinds of things that are possible in the scientific world with carefully encouraged transformations of certain types of cells, and the new achievements in genetic engineering and the combination of spores of vascular plants, and the complex molecular structure of lipoproteins.

I push through the plastic doors which slap behind me, and the waiting room for Emergency opens up in front us.

It's a nightmare, naturally. There's kids playing house in a broom cupboard opposite called The Fun House, a girl (12 maybe) is crying in the front row, the seats being arranged like this place is a Boeing. A guy with a tattoo on his neck (he's maybe circa 20 years old, hair barbered in a Bavarian crop, eyes like a tortoise, the tattoo looks like the bear in a vice from the album covers of the Super Furry Animals), is holding his left arm across his chest and there's just no doubt it's shattered into two trillion places. He licks his fat lips, looks up at the NO SMOKING signs which wall paper the walls. There's two lushlike nurses bent over trimming the plaster off a kid's arm. Where there isn't victims and mucus there's whole families who look like they come here every day to stock up on quantities of this pure clinical quality borefest.

I prop beside the Coke machine and compose the scene this way:

Crying girl, Furries tattoo, plastic falling from boy's arm, lushlike nurse adjusting her bra (turns out she's got teeth like a keyboard), gorm-free family of three, mother missing, two little girls eating Cheetos, Registration window . . . and now, closing up on STANDARD CHARGES and ITEMS OF IDENTIFICATION REQUIRED.

If you, like the rest of the civilized world, have been re-watching *ER* (except, of course, the episode in which Dr Greene goes AWOL to San Deigo to save his parents, because that is utter dog shit) you'll know that there are more ways to capture the sheer craziness of hospital environments than jump cuts and endless over the shoulder shots. Lens choice is an option, for one thing. I'm only sorry I don't have an Innovision or a Cine Photo Tech because then, with a beak as narrow and full-on as that, I could slip between the Coke machine and the payphone and film the whole shebang in a series of angular cutaways. And a man-lift would be nice, because a high shot would really add much needed weight to the sequence which otherwise, to my mind, has the potential to become too static.

But now the nurse in Registration (she's got badges on her hat, possibly a Gulf War veteran I figure) is calling out: "Hey, what are you doing there?" Followed by, inevitably, something like: "Do you have permission to do that?"

Fortunately, the elevator's opening ahead.

When we're in and the doors close, Ras peers down at the guy on the trolley beside us. There's no elevator noise: just absolute silence. . . . and motion. It's worse than *The Night of the Living Dead*. At least Russell Streiner, who plays the brother and also produced the film, moaned. But this trolley jockey, who must be 85 if he's a day, just stares up at the white cork lift lining and the male nurse with him, no Samuel L. Jackson that's for sure, is wearing headphones and listening to what appears to be the new Celine Dion album.

"Not feeling too well?" I say to the old guy, but he just goes on staring at the lift ceiling.

"Fine," I think. "Have it your way."

Instead of making dialogue in which I'm likely to be the only participant, I point to Ras and motion for him to move in close to the guy. I realize suddenly (and, frankly, I'm surprised) that this is the first time I've directly directed one of the actors in my film and, as if I've just put my finger in the wall socket and something absolutely extraterrestrial has come down the wire to me, I recognize that this might have been a mistake.

"Yes," I say, "Ras. Yes. Good. Now shake the guy's hand."

The guy's hand is buried under a hospital blanket and a sheet tucked in regulation (which no doubt is the handiwork of Tonto here in the green), but I tell Ras not to let that stop him. For a moment, however, it seems like he will not take direction—staring down at the guy with a half-grimace, lip-curling look.

"Ciaran . . ." he starts, questioningly.

But I stop him straight away and I point out that time is money and there is a right way and a wrong way to shoot every scene and sometimes, as an actor, you just have to go with the director's choice, the director's vision.

"Director's rules!" I say.

And though I can tell Ras feels unsure about this, cannot find the motivation, is suffering momentary angst because of this, I reassure him:

"Ras, look, think like you're Russell Streiner."

Being a first rate Horror freak he understands this and it sets him in motion. He reaches beneath the covers and feels about. Ras has a very full mouth, I suddenly notice, considerable teeth, and my phone seems to favor these. Strange how in a great shot an actor's features emerge, strengthen and then bloom. . . . Right, he has the guy's hand, I think.

I say: "Raise it up."

He struggles to make sense of the direction; then, trusting in me, slowly but stylishly follows it.

The old guy is obviously enjoying this. There's a kind of smile spreading across his face, and his feet which, after observation, remind me of Richard Wordsworth's arm in Nigel Kneale's *The Quatermas Experiment,* are kicking out from beneath the covers.

"Hospital," I say, doing my best *Movietone News* voice-over, "is no place for a talented young man. The world, after all, is his oyster. See here, Mr. Ras Bregendahl meets Mr. Walter Goldfaden in a moment when age is no barrier. Walter is on his way to wave goodbye to his kidney stones. It's a long time since Walter was as full of possibility as young Ras, but still here he manages a smile. 'Hang in there Walt,' says Ras, 'we're all rooting for you.' And can't you just see that he means it. That's a boy, Ras. And good luck to you too, Walter."

The elevator reaches our floor. The door splits both in front of us and behind and, as I have the age old problem of not being able to film two alternate actions occurring at once with a single camera, I naturally pause. The choices are pretty plain, but also impossible. I can shelve the rest of the walk with Ras and go instead with Walt. When I go back to Ras therefore (dissolving rather than cutting in this instance in order that the image of Walt is momentarily superimposed on the younger image of Ras and therefore picks up my theme in two parts: life is what you make it, and so on) I will have started an ancillary action featuring 85 year old Walt which I may or may not pick up later. If Walt's still around, that is: an old guy like him.

It's obvious now that I should have invested in a tripod dolly. If I had, I would now have the option of moving out of the lift in a gliding movement resembling (though not imitating, I must point out) Antonioni's penultimate shot in his 1975 stylefest, *The Passenger,* in which the camera passes smoothly through the narrow bars of a window, and does it when rapid zoom from one focal length to another was still experimental.

"Por favour," Ras is singing. "Mucho gusto."

I turn right. We're heading now in the direction of ICU with Ras singing kind of mournfully beneath his breath Sex and Candy by Marcy Playground beside me as I tell him to cheer up and enjoy things, and explain how great that last sequence looked, and quite a number of the nurses, porters and cleaners now passing us and smiling right at me. I don't want to be The Grouch about this but their subjective, intrusive approach, I want to tell them, is not particularly effective and I would rather they went about their business and there was some distance, some objectivity, at this crucial point.

Needless to say, the corridor is causing me no end of headaches and I know that no one will appreciate the effort I'm making to keep this whole thing composed. You simply cannot gauge the strength of an audiences' reaction and even though Ras is now distractedly whispering "O, man, I just think Jeremy Irons in *Dead Ringers* is so fit, you know. I am the biggest fan of Jeremy Irons," I am not necessarily creating *A Clockwork Orange* here or, more accurately, *Dr Mabuse, the Gambler*, but keeping my style entirely realistic and, using the fortuitously arriving non-diegetic sound which now is the sound of an alarm of some kind, a heart monitor or a respirator alarm or something, to add subtext ("life is always only one step away from death," that type of thing) as it's bringing from two plastic doors to the left three nurses (two of them being Nicole Kidman and the other one Olympia Dukakis) scurrying out and disappearing through the plastic doors on the right.

"There," I cry, pointing after them, through the doors which lead to ICU. "In there!"

"Right," says Ras.

I know if Ingrid Bergman were here playing Karen she'd want to take the lead, but having one of the nurses stand in for her is absolutely out of the question, because it is Karen's considerable emotional intensity which is difficult to emulate, her increasingly groovy handle on that forlorn Bergmann strength which would be alienating not only me but half of Southport as well, if not that she performs it so well. So I decide, instead, to play the entrance low key and the emergency at the far end of the room (doctors in white coats and nurses in green diving appropriately through the curtaining which is drawn) allows me to slip in undetected while Ras, who is thinking mostly of *esquites* and *tamales* or of the intrusions of the State Department in Honduran feature film production, or of his waning MS, is checking each cubicle in turn until, finally, as I begin to think I should have gone out to the fun pier to shoot some crazy night action instead, he whispers loudly: "Here!" Here!"

I'm onto this in a flash.

But "Wait!" I whisper. "I want to shoot this as a reaction shot."

"Such a poke!" he whispers loudly, holding the curtain.

There is starkness to the space between the left and right cubicles which suddenly alarms me and I wish momentarily for a pay-to-view TV to be wheeled in showing TV Classics: (a re-re-re-run of *Gilligan's Island* starring Alan Hale jnr as the overweight Skipper and Bob Denver as Gilligan and Tina Louise who was, at the time, extremely fit, as Ginger). Instead, I tell Ras to open the curtains at the count of three and, holding my breath, focus on a spot which should be about ten feet inside the cubicle.

"One," I whisper. "Two . . ."

When, on three, he opens it, I aim straight in there.

I suppose you could say this is not Steve Milroy's best angle. It's remarkable that I can remain so self-composed when I see laid out in front of me the guy who should be helping me produce my film ("the University of Southport will appoint a supervisor who is a specialist in your . . ." dee-dah-dee-dah-dee-dah), last year's Festival of the Waters Film Festival Special Award winner, so absolutely wasted; yet, I give him all the screen time he wants and all he can do in return is drift in and out of consciousness, making movements with his mouth like lost footage from the jewel in the oeuvre of Luc Besson, *The Big Blue,* and with his wrists bandaged right up to his elbows and his head fallen to one side and a bank of equipment behind him like he's orbiting the Earth and he's all frozen up, as wooden as a street sign, not an active movement within ten miles of him, and the steady, metronomic beat of the ECG monitor merely supports this point.

"I'm here . . ." I start.

The guy wakes and looks at me as if he recognizes me.

He draws in a shallow breath. " . . . Nell?" he murmurs.

"No," I say, truthfully. "But keep going . . ."

"Nell," he insists, rejecting the truth I guess. "I didn't mean it, babe."

"O?" I say, hardly equipped to disagree.

"I love . . . err, PVC," he says.

I have no idea whatsoever what he is talking about.

9

It is the year 2018 and society has gotten rid of war and poverty and the only violence left is to be found in corporation-controlled rollerball teams, who fight each other to the full gore finish with spikes and bikes in a sport which is part roller derby, part football and part hockey.

That, in a nutshell, is the premise of Norman Jewison's 1975 UA sports and scifi romp *Rollerball,* starring James Caan as the aging but talented Jonathan E. who has become so popular that the corporate executives want him to retire (played straight by Shane Rimmer: "No one, gentlemen, is bigger than the game."). Caan, however, has no intention of riding off into the sunset and just goes on winning. His performance, to my mind, is almost certainly the model for Schwarzenegger's *Running Man,* made twelve years later on a budget of $24 million, directed by Paul Michael Glaser from a screenplay by Stephen E. deSouza (and set, interestingly enough, in 2017); but Caan's performance is definitely stronger and *The Running Man* works only on the most narrow of action levels.

In *Rollerball* the inciting moment is established even as the titles are rolling and when we return to Caan's apartment where he is watching on the TV (a nice thematic flashback) himself winning the march he has just played, the contrast between the stomping and screeching of the crowd and the absolute silence of his own world simply reiterates the conflict between exterior demand and interior counter-demand which Caan is facing.

"A'you listening?" asks Ras, who is playing an arcade version of Kava: *Air Warrior IV,* holding the joy stick in his right hand and choosing, using the two forward buttons on the left, to equip his ground crew with Space Construction Vehicles, Spider Mines and Vulture tanks. He has a mint Ripple in his pocket and a Diet Coke sitting on the console next to a handful of coins and his bike keys.

"What?" I say. "What? Sorry."

"I said: 'Do you know what Goody is showing tonight?'' Goody Ansel, the projectionist at the Roxy Cinema.

"No," I say, precisely, "What?"

Ras is flying at some speed now through a fine strand of hyperspace. There are purple mountains which change, as he passes them, into the enemy, specifically and significantly Tiberians, who carry axes shaped like pendulums, have heads made of what appears to be arrow-shaped rock and hurl grenades which burst in great orange and red flumes all around him. As he passes certain points on the sky (which has three dimensions and four "location zones") he collects, using a well-placed fire button, a cache of what is registered at the bottom of the screen as Infantry L14A1s with a muzzle velocity of 160m.sec and a rate of fire of 6rpm. Something, somewhere down on the ground is shooting at him, but he avoids the yellow tracers automatically and actually has three hundred thousand points already.

"A Brooke Shields double bill," he says. "Woxy-loxy, hey! Get it?"

He's laughing now, looking sideways up at me. "It's a Brooke Shields double! Man, that's what Goody's gonna run tonight at the Roxy. Nasty, huh? Fook-hit, that guy is crazy. What a prize plum!"

10

Table 4.9 Exposure Adjustment for Low-Speed Filming

Frame Rate	Exposure Change
6	2
7.5	1 2/3
9.5	1 1/3
12	1
15	2/3
19	1/3
24	Normal
25	Normal

I I

I'm heading out later, just phone shooting some filler, some cut-aways, some night light, when I notice Ras's bike go past and catch it in three-quarter profile as it wheels around the corner of West and College, where I'm propped, phone shooting. And I follow.

In the bus, which is empty, the driver is calling back at me: "So, you're a film . . . err, student, huh?"

Reality alert, mister!

"What makes you say that?" I'm saying, slowly, hardly audibly.

So, realizing I'm dissing him, he's getting hot and, with his big head in big close up and my angle made hard by the corner of the glass that should separate him from me but doesn't because he has the glass open in order to talk to his passengers, I guess, to be a friendly guy I guess, and that allows me to catch the green glass edge in the left corner of the frame, and I'm telling him:

"Just keep up with the bike, will y,' bud?"

. . .

"Is that okay, man?" I'm saying, not threateningly really. "That's all I need you to do."

And he's saying, whispering in fact: "Creep kid."

Then, louder, shoving the bus, which is not a big bus but one of those mini-buses that go up and down the escarpment all day, from the university to the town and back again, around the corner of College Road which leads up the escarpment to the university: "Listen, kid, this is my bus."

And: "Look!"

That's him yelling now.

"Get that frigging thing out of my face."

And I'm saying: "This is great. Real nice. All nice. Keep going. This is perfect. Really."

I'm shooting him like my life depends on it because this guy is terrific and, because he's such a natural, I want to say how pleased I am that film is a naturally generative medium, that film generates other ways of seeing things that otherwise no one would know or realize, and I want to say this to this guy, this mini-bus driver whose wife is probably some fat soap-headed mama, whose kids are probably complete shoe-less morons, whose life is probably so incredibly shit, so awful, that I'm changing his life here, that I am generating a new life for him here.

I'm reminded of that terrific scene in *American Pie* when Jodie and Sammie go ape over winning three free weeks of meals at Taco Bell and Kelly says she doesn't know if she could eat that much and Sara says that free food worries her, the concept of free food, and Billy says he doesn't know about that but has anyone tried one of the new chili lemon burritos and Heather says she's tried one and it was magnificent and I feel, thinking on this, my eyes welling up, my throat growing dry, and I tell myself to focus, and I shoot on.

I'm trying to work out why Ras is heading west when the Roxy is east. When the Roxy, because it is this great old cinema down on the beach, because it was built like a century ago down on the seafront so that from the balcony of the Roxy when the films are playing, if you somehow manage to step outside, if you've stepped into, for example, by accident, some dire pic directed by a director like, say, Tarkovsky or Potovsky or someone, and you just have to leave the cinema and step outside, you would see the sea . . . dark and open and wide. While, inside, on the screen, on a good night, a great night, a whole new and wonderful world is expanding.

We pass the Southport halls on the hill where all the USP freshmen have rooms. There's a bunch of them out on the floodlit front lawn and I catch them in the upper right of the frame and they jump and cry out and wave their hands in the air (or, at least, they should). And we pass by Gilvert Hall for women and Smithson Hall for men and The Halls of Montezuma (whatever). And then it's a dark, and the road is narrowing. The next thing I see is what I think is the Maldon Building looming, and then, I think, the Plumpton Building. And I realize, as we pass each of these, that I have no idea whatsoever what happens in these buildings. That, in fact, I have never been to this part of USP which is devoted to Chemistry and Biology and Botany. That it might as well be another world, and the shape of the buildings with their giant stone facades, and the floodlights which beam up at hem and the bus driver dribbling something about how the next stop is pretty much the last stop on this route and . . .

And then Ras disappears.

12

Down along a path which is threaded with yellow light from the windows, it's difficult to make out anything at all. . . . except the bus disappearing behind me. The strange crashing! of the leaves over the lens.

This is almost surreal. Almost avant-garde. A thought which does me no good as I try to work out, for no reason at all, which light streaming across the track is the light of the Maldon Building and which is the light of the Plumpton Building. In fact, this puzzle occupies me long enough that, when I emerge into a courtyard and catch sight of Ras's bike over by two huge yellow dumpsters, I am suitably thoughtful and phone shoot the bike in a long slow zoom which cuts away at the seat where, perhaps, ten, perhaps fifteen minutes ago now Ras was sitting.

That's the thing about light says Leonard Nimoy, who's terrific in *The World's Greatest Mysteries* and *More of World's Greatest Mysteries,* in his low Spock voice, entering my shot in a smooth, loping walk, left, and positioning himself beside a dumpster with his left elbow—because he is so tall, and elegant that way—leaning on the lid and smiling into my phone.

"Light is the child of its origins," he says. "A light generated by a low power source is yellow and deep and gives the impression of being mixed with a kind of sweet cream, while a light sent out on the back of some great electrical surge is white and as hard as brittle as glass. The sensitive emulsion of celluloid picks up the mildest difference in light's intensity or the smallest change in direction. Light, therefore, can rightly be said to contain 'pieces'; and each individual piece, some more intense, some creamier, than others, can thus have visual character, can give real character, to the direction of any scene or situation."

All of which, of course, is true.

So I follow a yellow shaft of it up the building and can see in one of the low lit windows above a guy at a filing cabinet rifling the papers and pausing, and rifling and, in a window opposite, two middle-aged den mothers in white coats, talking about . . . about fiber, about which of them gets the more fiber in their diet than the other one, and whether this makes any difference one day from the next, which of them eats Hi-Fibe, and which New Improved Bran Flakes, whether they will live longer because of it and so on.

When, finally, I manage to drag myself away from this staggeringly riveting conversation ("Yes, but I take three spoonfuls in my milk" . . ."And me. But I even bake it in biscuits" . . ."How wonderful!") Wonderful. I notice a set of stone stairs nearby and carefully bracing myself against the old painted railing, so as not to jerk my phone, descend them until I am below the level of the grounds and the buildings are massive against the night sky and the windows above are like windows in the sky itself, the frames all gone against the black, and the characters once in the frame are floating freely in the air, and I crane down, right down, until, in the distance, I catch sight of Ras.

This is a Vista Shot. At least, if I am to describe it, catch parts of it and edit it together into one whole comprehensible motion picture, an establishing shot, then I like to think it is a Vista Shot, a meeting of things. The walls of the courtyard are made of stones cemented together and the ground is paved in slate chips and my footsteps sound heavy and clumsy on it. Ahead, passed the tangle of cotoneasters and plum trees and pines, there's the hard peak of a glasshouse. Then another. Then another. Then another. Seven glasshouses in total. And stepping down two further stone steps (Am I going into the earth?) they abruptly spread out in a line and, suddenly, I can see, through the cracked opaque glass of the first one, Ras inside.

But what is he doing? Though I go close to the glass and focus deep into the interior I cannot work it out. Ras wandering between the plants that are just crazy huge, their leaves like pillows, their tendrils like snakes, their roots rising up from the thick black soil. The whole place seems to be growing up and out of itself, the walls dripping with moisture, the light white and strong, and that steady weird whirring of something electrical nearby, something completely unfathomable, and Ras there, right in the middle of it. But he is not alone.

I zoom in. Steady. Shoot. There's Monika and Cole and Kevin and Grace and Alice and Colleen and . . . Karen, I think. I think I see Karen. But the impossibility of this, the strangeness of this freezes me entirely and I phone shoot like a fool in a long fixed frame, unable to move or comprehend how awful, how incomplete and crap this all looks.

13

On the bus back, all the seats are empty except for one in which is sitting a guy in a tuxedo whose bow tie hangs loosely hanging around his neck and his collar is undone, a cross between some upper crust poke, Hugh Grant or whoever, and a wedding singer (come to think of it . . .). Seated on the back seat, I let my phone run in lighting mottled by the street lights and, now and then, the blues and greens and reds of the stores.

What Ras was doing with Karen is difficult to understand, and why he hasn't mentioned it makes no sense at all. That Karen was supposed to be, at the time, in my film only makes it worse and with the others there too and Karen seemingly screaming at Kevin, who almost breaks into a fight with Cole while Alice and Colleen sob nearby and Ras, grabbing Monika close to him as she lashes out with her fists, and I get a brief but poignant sense that they're replaying the escape plan scene from *Confessions of a Trickbaby,* but why they would do this, and why they would do this without me, equally escapes me, so the whole thing reeks of something I was not supposed to see and, aware of how bizarre and how cruel that would be, I can't help wondering if Kevin is somehow behind it, being as it is him who most resents what I do and how I do it.

The driver lets me out right on the corner of the Halfmarket and tells me to have a good night. I don't point out to him that it's three in the morning. A mist is rolling in from the sea, pitching up onto the Halfmarket, making ghosts over the potted palms and the pattern of paving which features the crests of the city fathers or something, a fountain further along was erected in celebration of the International Year of Children and spouts water in three thick blades twelve or so feet into the air.

I slip in quietly into the Langford stairwell and tilt my phone upward. I imagine I have the full night's shoot in a canvas bag on my shoulder, along with a suspension ceiling clamp, some wax spray, a roll of double-sided adhesive tape, and a notebook in which I write:

"Tomorrow: collaboration, parallel story."

"Crew?" I write, quickly. "Who?"

Also: "See university regarding more equipment."

Finally: "Find Karen"—underlined in bold hard Claude Van Damme-like strokes—"at all costs."

I should light the terrace hall with at least 200w Inkie spot because the stairwell is barely 40w and the flat itself seems to be lit only by the table lamp which Karen has in the corner by the stereo so that she can both watch TV and read at the same time, but it's late and the possibility is I won't use any of this and I want to watch, before going to bed, the episode of Jerry Springer I DVD-ed this evening in which Jerry is talking to several guys who admit to sleeping regularly with their grandmothers. Jerry, of course, was signed to do a movie (going price: $2 million, which makes him a seventh of Willis and only a tenth of Cruise), produced by Steve Sabler who also produced *Dumb and Dumber*. This I've got to see.

I push the door open smoothly with my foot and follow it immediately into the flat, panning left to right in the direction of the venetians which are open and let in bars of white light from the street. But before I get half way I stop. On the lounge is Duchovny seated upright watching the TV which is tuned, I think, impossibly, to an episode of *The Rockford Files* in which James Garner solves the mystery of three murdered cowgirls in a situation which takes him back to familiar territory and his days as Sheriff Maverick. Stretched along the lounge is someone I think, at first, is Ingrid Bergman but realize quickly it is not. It is Helena. With her arms stretched right up above her head and clasping the thick arm of the chair she is nodding her head into Duchovny's lap from which his cock rises obediently into her mouth.

"Seen Karen?" I say, phone filming in what I suppose is essentially a phone two shot.

I'm thinking this would look better with cyclorama lighting, a 2kW Fresnel on a floor stand and I would like to dub in The Sound of Drums by Kula Shaker. There's a slight sense of Russ Meyer's *Beneath the Valley of the Ultravixens* about it and also, I swear, something of *With Six You Get Egg Roll*. I look at Duchovny, who laughs lightly in the semi-dark, crossed by the light through the venetians, and, much to my surprise, he gives me the thumbs up.

"No," mumbles Helena, but she is not essentially stopping what she is doing and I go around behind the lounge now so that what I am getting is a shot-reverse shot, but from the top down; and now, from the floor up.

"Are you sure," I ask, lying below him on the carpet.

Duchovny, who I must say has always struck me previously as a fairly dour bastard and not the sort of guy I would want to spend the night with, suggests I would do better to take myself over to the kitchen in a cutaway which could have me resurfacing on the other side of the breakfast bar. This works and, picking up on the glow from the TV has a very appropriate '70s feel about it.

"Thanks," I say.

"That's sound," he says, "But Karen's been here . . . and gone"

Helena, continuing, inhaling, exhaling, raises her right hand and, waving slowly, then points towards the door. At which point Duchovny, giving me a smile that would melt a Vulcan's heart, adds: "So maybe you should . . ."

"Yes," I say. "Sure. Uh . . . good luck."

14

The first picture opens something like this: Brooke is standing in full view. She is twenty-two years old, but looks much younger, her naturally blonde lit hair rolling over her shoulders effortlessly, and wet on the ends. She is standing waist deep in seawater wearing what looks like a loin cloth. There is a very full sun in the frame right and a pair of coconut trees tight on the left. The sand of the beach is the color of New Light Spread and the ocean is loaded with cyan, like that blue glass Macy's was importing last season from Israel. From the left, across the beach, enters Christopher Atkins, who is wearing, not surprisingly, a kind of loin cloth. There is, at this point, a fairly strong feeling that the Basil Poledouris score is going to overpower everything, but the music holds off a moment and the sound is only of Brooke and Chris moving through the water, moving toward the beach where an old guy sits by a fishing boat drawn up on the sand, untangling from a fishing net, hundreds of glittering silver fish. The producer-director is Randal Kleiser. The film is shot by Nelson Almendros.

I sit back and open a packet of Maltesers. When the Festival of the Waters Film Festival opens The Roxy will be packed, but tonight it is just about empty—except for a couple in the stalls over yonder who are not, needless to say, watching the film.

three

Pulp Fiction
1994, 149m, Color
Crime/Thriller, R/18
Jersey Films (U.S.)

I

I have made up my mind that I have every right (an obligation, in fact) to include in my film something befitting each and all of my moods, including this one which is not good but instead finds me tugging at my eye teeth as if I can turn myself into Lestat the vampire and suck the whole place dry.

"But why," I'm wondering, "would they do this to me?" (and, cheesing it up in wonder, adding, "when we share a terrace, a sense of purpose, our lives"?)

I am sitting in Candia drinking a straight black Kona Kai while Alec Baldwin, whose brothers Stephen, William and Daniel are nowhere near the actor he is, is sitting close by wearing sunglasses which are definitely not Bausch and Lomb and, would you believe, a red Hawaiian shirt, and picking his way quickly through an Egg Benedict. There's a storm brewing out of the ocean, which looks like Jack Nicholson's mixing it, turning it round and round in Devilishly clever Nicholsonesque swirls, so that the layer below is growing blacker than the layer above and the whole shebang is becoming so heady and rich it could well be a . . . a great chocolate gateaux, maybe, with a genuine guaranteed minimum of 50% cocoa solids. At least, it feels heady enough for that.

Just my luck now, and who should walk in but Kyle (surname irrelevant), a poor man's Ethan Hawke poke-a-like, minor animation student and major ass-hole, who lives downstairs from Karen and I with Fynella (following), who is a brand new house office in general surgery. They enter with Kyle leading and I can see that, although Fynella is undoubtedly the superior and more upwardly un-stupid partner, she is following his lead as he finds a seat in the corner by the fish tank in which there is, among other things, a spiny Australian sea urchin which may or may not be dead.

Before Kyle's even gone to the counter to say "Hi" to the waitress who is not Denise Richards, Fynella has lit an Embassy Light and started talking, fairly loudly in fact, about something she was told during one of her regular frantic calls to Careerline or Lifeline or Helpalongline this morning which proves she is almost certainly going to become a neurosurgeon before she's thirty.

"And," she says, leaning forward somewhat onto her wrists, like a sphinx, "I'm going to use some simple keyhole surgery on both your temples and, drilling in there, find out what makes you tick, Kyle." (Well actually, she doesn't say this exactly; but it requires no leap of imagination on my part to see that the guy is three parts baboon and that his animations, which are largely poor manga leaning imitations of the fantastic work of Ralph Bakshi, would drive anyone over the edge. So there is good reason to believe that this is what she's thinking.)

I have a sudden urge to ask Fynella what she thinks of So, for him, or whether she really prefers men who wear Joop!. Likewise, does she or does she not think the rumor that Pearl Jam's drummer, Jack Irons, is sick with a "mystery illness" really means the band is about to split up? But now she sees me and, ignoring the fact that I'm using the manual focus, she points in my direction and, not taking her eyes off me, in this way signals Kyle and he comes directly over.

"Uncool," he says, with his voice that sounds like a hedge trimmer.

I have no idea what he's talking about so I simply shoot over the mirror top Laminex and in this way split his head completely in two, the reflection on the bottom and his head on top, like a pair of ripe melon halves

"I mean," he says, "what was that with Milroy this morning?"

"I have no idea wha . . ." I begin, but he cuts me off.

"If you think you're going to get any sort of screening at the Festival just because you're a friend of Steve Milroy's, think again Ciaran."

"What?" I try to ask again. "What was that what?"

"You know," he says, as if I haven't even delivered my line at all, "I hate people like you who denigrate film. . . ."

Though maybe what he really says is "I ate peas like glue with a dentist named Phil" and I just transposed his words.

But he then goes on seriously to describe this outrageous scene in which Steve Milroy was at my door earlier this morning with Karen and others—LK, I note, was there—and the great argument that broke out, and how this disturbed his life, not quite getting the point that his telling me this is significantly disturbing mine, though momentarily I don't believe a word of it. Why, for a start, would Leesa Kennedy be at my door? She's not known for being "social." In fact, some people say she is genuinely bizarre. That she spends all her time trying to follow her creepy hippy mother, and . . . well, they just figure she's a creep queen and has no place in our social circle.

I let him slip right out of focus so that his head could be a cauliflower or cabbage for all anyone can tell, and I don't let on that some parts of his story disturb me.

"Do you know . . . err, Nell?" I ask.

He laughs through his prosthetic Ethan Hawke nose and the effect, which is not uninteresting, is to dislodge the calm, Hawke-like exterior and reveal the ranting fool within.

"Whatever!" he grunts. "No."

"Then the plot, in my view," I say loudly, "thickens."

"But let me say this," he continues, unhearing, "Fynella's got registration exams tomorrow so if you could just . . . well, keep your head on, Ciaran."

Then he's gone, back to the table where, no doubt, they're discussing the fors and againsts of that well known Timotei body wash with natural herb extracts versus Corell foaming bath essence with essential oils of ylang ylang and sandalwood, and I'm left with this even greater sense of despair than before as I try and place this dubious piece in the bizarre jigsaw of the last twenty-hours.

I have the feeling that at this moment I would like to show this scene in full as Candia is beginning to fill up with cashiers, in cute black and white pinnies no less, from WalMart, a couple of C-Hair hairdressers drinking Turkish and discussing (no doubt) deep conditioning, some undergrads, a lot of undergrads, saying "Gomez are skank," and "Hey, I've got tonsillitis again." and generally ordering *au lait* (large) and blueberry muffins, a guy who is reading a Disc Emporium catalogue and impersonating Edward Scissorhands, and two fit fans of the Melia Ample Size Collection, fresh from the Solarium (revealing that I am not prejudiced against any woman over a Size 12, only that I consider the rest of the package has got to match and balance and therefore that the shape of someone like, say, Kirstie Alley, whose role in Cheers suited her perfectly but who was seriously overstretched in *Village of the Damned*, is not so bad), and I just want to say:

"Excuse me. Just excuse me, this is my life! My choice! My film!"

Leaving Candia, I go to Supa-Video, which is now open, on the way filming two nuns of some unknown and unknowable order waiting in their long grey habits at the bus-stop, clutching shopping bags from the Circuit City no less. The mind boggles.

Nic Cage, meeting me at the door and pointing at my phone, says:

"Karen's not due in today."

"Figures," I say, "any idea . . ."

And he claims that the last thing he heard was that she was meeting her Professor at the Roxy Cinema which, of course, is either untrue or inaccurate. Yet he plays this absolutely dead pan and, though I have always preferred him in comedy, I can't help thinking that at this moment I'd like to cast him as a child killer in a 160 minute summer release about the Ku Klux Klan, a mass terrorist supermarket food poisoning, and Columbian gun running.

Of course, I'm about as sure of what he is telling me as I am that Karen has been spirited away from me by a phony evangelist driving an all black Audi (pronounced *Owdee*), heading fast in the direction of peninsular which winds away in high shot towards an open and wind-swept black bay . . . while somewhere back in the city a millionaire tobacco planter, Jason Channing, haunted by memories of surviving an appalling plane crash, stands in his office overlooking the city (neons, office lights, mad homebound traffic) and is being told by a cop (who himself is taking pay-offs) that his son is actually an imposter and is truly the offspring of the lethally paranoid mob boss, Joey Bracco, who wanted the kid to grow up straight but now wants him back, while Karen is arriving at the home of downtown jazz musician, Dwight Troy, whose own daughter has been missing for a month after a long session at the Sacchetti Club with a known young S&M kook, Rudy Sheridan, whose hands are delicately manicured and whose connections with silver-haired Senator Clark Addams are . . . and dah-dee-dah-dee-dah-dee-dah . . .

Waiting around until Cage goes back into the storeroom (panning across Self-Help and Exercise, Action and THIS WEEK'S NEW RELEASES) I spot Neve Campbell and ask her:

"Where's David?"

She looks at me like I'm speaking Tibetan, but answers eventually: "Sick."

By this time my head is spinning and, forgetting about trying to find Helena (who I think for a moment might hold the clue to these clandestine meetings), I'm making my way out into the

Halfmarket, shooting anything that gets in my way, feeling the wind thick and wet, and hearing my breathing which the microphone picks up too easily, being electret and unidirectional. And I'm wishing for an electrostatic condenser with a frequency response of between 20,000 and 18,000 Hz and no top loss, attached to a fish pole, which can be equalized and faded, grouped and mastered. I want to mix it and key other sounds into it. I want the bus which is now approaching through the storm, that hangs low over the beach and bellows and grumbles, to sound out its engine above the wind and the rush of people going past under the marble portico of the Serpico Mall and the more distant but not forgettable rattle of rigging of the sailboards and yachts in the harbor to grow louder until the crowd becomes bees prodded and poked from their hive . . . because this week is Freshmens' Week and it is also the week of the opening of the Southport Arts Festival and the Festival of the Waters Film Festival which means the Halfmarket is overflowing with people. This I want the soundtrack to reveal.

I pay too much for the ride to the university but I'm already drowning in a bus which is sinking down below grey and the wipers are shifting rainwater like bulldozers building the road out front as the driver (whose eyes are missing completely from the picture) drives on (toward the mothership).

Expressionism in film is anti-bourgeois. Oblique camera angle. Bizarre settings. Dramatic shadows. Unnatural realities. Distortion. Tyranny. Madness. Death. The Halfmarket gone now and a mist on my lens which no amount of rubbing with tissue will take away. The whole bus smelling of sweaters and coats and the weird way the undergrads are not speaking. Not saying anything. Struck by the sight of the university which is washed over now by so much water that this whole underwater scene is turned into Atlantis and the main building, with its sandstone turrets and endless tracery, its dosserets and capitals, its orders in everything from Corinthian to Tuscan, is a shipwreck, which my phone explores.

In the long green corridor of the university's College of Arts and Sciences everyone is crying. They are bawling their eyes out like they've just watched Demi Moore in *Ghost* for the first time, or their mothers and fathers, best friends and any number of true sage musicians have been hit by the 8.15 from City Central to the North West and died instantly in jumbled meat sandwich, all at the same time. Or, at least, that's what my film is doing to them, being badly affected by the rain on the lens.

I stop and try and raise Karen, but there's no answer. So I try Ras. But his phone rings out and all I can say to myself is, low and slow under my breath:

"Ditto.

"Ditto.

"Ditto.

"Ditto."

I'm wondering what Tommy Lee Jones would do in circumstances like these . . . because he is so established and respectable that, although you could say he is the idol of the *Charlie's Angels* generation, he is made well enough that even his age, which is something like 50, is no restriction from wondering what he would do in these circumstances. More absolutely than Matt Damon, who lacks dramatic range in my view.

I can't help thinking as I'm heading up the stairs: "Oh, there is something about Gwyneth Paltrow which is unavoidably brilliant, isn't there? I mean, her hair is not so perfect and could be thicker, and her face is kind of round which makes her mouth seem thin and her eyes too wide. But that is absolutely not her fault! I don't think they're using the Pan-Stik in the right places or powdering her up properly. Has any Gwyneth Paltrow movie won an Oscar for best make-up, for instance? Just a thought. It's jealousy on the part of the make-up artists and costume designers who leave her with apple cheeks and encourage her to conceal a lot which should be boldly out there. Because of this she is not ever given the BEST DRESSED nod in the Pizzazz column of the

77

National Enquirer, for example. But Gwyneth Paltrow is superb. You'd have to blind not to see it."

2

Some cell phones I've heard a lot about recently:

Audiovox 8410	Kyocera Blade
Audiovox 8610	Kyocera Cyclops
Audiovox 8920T	Kyocera Dorado
Audiovox CMD8900	Kyocera K132
Audiovox FlasherV7	Kyocera K342
Audiovox SMT 5600 I-Mate	Kyocera K9
Audiovox Snapper	Kyocera KX2 Koi
HPC Ty Tn	Kyocera Slider Remix
BenQ-Siemens CF61	Kyocera Slider V5
BenQ-Siemens CL71	Kyocera Strobe
BenQ-Siemens P51	Kyocera Topaz
BenQ-Siemens s81	LG 210
BlackBerry 6230	LG 6070
BlackBerry 6710	LG 6200
BlackBerry 7001i	LG 8100
BlackBerry 7001x	LG A7110
BlackBerry 7500	LG AX355
BlackBerry 8700c	LG ax355
BlackBerry 8707v	LG ax490
BlackBerry Pearl	LG AX5000
BoostMobile i835	Mitsubishi m21i
BoostMobile i875	Mitsubishi m420i
Cingular 2125	Mitsubishi Trium Mondo
Eton glofish x500	Motorola 120t
Handspring Treo 270	Motorola a840
HP iPAQ 6920	Motorola c330 series
HP iPAQ hw6510	Motorola E6
Jam LG 8600	Motorola e1070
Kyocera 2325	Motorola i30x
Kyocera 5135	Motorola Pebl
Kyocera Activ	Motorola RAZX MAX

And that's not even half of it. . . .

3

LK's mother, Heather Rebane, the '60s artist and recently appointed Honorary Fellow of the university's School of Arts, who is incidentally both Kyle's animation supervisor and extremely short, approaches on the stairs in the company of Professor Krotow, and I am struck at this moment that it is patently obvious that at some time in another life, at another time, I have been in a room with Steven Spielberg, right there in the MGM office when he first cast his eyes on the similar sized Zelda Rubinstein, who plays the clairvoyant Tangina in *Poltergeist* (or maybe, just maybe, I read about this meeting somewhere; in *Cine-Magic* maybe), and realizing that with a person like this, with a person with so few star qualities, so little cinema stature and so few future prospects, that she can be anything a director wants or a director needs.

For example, there is no reason to suppose, as Heather Rebane approaches talking to Julian Krotow (who may or may not know where Karen is) about her forthcoming Festival exhibition, which apparently will be her last Southport retrospective, that I have to present her as the four-foot nothing, 50 zot, animator and installation artist, whose '60s *oeuvre* is represented in major private collections in Amsterdam, Tokyo and London, and who just signs her works REBANE. There is no reason, if I so choose, that I can't make her a Jewish Hungarian immigrant arriving in New Jersey on a steamship in 1938, barely alive but dreaming of starting a chain of automatic laundromats named CHINZY-CLEAN. If I want I can turn her into a dwarf Tippi Hedren, a conveniently sized Janet Leigh.

Oh, that would be so Spielberg. So incredibly S.S.! As imprintable as the mud mountain Richard Dreyfuss builds against his family's wishes in his lounge room in *Close Encounters of the Third Kind*. As totally Spielberg as Richard Attenborough's big roaming lizards in *Jurassic Park*.

Man, I can send her Spielberging down the yellow brick road singing "Welcome to Lullaby Land" in thoroughly modern munchkin with Ray Bolger and Bert Lahr nicely typecasting themselves forever beside her. I can Spielberg her into *Forrest Gump* as Mrs. Gump who has a slow, steady love of her dumb son. And though I know these are not his films, not Spielberg productions at all, they are so very Spielberg that this doesn't seem to matter at all.

There's no place like home. There's no place like home. She is, at this point, completely at my Spielberging command.

Krotow is saying something to her, whispering it forcefully so that the strength of his voice breaks through his whispering and he croaks out something which sounds like: "It's getting out of hand, Heather, that's why."

She replies: "Hey, it's not us that are getting out of hand, Julian. We have some developed sense of the real purpose of a liberal education I would have thought. Don't we?"

Him, pacing, almost skipping, ahead of her. She turning to clasp him weirdly by his two hands.

"It's certainly not that we haven't already been pushed to the very limits of the human project for God knows how many years now. Look around you, Julian. The beach has become a nightmare. The town's full of . . . yuppies! You call Southport a creative environment these days? We need you. I need you, Julian."

I don't have time to consider the implications of this; Steve Milroy's door is ajar. I stick my phone in, expecting him, but the room is dark and I don't immediately sight the character in the corner who is ducked down, I might add, behind his desk. Instead, I whip pan to the window and take the colors of Milroy's books with me. Kind of psychedelia. Kind of Grateful Dead. Kind of Monster Magnet or early Bowie (his Stardust period). It's only now that I pick up the person knelt down on the floor and it—I can't tell whether it is man or woman yet—it slowly begins to stand up.

Pointing my phone at its silhouette which is now, because I'm tilting upwards, rising into the frame, I say: "Just slowly . . . raise your hands." Which it, now she (but still not easy to see), immediately begins to do. "Slow. Slow. Great!" This is great.

I can't believe how good this looks. The whole thing is getting better. Better than reality. She is lifting her hands and in them— What's that?—Jesus! She is lifting her hands up and in them there is a knife and now—you won't believe this—it is catching the light coming through the venetians and, even though I am not in possession of a star filter, have not planned this at all and am really getting closer without thinking or planning anything, the knife, that beautiful, moon-shaped knife, that emerging-from-the-dark-of-the-storm knife, that knife of knives—unbelievably!—is glinting.

Absolutely, the knife glinting in the daylight and the striped daylight behind it, and the dust rising from the books all around, and the desk cluttered with letters and books, his book *The Film Revolution* included, and coffee cups from the Cafe-Bar, the low chug of undergrads in the corridor way, way behind now, the rattle of rain against the windows . . .

Stepping slowly out from behind the desk, she is tremendous, stupendous, scene stealing.

"You're looking for Steve, right?" she says.

What I reply turns out to be inaudible.

"Well, he's not here," she says, as the knife somehow turns in mid-shot into her slender reaching hand. "I'm Leesa."

And, for reasons which do not appear clear to me, I run.

4

Morning. 5.00 am. The sun achingly red over the beach. Light like a bloodbath broken open on the promenade and flooding Ti-tanically into the mall. And I'm phone shooting down the Half-market, hanging out the window of a cab doing twenty or more with Ras running in front and everything is going past so fast that I'm not sure I'm getting any of this in the way that I want it or in a way that reveals the real extent of my subject or emphasizes planes of depth or that will bring to the minds of the audience the fact that Karen will not answer the door, even though I know she is in there, in our flat in the terrace, and that she has dead-bolted the door from the inside so that my key will not open it, and that she will only shout at me:

"Go away Ciaran. Go away!"

"You're not being rational, Karen," I shout, generously. "Listen to yourself."

"Ciaran!" she shouts, "I cannot cope with you right now!"

Oh, so it's Vivien Leigh in *A Streetcar Named Desire*, Jodie Foster in *The Accused*, Isidira Vega in *Hurricane Streets*.

But when, even with this kind of simple, direct pleading of the kind so many film-makers have used before, and succeeded, she doesn't answer, then I'm forced to go ahead and reveal to her that Ras has told me this morning that she has agreed to be in another film. That, actually, they have all been working on a project with Professor Krotow and Heather Rebane, which apparently has everything to do with the exhibition that is opening the Arts Festival, and whatever I think I've seen I haven't seen, actually, at all. That Ras would have told me sooner, but he and the others were worried about how I'd take it.

"Well then," she says, after a long, revealing silence from beyond my own door.

"Well, you can't," I say.

"I have to do it," she says, hardly loud enough to register.

"Of course," I say, "you can't."

Still nothing . . .

"Okay, let me follow," I say, "a train of thought. Will this, for instance, lead to employment? No. Will this, for instance, prove that you are capable of acting independently within a limited budget and with few of the usual industrial safety nets, completion guarantees, vertical company integration and so forth, which today's mass media industry provides for its privileged insiders? No. Will you be offered, because of this, a deal by Kevin Smith or any other contemporary director associated with the currently popular new school of American cinema known as New Brutalism? No. Will any moment or mere flash of real fame or actual wealth whatsoever, however, or in any fashion, come your way because of it? No. . . ."

My train of thought lurches powerfully forward, quickly gathers steam, blows its shrill whistle, and soon begins to reveal plainly that the only way anyone ever gets into the film industry these days is through bold, personal achievement and disregard for the kinds of restrictions which the old world of the studio majors once imposed. This, I note, is why we all came here to Southport: to be as bold and as successful as possible. Why is Cole here, for instance, if not that he wants to get a position in a big city museum or something and to spend the rest of his life on pre-paid holidays tracking down and bringing home ancient relics from remote but now conquered ancient civilizations? Like Harrison Ford.

"Something to do with his French parents," I say, tracking the logic. The French love Harrison Ford apparently.

And why is Alice here if not that she seriously believes she will one day solve the problem of inner city homelessness? Why does Kyle persist with those atrocious animations of his, even streams them like King Poke calling cards on his web, if not that he has always had this thing about Walt Disney's wealth, which comes about from finding out that virtually the whole Disney World empire is actually built from the proceeds of one Mickey Mouse cartoon? Why is Monika here—not, of course, to work in Pencils but to capitalize on her natural but sometimes off-putting elegance and mathematical prowess to get a job at BOL, initially in PR, but, with her Southport graduate diploma in tourism and marketing to draw on, soon becoming both their international marketing manager and the driving force behind BOL's future and predictable move into virtual holiday packaging?

"So, you see what I'm saying, Karen? The chance we've got here is your chance to get a real production job and mine to make it too and right now, quite frankly, you're blowing it not just for you but for both of us. . . ."

83

If I hear the TV now going on inside the flat, and pick up the strains of a National Geographic Special on endangered Southern African white bats or White South Africans in danger, and their bats (don't know?), it is only because she is looking for a moment to compose her thoughts, a distraction to lead her back to the obvious significance of what I am saying.

"I love literature," I say, with some feeling. "Books. I love paperbacks. Web-novels. Audio-cassettes. Absolutely all of Elmore Leonard."

"But that doesn't mean," I explain, "that I am unaware of the passage of time. That I can't see that the old world of book culture is giving way to the new world of visual imagery, and that to make it in this world, our world after all, Karen, we have to devote ourselves to exploiting to the fullest extent the truly cinematic experience which is constantly and relentlessly unfolding around us.

"I know you understand that, Karen," I say, into the hard, thick silence.

I suddenly feel very awkwardly, impulsively, that I would somehow like to hurt someone with my camera phone. Not by physically wielding it or anything; nothing so crude. Just, somehow, by how I handle it, its murmur and its focus and its steady undaunted forward cogging movement. Just to over-crank the thing so it so that it slows the action down so much that gradually but inevitably it completely absorbs all that is around it, draws it in, freezes it and slowly but surely dissolves it.

"So, you see," I say, controlling this feeling and rejoining my train, "If you're just trying to please Julian Krotow you're wasting your time. We are the film generation, Karen. Literature is . . . How come there are so many screen adaptations and . . . remakes? Tell me that. Not that I don't appreciate . . . err . . . medievalism. I said before that I see your point about her . . . Joan of Arc's bravery and so forth. Her miraculous . . . visions and . . . greatness. But, as Colleen has pointed out, I just don't get what's so great about Krotow. He seems to me to be . . . well, a bit of a poke, actually."

"Money," she says.

"Money?" I try the door handle but it is still fixed.

As anyone who has watched *Cliffhanger* will tell you, silence truly can be deafening.

"We're broke, Ciaran."

"Fine," I say finally, to fill the void of silence which suddenly we're in; but, instead of Karen answering the TV volume comes up, "the white bat is a stark survivor in this stark African climate, so stark it is, in the stark politics of starkest African . . ." and so on.

"I need the money," she says again, quietly, unseen.

Fine, but hardly unique.

"Just let it go, Ciaran."

And I realize, in an instant, that all of this may have something to do with Helena, who makes such a packet at Lystead and Wishhart, even though she abandoned any thoughts of a serious education, left her place in Langford Terrace to us, rented a place overlooking the Aqua-Park (a Pisces maybe?) and innocently but determinedly began her well-paid Miss Marple job. That Karen, who has entrusted her life to Southport U, taken a loan against her parents, her bank, and her future earnings, can feel in her Joan of Arc thing some obvious cracks forming. This, and perhaps her envy of Helena's Irish family life. I mean that Meryl Streep mother; that Richard Harris father. She sure does have a thang about families, does Karen. But I can't, at this moment, spend time on such a bizarre Hitchcock sequence, with accountants and cops and a vengeful Missy. My film is getting behind schedule and no matter how much I tell her this, how much I plead with her through the door to come out and forget this other waste-of-time college film she will not acknowledge my point of view. She will not participate.

Her attitude stinks.

"Yes," I say sublimely, finally, like a powder keg, slow. "Yes, you're right, if there's one thing no one should do it is wear a yellow fringed dress and tan horsey cowboy boots and a necktie featuring a cow's skull in silver and copper. Or carry a knife. Shoot the breeze with an old Apache. Drive off a cliff. Sing a love song to John Travolta. Eat breakfast in zero-gravity. Hunt for gold in the desert. Adopt a mouse. Bathe in rose petals. Impersonate the President. Become invisible. Front a mob operation. Fall in love with The Devil. Make an alternative life choice and therefore experience an alternative personal reality. Meet your new parents-in-law. Go on the road with a killer. Impersonate a nun. Get involved in kidnapping a rich but mouthy socialite. Attempt a graveyard stand-off with a voodoo doll. Underestimate a dystopian technocrat Artificial Intelligence. Infiltrate the Hong Kong garment market. Try to salvage a small vessel adrift in a remote part of the Pacific. Assume a vampire is an old, unfocused poke.' Write 47 love songs to your ex-lover. Claim to be dead when you're not. . . In a word: be in The Movies."

"Incidentally," I say, "do you think Leesa Kennedy is a bit like Gwyneth Paltrow? I mean, I'm only asking, but it seems to me she might not be as weird as everyone says, you know? That she might have that same tough, cool quality. . . . What do you think?"

5

Green Beans, Chicken, and Cheese soup

(Serves 6) This is a cost effective recipe for a shared house, because everyone can share in the purchase of the chicken, and the rest is made up of things mostly already in the house. Any kind of cheese will do; though if you enjoy those blue cheeses, they're not so good in this dish. Green beans can be purchased in their pods very cheaply at markets or from farmers, if you happen to be in a rural area. Beyond that often cans of these are heavily discounted.

2oz butter
4 medium onions, chopped
I large chicken

1½pt boiling water
4oz of cheese, grated
Black pepper
2fl oz whipped cream
2tbsp olive oil

Cooking Time: 35–40 minutes

1. Heat the butter in a pan. Add the onions and cook on a medium heat for 2 or 3 minutes.
2. Chop the chicken as much as possible. Some people prefer to tear it into strips. Add the chicken to the onions and pour in boiling water. Simmer for 30 minutes.
3. When the chicken is tender, add the cheese, and the black pepper, to suit.
4. Use a food processor, and add the whipped cream, to give the soup a smoothish texture. Ladle into bowls and pour over olive oil before serving.

6

"A tracking shot," I tell myself, plainly, "creates parallactic movement. It is a monumental moment for a film-maker. The smoothness. The concentration. The precision." And though I get the feeling that my voice is a voice in the wilderness, going out into the mall which is weird and misty, gothic, over-stylized, I know that something significant is happening here and that I am making it. I am in charge.

"This right?" the cab driver's shouting over his shoulder at me. "Slow enough for you?"

"Don't speak," I tell him: "Okay? Just drive!" He'll get his money.

I'm passing NEXT, BOZ'S BURGER BAR, COLLINS SHOES, EXCALIBAR, RUFUS FOR MEN, APPLEYARD KIDS CLOTHING, WOOLWORTHS, CENTER COFFEE LOUNGE, KFC, WATERSTONES, GO SPORTZ, THE HEART FOUNDATION, VIRGIN MEGASTORE, THE HALIFAX, RIVER ISLAND CLOTHING, HMV, MCDONALD'S, HABITAT, FOODLAND, RAGWEED, PEPE, PROVOCATEUR'S T-SHIRT, MOTHERCARE.

Ras is running like a heathen. He is absolutely seeded on amytila (suggested), Big reds, Codx, C feed. Feeling guilty for ever having held back that information about what the others are doing, he's running like Godzilla's lumbering hot after him, on his tail, on its tail. The look on his face: it's priceless! But the fact is; it's me that's chasing him. I'm the one who's Godzilla: one monstrous big poke with a camera. I'm working up to something. I figure I can surely build up to it before the garbage trucks come onto the Promenade and into the mall to extract their wire baskets, hose up the vile night puke, the Technicolor spray paint, Burger Bay backfire, vacuum, scrub. I want him to look like, to believe, he will die if he stops running. I want his face, already narrow, like the face of a mantis, pointed to a jaw that now hangs brilliantly open, eyes thin and glass edged, thinking maybe of Honduras, I don't know, building on whatever's driving him to run like this (as if I screen tested him for *Chariots of Fire*). Drugs, guns, helicopters. Could be anything. The audience will appreciate this. I've told him to keep running until now, backed up against the front of RAWBONE, there's nowhere else to go.

"So this is when," I say softly, under my breath, maybe to the driver, maybe to the drunk who is stumbling onto the step of NEW LOOK shouting Christmas Carols at his dog, "the real fun starts."

I phone shoot down the mall past the terrace toward Ras, meeting the molded white seats and brushing past them, the spotlights of shop fronts, tom-peeping into windows full of SFX (I see entire families living entire lives, kids skiing on Mt Bitzo, beach parties, ideal kitchens, double bunks in honey finish with under-storage, Aqua Vacs, Sega, CD midi and mini systems, hi-fi separates, Nicam stereo sound, beautiful stuff, three-way exercise cycles, alpine ski walkers, Beast Wars, Action Man), all in real time, fading against the half light.

Holding my phone against the window frame and, bracing myself against the door, I'm counting down the last five beats . . . until he picks up—I know! I know! He's absolutely Stal-

lone in *Rocky!*—and there, left of frame, postured exactly, shot
from below, to the side, and therefore growing in size, he throws,
no he pitches with both arms over his head, a stone, a garden
stone, which someone has placed at his feet just for this purpose
(I blush with guilt because I cannot tell a lie), at the window of
RAWBONE.

Which explodes.

"Holy shit!" cries the cab driver (on cue).

I tell the guy, naturally: "All part of the show, buddy."

But as this is having no effect I tell him also: "Hang on to you
goolies."

Ras, arms flaying now superbly, jigs from the shop window:
a Bathing Ape camouflage jacket, a pair of orange jeans, some
Wind Bloc fleecy gloves, a Red Oylam swear top, leatherette hat,
a pair of chalk stripe jeans, a red cotton shirt, a denim pencil
skirt, a vintage '70s Rockit t-shirt, a v-neck cotton sweater, a pair
of Silver Rider pants, a satin slip dress, a grey Exco jacket. The
alarm is blaring.

"Go! Go! Go!" I scream; but the cab driver has gone to mush.
So we run for it.

Cue: soundtrack. Cue: Vangelis. Cue: running shorts by Mile-
na Canonero.

I've got 30 full flow minutes of pure adrenaline and Ras,
whose eyes are shining like full moons, isn't finished yet.

"Wox!" he's crying. "You poke. You fooking poke! Extreme!"

My heart is purring like a Corvette.

7

In *Bob and Karen and Ted and Alice* (1969) Karen is played by Natalie Wood. That is, Natalie Wood, the child actress, child star of
Happy Land (1943), *Tomorrow is Forever* (1945), *The Bridge Wore Boots*
(1946), *Miracle on 34th Street* (1947), *No Sad Songs for Me* (1950),
The Blue Veil (1952), *Rebel Without a Cause* (1955) and *A Cry In the
Night* (1956). Born Nastasha Gurdin in 1938, and twice married
to Robert Wagner, she died of "misadventure" while boating.

Karen Channing, on the other hand, was nominated for an Oscar for *Thoroughly Modern Mille* (1967) and is never known to be off duty. Karen Burnett starred in *Chu Chu and the Philly Flash* (1981) but is much better known as a TV comedienne and, quite honestly, is no Buster Keaton. Carole Lombard died in a plane crash but made her name in *Rumba* (1934) and *Nothing Sacred* (1937). Carroll O'Connor, from *Law and Disorder* (1974), is a man.

I'm sitting in El Monkey forking a decent vegetarian Kofta Mabrouma in which the usual mince meat has been replaced by a mixture of soya protein and caraway, and my phone is fixed on the table, just waiting for someone to pass by it, sometimes zooming searchingly, but never moving. Already Kyle, who is working today, has looked at me twice as if he would like to throw me out but as I am eating, have ordered my third Kona Kai coarse grind Turkish, and am not disturbing anyone he can't do a thing. I recognize, also, Eva who is studying for a certificate in . . . necrophilia, embalming, taxidermy and the like, and Piper who spends her winters in a Coke t-shirt and tights jockeying ski lifts up and down remote and snowy mountains in the Pyrennes or somewhere, and Professor Krotow and someone, I think, in a booth over by the Fire Exit, who is definitely Heather Rebane.

I watch the two of them now like a hawk.

Whatever they are saying or doing the lunchtime crowd doesn't notice and I feel it wouldn't hurt at all to let the everyday lives and sounds of ordinary men and women just take over things (ala Jennings, ala Kopple, ala Rouch). Surreal, poetic, montagesque flashes of Krotow and the dwarf artist.

Colleen and Alice and Kevin and Grace have just left (to go to Plexus for the lunch time pick-n-mix salad bar specials) and though I tried my best to open up some kind of positive dialogue between us, to make my case against them as plain and as unadorned as possible, they acted as if they barely knew who I was, would barely acknowledge my phone and me, and chose instead to repeat a version of Karen's previous mantra:

"Please, Ciaran," said Grace, grimacing and squeezing Kevin's hand, "don't hassle us at the moment."

At which point I lost my composure and, breaking out of character, tried to fill in the gaps, all the gaps still left in our lives, the half-formed aspects of things which make up the moments of any young person's day-to-day world as we each move toward finding our true and active place in the poke,' poke,' poke,' dee-dah-dee-dah-dee-dah-dee-dah . . .

"What is it with you, Colleen?" I said, and wheeled out a fact or two about her place in the terrace.

"You have never," I said, corning it up, "been known to reach out to others."

She blushed every weird shade of crimson, but I went on, at first figuratively then more directly. Her arrival being, I said, a fairly "underwhelming" experience for all of us, the burbling disregard of her mustachioed father for the terrace, the chirpy squawks of her lemon-frocked mother, as each carried box upon box up those old Langford stairs. Them dwelling in her "new room" just long enough to leave the scent of Pine-Fresh, test the reception on her own phone, hover at her door filling the stairwell with a nice little story about how Aunt Rhona once camped out on a beach in Bolivia and survived. And then what? How neat you are, Colleen. Who hogs the bathroom on the second landing, complains about sand on the bathmat, pins the shower-curtain up with a hair-clip, orders milk for poke' sake, from the delivery man, and expects us all to guard it? The way she has suspiciously come to know things very quickly around here. The influence she's had over Karen— who did not, incidentally, know what a phallic mother was before she met you or talk about "*jouissance*" or read book about Dinnerstein's problem with Irigaray and decentered flux (who the Hell knows?).

"Nothing seems too messy to make sense to you, Colleen," I said, "and your theories. As to you, Alice . . ." I began.

Kevin, of course, got hot at this point, figuring (rightly, in fact) that he and Grace were next on my list, and so threatened to thump me to death and bury me out back, behind the big dump-ster and an old cardboard cut-out of Iggy Pop that someone from the BOZ store had dumped in the alley. But I didn't let up.

"Kevin," I said. "You are the man. You are the guy. We all know that. You are Tom Cruise."

But we all know likewise, I went on, that it was him and Grace who tried to keep me and Karen out of the terrace. It was them that told Helena that she couldn't give her place to us and, though he'd deny it now, this was because he wanted him and Grace to be the only couple, the only pair in the terrace.

"Oh, bullshit," he said. "What about Kyle and Fynella?" But the way he asked this only confirmed what I was saying.

I said: "They're new. But, okay. Fine. Then tell me who is a climber, who windsurfs, around here?"

"You are our leader and our Champion," I said. "Tom. You are the future father of our children. You . . . You know that."

But as if I had struck some high tight string on his tanned fret-board he then went ballistic, his voice up an octave and a half at least, and he spieled out this terrific speech about responsibility which I'm sorry to say I cannot recall, except in its most rappy parts: " . . . wonder what you gonna do; you don't know what's real or true" and "be a man not a moron; you, Ciaran, are boring" and some ticky line about "pills, pity, the city, responsibility" that seemed to gather up a whole range of his own personal traumas and attach them somehow to me and my film.

It was quite a stand-out thing, and I think it's just a shame he delivered it with a bead of El Monkey's creamy Horseradish Mus-tard bulging like a zit in the right corner of his lips.

Finally: "Then they," he said, looking over at the Professor and the artist and changing tack, "we're going to make some bucks."

"They," I cried, watching that mustard shimmer and shimmy, "what they?"

"Postmodern ar*tees*ts," he said, deadpan man, shooting a glance at Colleen.

With his Tom Cruise eyes he drew in the rest of his harem.

"And then," he said, pulling Grace to his side, "we're going to get on with our lives."

I suddenly felt that this was a moment for them, a defining moment of some kind, and the thought, quite frankly, made me nauseous.

He then joined the others as they shot back, I've got to say, as good as they got. They said I should finish my film and leave them to Hell alone. That if I wanted to stay around the terrace I was going to have to learn to respect their privacy. They said that all this stuff about making a film was just an excuse to distill their problems into something so trite and so crap that it ignored the nature of being part of the new global experience. Kevin did this great monologue on twenty-first century American politics and its influence on the popular cultural icons of our times (?), before adding his weight to the general opinion, expressed first by Grace, supported by Alice, and then echoed by each of the others in turn, that they were no more than my imaginary friends, ghostly inventions with which I peopled my otherwise demented film world—ignoring completely, of course, that it was me, me and my commitment to filming them, who had in fact made their lives flesh and blood.

"Personally I think this whole other project thing just comes about because of your insecurity in what your own individual roles in the world might be," I said as they left.

Whether this ad-lib of mine will have any impact remains to be seen.

8

It is cliché by now to say that we live in a postmodern world, and indeed "postmodern" has become one of the most used, and abused, words in the language. Who has not heard the phrase "that's postmodern" applied to some occurrence in everyday life? And doubtless replied with a knowing look, smile or laugh. Yet it is striking that few people can say with any sense of assurance what the term "postmodern" actually means or involves. Some theorists have suggested that it is as much a mood or attitude of mind as anything else, but one nevertheless wants to know what constitutes that mood or attitude. . . . In a general sense, post-modernism is to be regarded as a rejection of many, if not most, of the cultural certainties on which life in the West has been structured over the last couple of centuries. It has called into question our commitment to cultural "progress" (that economies must continue to grow, the quality of life to keep improving indefinitely, etc), as well as the political systems that have underpinned this belief. Postmodernists often refer to the "Enlightenment project," meaning the liberal humanist ideology that has come to dominate Western culture since the eighteenth century; and ideology that has striven to bring about the emancipation of mankind from economic want and political oppression. In the view of postmodernists this project, laudable though it may have been at one time, has in turn come to oppress humankind, and to force it into certain set ways of thought and action.

(Library Shelf: Short Loan. Sim, Stuart
(ed). *The Icon Critical Dictionary of Postmodern
Thought*, Icon: Cambridge, 1988)

9

I have promised Ras I'd meet him at 1:00 pm at The Roxy where he will introduce me to Goody Ansel whom, he says (though, following the outburst from the others, I'm not sure now whether this is just some weird kind of venom on his part because I've said I really can't say at this point if I will go to Honduras with him, the *albergues,* the *cervezas,* the *cantinas,* the *sangria,* and so forth. The only thing I'm sure about is that I never want a job in Supa-Video:

"Two dozen take outs of *Lorenzo's Oil*," I said. "Man, I would be absolutely barfing.")

Goody Ansel is looking for someone to assist him during the Festival of the Waters Film Festival and because Ras will by that time be somewhere south of San Miguel De Allende looking for all-nite mariachi probably and holding a stone Chihuahua he plans to send home, he is planning to recommend me.

Suddenly, while I'm focusing hard on Julian Krotow and Heather Rebane as they stand up to leave, trying to read their lips which are hidden by the soft brown shadows of the cafe exit, into El Monkey walks Helena and comes straight over to me and says, Irishly, exhaling smoke:

"Mind?"

She is dressed in a silver grey suit and is wearing, I notice not disinterestedly, an antique gold locket and matching earrings, and her lips are painted with a color which I believe is called Paradise Pink, and she seems distracted.

"Any friend of Karen's . . ." I say, and she sits down at my table.

Lighting an MB Light Tar she sits back hard in the seat and tries to get my attention for what is probably only a few minutes but feels like weeks.

Finally she says softly, into her leberknodel (which has now arrived), speaking forward as if her leberknodel is some kind of anchorwoman's desk mike: "Go on then. . . . You got all that, I suppose . . . on film?"

"What?" I say. I am already, mentally, in Supa-Video sorting through twelve dozen bottom-shelvers ranging from *The Age of Innocence* to *Zorba the Greek*. A complete nightmare.

"Julian Krotow," she whispers, inhaling, leaning forward, "and that bitch's mother."

"Doh!" I say, lightly. "Which bitch, sis?"

Exhales. Pan-scans the room. Answers: "Leesa Kennedy."

"O, boy," I say, "there's a twist." Genuinely surprised that she feels this way about Leesa."

"Yeah, well, boom! Ciaran," she says, inhaling, "artist girl is a rock slut, in my view."

I realize she is plumbing for something, but as I am sitting in El Monkey with Jon Avnet, the *Up Close and Personal* director, newly arrived at the table to the left of me and Jennifer Jason Leigh who starred in the new sci-fi thriller, *eXistenZ,* which Cronenberg shot in Toronto only for economic reasons, slipping now into the booth to the right, I just don't want to answer.

I want to say to her that the footage I have of her with David from Supa-Video in her old flat, our flat, is not a final cut. There is so much still to do; a reverse shot of our door in the terrace, for instance. Likewise, I might dissolve her into a picture of Sarah Michelle Gellar because, having viewed the phone rushes so far, as she is going down on Duchovny, I have this truly miraculous vision of her being some kind of vampire slayer and I might just dissolve her, slowly, into that.

Makes sense.

Or, I want to say, alternatively, I might wipe her away, and Duchovny too, and replace them, wiping downwards, with the charge of the Light Brigade. Horses falling. Men screaming. The inevitable heavy clashes of sword against sword. If I want to— and I want her to realize that it is only my sense of responsibility that will prevent me from doing this—I can superimpose the su-perb Kermit riding a bicycle sequence from *The Muppet Movie* on her blowing pink cheeks ("It ain't easy, Helena, being green."). I can create a whole new cause-and-effect in which it is suggested, through the careful insertion of several library shots featuring Robert Duval, that what her scene is really about is the unstoppa-ble power of the wrath of God. I can cut at a rate so deliberate and shocking that she will turn into just one of a dozen related im-ages, one kicking off another, background becoming foreground, sometimes sequential, sometimes not, until it is impossible for anyone to know what came first, what was in the middle, or what came last, to even speculate what has come out of the studio and what has been made on location, to know if she is really there or not. I want her to know this.

She pushes slowly at her leberknodel with her knife, separat-ing the bacon from the liver and both from the potato, but finally decides not to eat it at all, and lights a cigarette.

"I am," she says loudly, exhaling, directly to my phone, "quite serious. About Krotow, I mean."

"O," I say," doing my best Dennis Hopper VO, "why's that sweetie?"

She inhales long and hard on her Light. "Steve," she says (Steve being Steve Milroy I assume), "thinks he's tied up in this arts festival business."

"Well, well," I say, slow and steady as a gun-fighter.

So that's the way things might be going.

"Can we see it?" she asks, Miss Helena Marple.

Alternatively, of course, this whole part of my phone film might also be no more than a collection of stolen sub-plot elements stolen from *Murder, She Wrote* and *Law and Order* and, in truth, Helena is actually a choir girl from Vermont who is travelling around the world on a New English Bible scholarship, working her way through college in the direction of an Archdeaconship in the Church of the Apostle of St Maude Red Mondial Ferrari, who is not one of the Golden Girls but merely a saint whose disciples wear only mauve, refuse to eat eggplants, and believe that speaking during sunrise or sunset is a sign of disrespect for the Earth mother.

Durrrr!

"You know," she says, exhaling, calling for a Viennese which Kyle brings over more quickly than you'd imagine, "I was wondering if Steve had time to talk to you about his films before his . . . trouble."

"Not really," I say, truthfully.

She pauses over her Viennese, pushing gently but persistently on the cinnamon with back of a teaspoon, as if she's trying to drown an insect in the cup.

"Well," she says finally, drinking, "no matter. I would really like to see what you've been filming, Ciaran. . . . . anyway, I mean." Inhales. "Amateur interest, you know?"

Around the international salad bar the crowd, who are all dressed in green and yellow and look like they must certainly be

from The Body Shop, is breaking into a rendition of "We Shall
Overcome".

"I don't know," I say, truthfully. "It's not finished." I'm imagining what Karen would say if she found out I was thinking of
superimposing another woman over her sequences. LK maybe.
Probably. Or, perhaps, of simply replacing her head. Even better:
her head and neck perhaps, with the rest of her remaining, still
acting away unknowingly. What a director's coup!

"L&W might want to buy it," I hear Helena say.

"What?" I have the stupid idea that she has just said: "I want
to buy it." but as this is impossible I don't say a word but instead
imagine the sequence in *Network* in which Faye Dunaway, playing
Diane Christensen, a programming executive at UBS, tells William Holden, who is Max Schumacher, the head of network news,
that she wants to sign Howard Beale, a veteran newsman on the
brink of insanity, played by Peter Finch, to present a weekly show
where the audience "lets it all hang out." Despite Holden's pro-
tests the show goes ahead, and turns out to be a major winner.

"Can I see it?" Helena says again, exhaling, and I hear her perfectly this time. "If I can just see it, chances are that L&W will
probably buy your SD card, Ciaran."

I swear that as I watch through the viewfinder, the space
around her lips begins to quiver, and then glow. A kind of diluted
red.

"Film, actually," I say. "Buy it? How do you mean?"

"For evidence," she says.

Feigning full-blown stupidity, I completely Sean Connery the
line: "Espionage, Miss Marple?"

She leans forward, into center frame, widening her eyes as she
does; eyes which are, incidentally, an Irish green.

"No," she says, inhaling, deadpan, "theft."

I'm thinking: maybe I should include a frame now containing
fetching cameos of Matthew Modine and Denise Richards, whom
I can see sitting two tables down, sharing a couscous.

Perhaps also I should raise my phone up, I should elevate, arc, zoom. It is a matter of getting the composition right; though in post-production a great deal can be corrected. I might make and break continuity, sweeten the audio, juxtapose new words to established shots, disrupt time, alter performance rhythms, tighten transitions, decide what needs post-synchronizing, counterpoint. Only now, inexplicably, Helena's Viennese is beginning to bubble and foam right in front of my phone. It makes its way out of her cup like an incoming sea. The skin around her cheeks is rippling. There are green scales below. And her skin . . . now . . . breaks open. Her forehead begins to transform in a way I can only describe as volcanic. I'm getting all this. Close. Hand-held. I'd say: moody. But unobtrusive. Nice. I shoot her eyebrows emerging like rabbits. Her cheeks are coming alive with cancroids and worms. Her ears sprout long bristles from their now extending tips. There are welts appearing in her scalp which has split open to reveal a primeval swamp-like ooze. Drool-dripping, fang-shooting, black-gummed, her mouth transmogrifies. Her blue tongue flickering. Hissing. Spitting. Yellow-eyed. She screeches.

CUT TO.

10

Next month, next week, next time I get a phone plan, maybe, just maybe, I'll try this model:

The SYNConi x333

by Anthony Barrittz
for Axis.com

The Synconi x333 sports many fine features including: a high volume speakerphone, CONI high speed WIFI data, plane mode and predictive synaptic Bluetooth.

Synconi x333 Specifications and Key Features

Size:
• Weight: 1.3 ounces

- Dimensions: 2.3 x 0.9 x 0.6
- Form Factor: Flip
- Frequency Band(s): 700,1500,1800

Cellular:
- Cell System: GSM
- Downloadable Applications: K2MEMEME

Phone Features:
- Built-in High Volume Speakerphone: yes
- Automated Call transfer: yes
- Caller ID: yes, memorised

Capacity:
- Phone Book Entries: 10000
- Is a USB Mass Storage Device: yes

Main Display:
- 4D Graphic support: yes
- Display: TFT
- High Resolution: 158 x 270

Custom Opportunities:
- Ringtones: choice of 350000 • Customized Graphics: yes

Comms:
- Synaptic Bluetooth: yes
- WAP: WAP 3.0
- Advanced SyncML: yes
- WIFI Data Protocol: CONI, GPRS

More Fun:
- Games: 38
- File Formats: AAAC+, MP3, MPEG4, MPEG4+, WMA, ACC, e-AAC+

Visuals:
- Camera: 5.8-Megapixel
- Camera Options: Super Brightness, Automatic White Balance, Triple Timer, Nightvision mode, Friends shot, 3D Photo effects package
- Streaming High Speed Video: yes
- Film Recorder: yes

Music:
- Sound Enabled: MuSic AAC, MP3+
Fingerfood:

- Predictive texting: yes
- SMS: naturally
- MMS: certainly
- EMS: of course

Simple tools:
- Scientific Calculator: yes
- Your Voice Recorder: yes

Performance:
- Stand-by Time: 630 hours
- Talk Time: 512 minutes
- Battery Type: Li—Ion
- Battery Power: 900 mAh

Other Features:
- Go Flight: yes
- Exercise watch: 5 aerobic modes

(From: http://cells.axis.com/od/synconi/x333s. htm. Last accessed: November 29th 2009)

11

"How much," I ask myself, "is it worth? And do I want to sell? Could I remove a sequence like this and my film still make sense? You would, Helena, have some personal knowledge of these questions. Questions like: would it stand up? Would any film, for that matter?"

But then, if she's right, how can I not? Can I lock it away in a safety deposit box? Send it to an honest LAPD detective? Screen it for a table of mobsters in a private, underground session?

This whole list of possible scenarios start to confuse me and I begin to track back through the scenes, the sequences, the set pieces I've phone filmed to see if back there in the narrative of people and things there's some finer point that I am missing.

This takes some time. The sun kind of shifts up over the beach, hovers over the pavilion which apparently used to be a surfer hang-out years ago but now houses the truly great El Monkey cafe, over the new groyne that protects the yachts in the South-port boat harbor, and the old run of tobacconists and blow shops and Asian Wear Emporiums that hang on pathetically to the end of the real stores. Then drifts down onto the mall, catches the flags of many nations along the Promenade as the wind gladly dies into the early evening and let's them loose, skirts the shops on the beach front as they roll down their shutters, weaves in and out of the neat little pines on the mall, the electronic billboards as they flicker from iron beds to complimentary medicine to the new VW Beetle to posters for the Festival of the Waters, the shoppers as they crash with the shop assistants from clothing stores and cafes and great little flurries of office workers all cold for the day, until gradually, but relentless, it spreads itself in a powdery orange glow along the entire façade of Langford Terrace.

I can't wait to tell Karen.

"Your professor," I'll say, "is a complete thief."

The more I think about this the more excited I get. I put on a copy of Holy Wood (In the Shadow of the Valley of Death) on the old CD player. I put on the TV and turn the sound down to nothing so there's just images. I turn my mobile from "vibrate" to "chime." And I dance around the flat in my *Bicentennial Man* t-shirt and pure black jockeys until the sun finally goes down on the Halfmarket.

12

A film producer does not necessarily have to be a monster. Take Walter Wanger, for example, who produced Victor Fleming's *Joan of Arc.* What a guy! He also produced *Stagecoach, Riot in Cell Block Eleven, Cleopatra,* and *Invasion of the Bodysnatchers,* the original starring Dana Wynter.

A film producer's role is to assemble and administer the necessary funds. The ideal producer is cultivated and intelligent. Also, though the producer provides and, to a large extent, controls the money, the best producers sublimate the impulse to interfere with the artistic identity of the work. The producer's role is solely fiscal. The danger signs that all filmmakers should be wary of are: Impatience with the Film process; An Inability to Listen and Learn from the Filmmaker; A high Level of Distrust; A Drive Toward Micromanagement. Some notable recent examples of first class producers include: Steven A. Jones and Rodney M. Liber (*Wild Things*); Michael Bay, Jerry Bruckheimer, Gale Anne Hurd and Barry H Waldman (*Armageddon*); Bob Weinstein, BJ Rack and Ole Bornedal (*Mimic*).

"You're crazy," says Ras. "Don't sell."

He studies his boots peddling on the step below us.

"Why would you?" he says. "How do you know he's done anything?"

"I don't," I say.

"Anyway," he says, "I hear he's also a filmmaker himself, and a . . . poet. Maybe that other stuff's behind him now."

"A filmmaker? I don't think so. How's so?"

"Well," he says, "he is on the Film Festival Committee."

He lifts his eyes and stares out over the roof tops of Southport.

"Sorry. Sore point, huh?"

"Look," he says, "do you know what I think? (no pause for an answer) I think it's cool, Ciaran—a straight old guy like that into film."

"I don't know," I say, voice noticeably shaky, but Ras seems to miss the intonation.

We're sitting on the high back fire escape of The Roxy. It's six in the evening. Dull. No breeze off the sea. The traffic from the city, stinking like industrial welding, is passing in a slow crawl below us now toward the ring-road which will take them up the hill, away from the Halfmarket, past the gates of the university with its rampant cavalry horses, in greened bronze, and its wrought iron, its o-so-filmable facade of turrets and entablatures, pedants and columns and domical vaults.

"You know," says Ras, pulling him up by the wooden rail to stand on the top step of the fire escape. "It finally happened (no room for a question). My parents are coming up next week."

"That bad?" I say.

"Ain't good."

"What are you going to do?" The place, I figure, for a scenario.

He makes no attempt to answer.

13

Ras and I have counted so far, here on Southport beachfront, in the mid-evening glow, eighteen BMWs, twelve Mercedes (classes:C180 through C280 Elegance, E430, SL500 and CLK230), four older Porsches (one with "lightweight Carrera bolt-ons," Ras tells me), one Nissan 300 ZX (almost vintage), two Honda NSXs and a Replica SVT Cobra. Ras is wearing a black Victorian frock coat and a black Stetson. I'm dressed in a pair of cream Lee Riders that I bought from an "Animals Have Rights Too" shop and a Wonderland bomber jacket that I got for Christmas two years ago.

After a long time, in which I create a visual rhythm resembling a drum solo (which I will, in fact, dub in spectacularly later), using the smooth white columns of the Roxy's Roman colonnade and its lancet arches, Ras continues: "Anyway, about that Krotow thing, do what you think. I'm certainly not going to try and change your mind."

"Well," I say, shrugging my shoulders and acknowledging that bumming around Honduras does not sound so bad, it does not entirely disinterest me, not least of which because Buñuel's *Los Olvidados,* spreading over Honduras like a handwoven blanket, contains the most amazing movement between gritty realism and disorientating surrealism . . . only I can't go. I absolutely can't go because I have to finish my own film.

He lights an Embassy Light Tar.

"Do you realize," he says, "in Honduras life expectancy is just over half that of most mainland American States?"

Fortunately we do not have to wait too much longer. A bicycle made for two, a tandem, sweeping into the car park with a guy of maybe 50?, 45?, on the front seat and nothing but a grocery bag from Wal-Mart on the back tells me Goody, the projectionist, has arrived.

For some reason, back in his prime, which sure hasn't occurred since they invented video, not in the last thirty years, before it became the norm to produce films which contain both authorial dialectics and pure action, his friends (named Jane, Pepper and Wyatt, no doubt) decided to invert his name. So what was in the '60s an Ansel Goodman became a Goodman Ansel and, I'd bet, they still remember the day they turned his world, and theirs, upside down, the day it all made perfect, inverted, sense.

So here he comes: Goodman, Goody, Good. I try to shoot him to reveal this upside of him, but seem to be getting only a slightly built 50 year old guy with, admittedly, a good sense of balance, wearing a Lakers baseball cap, reversed, and having a full set of teeth which appear, though it's really amazing what they can do with dental prosthetics these days, to be mostly his own. He is wearing a long khaki ex-military coat, cheap t-shirt, sneakers. I know he is on the Film Festival committee but I try, largely, to forget this because I want to act natural and I know if I think about it, I won't.

Not smiling, he says: "Been waiting long?"

"No," says Ras, which is an outright lie because we have been here for at least forty minutes and I have twice now phone shot a sequence of the kiosk woman (35, two kids, blue stockings, heavy coat of liquid foundation in honey bronze) going in and out through the glass doors to wash out the Pepsi pump, just so that I can drop these in somewhere later, between shots of geese in formation, flying over a pine forest, and a whole sequence featuring Kevin Costner and Jennifer Anniston changing from lovin' father and daughter to fang-faced bloodsucking vampires (Not!).

"What's with the camcorder?" Goody enquiring as he dismounts the bike, coughing deeply, and locks it to the fire stairs.

As Ras doesn't reply he turns to me and, as he leads us up the whitewashed fire stairs, which are lit by PIR floodlights that ignite as we pass, continues:

"You a shooter?" he says.

I guess he means film-maker.

"That's right," I say.

"You know any of the greats?" he says.

"I . . ."

"The greats," he says, "Cassavetes, Nichols. The greats."

"Oh, sure," I say. Greats?

"Yeah?" His face likes up like a whole pooting firework display. "You involved in this Festival of the Waters gig?"

"Kind of," I say. He doesn't know?

"You want to get involved." A statement.

"I do?"

"You do," he says, finding the keys in his long coat to unlock the Roxy's back door. "If you love the greats. You like Hopper, Warhol, Antonioni? You want to get involved. Speak to Leesa."

"Kennedy?" I ask, unthinking, not pausing.

"Yeah," he says. "Cinema ain't gonna last forever, kid."

"*Easy Rider,*" I say. "Jack Nicholson. That great scene with the coke scoring in the junkyard." LK? I'm thinking.

He lets his spidered eyes spin a web all over my face.

"That's it," he says, finally. "Speak to Leesa; she's our scheduler."

"Sure," I say. "Sure." My God! I'm thinking, is it this simple? This easy?

"Mighty fine," he says, staring me down.

By the time I'm in the projection room I'm thinking: when I finish here I will have a full 36 hours in the can of which about 20 minutes is definitely going to be very usable, very Festival-screenable (but I'm guessing). The stillness is incredible. I absolutely feel all of a sudden like the room is building itself around me, brick by exposed brick. "It's amazing to think that from this, comes that," I say to myself (though I half hear the words come out aloud, and can't be certain they haven't), staring out through projection window toward the screen, across the seats which are low lit because two Asian women are currently vacuuming both them and the carpet, both of which is a deep rich crimson reminiscent of most slippers. Heads down, they vacuum, backwards and forwards where whole families would usually be watching something twee by Disney. Suddenly I'm overcome by the urge to cut to a shot of the African savanna, wildebeests, loping giraffes, or simply desert, hard lit, featuring a dusty Sir David Attenborough, a Knight in a zebra striped "Land Rover," speaking about "nature's poetry" and "what we have done to the great beasts."

Goody leans, coughing a little, back in a deluxe high-back operator's chair, putting both his sneakered feet on an oak and ebony laminated work center which holds an answering machine, a plain paper fax and a Canon compact copier. "Pretty soon," he says, "all this will be gone."

I look at him thinking, for some reason, that he means his legs. Of course: cancer. God, it's cancer, right? The guy is riddled with it. He's been smoking the reed weed for a lifetime and now he's just one great seething, coughing tumor. I don't know if I feel sorry for him or not. Mainly, because he reminds me for some reason of that great character actor, Bruce Dern. Ras fingers the can on which is written *The Real Blonde,* Distributor: Metrodome.

"Digital," says Goody the cancerous projectionist, "that's what," smiling at me directly with his prosthetics shining like stars, "marks the end of cinema."

At this point, and I shouldn't really be surprised considering I've now noticed he is wearing a pedometer sports watch and an engraved copper bangle from Thailand said to cure arthritis, cancerous Goody begins to go into a trance of some sort, saying something about the future of cinema. I am only half listening, because I've decided instead to create what is undoubtedly a unique piece of cinema in which Ras becomes, right before your very eyes, Robert de Niro, having entered the projection room to confront Bruce Dern (sitting where Goody once was, chewing the edges off his lips) about laundered money and some business involving a list of known transsexual Chiefs of Staff. . . but it gets worse. In the cinema itself two escapees from some privately financed scientific facility (underground, naturally), the kind that is currently producing identical twins from the eggs of dead women and the spliff of insane but brilliant astrophysicists, discover the wife and daughter of a Chinese warlord tied up, with, naturally, their throats cut beneath the seats where three young, soon to be famous, band members from the Boston college rock group Putrefaction had been sitting having an argument about whether the guy with the hockey stick in *SubUrbia* actually *was* Ben Affleck. There is a sub-plot, merely hinted at by the photo of Spike Lee, actually not wearing a striped t-shirt, on the wall above Ras/De Niro who is now shaking (his hands, that is: because he has a serious mixed drinks problem), involving basketball, Toyotas and a Central American gang wearing antique brown leather blousons, but the full gist is not a prerequisite for this sequence and I cut quickly back to the action.

Goody stands up. He's pushing open a window way above the car park and, standing below it, he lights a Wilhem II and draws back hard, not making but rather encouraging his coughing.

"Yep," he says, and I realize that he is not only dying but wants to go out with a long speech directed, it seems, at camera:

"Digital's here," he says, staring out the window, smoking his cigar, overacting considerably. "Luminance," he says (the ham!), "and chrominance. They don't record the picture, you know. They record picture information."

"Really?" I say. I am able to shoot his head in the frame of the window and, because the sky is blue, and the window is reflecting him into it, the effect is to predict his death without necessarily saying a word about it.

"Oh, yeah," he says (Peter Fonda), "Digital. Man, you can download it with no quality loss whatsoever. Can you believe that?"

"Incredible." I say.

"Sure it is. No more 35mmm stock. Just a JVC and a datalink and . . . It's the end of cinema as we know it, man! This year'll probably be our last Festival of the Waters."

Playing this for all it is worth, he now turns to Ras.

"For the late show tonight," he says, "I'm screening *Humanoids from the Deep* and *Chopper Chicks in Zombietown*." He flicks his cigar from the window. "Now that, I'm sure, you boys ain't going to miss."

14

Out through the projection window I pan. The Asians are leaving, dragging their vacuums smoothly between the seats and up the crimson aisle, talking about what happened on Open House with Gloria Hunniford this afternoon on which Gloria's guests included two former school teachers who run the electrical appliances in their house entirely on the gas made from chicken shit. "The smell," they said, "is not the issue." Their school subject, apparently, was mathematics. Then the footlights come on. Somewhere behind me Goody has loaded one reel and he's now dragging his cancerous fingers over the can of *The Real Blonde* which he's going to load now for the seven o'clock screening (saying, as he does, that with digital there'll be no loading involved, no film, no anything, it'll simply all "come down the line".

Would it be too much to describe his words falling from him like . . . well, like his life probably? Too bad if it is: I just luuurve melodrama!

"There'll be no nothin'," he says as he loads, thumping and slamming around the projector. "No hands on. No home-grown decisions about what we gonna screen or not screen. No late night free shows. No local reelers. No travelling shows. No kids doing their Halloween fund-raisers. No you write-in type re-runs. No

USP sponsored arthouse. No surfer shows. No college all-nighters. No cheap seats. No great little matinees. No nothin'!"

The first reel starts rolling. Some ads (high production values) for Whoppers, Kenco, Canon Advanced Photo Systems, Cherry Cocktail, Dodge 4x4, Kelloggs Healthwise Bran Flakes, Kronenbourg, Hewlett-Packard, Whiskas, McDonald's Restaurants, Abba-Zaba, BASF, Seaworld Adventure Park, Safe Sex. DVD release trailers following include those for *Matrix 4* (sci-fi action about a computer generated dream) starring Keanu Reeves reprising, *Devil's Agency* (road movie about renegade angels) starring Matt Damon and Linda Fiorentino and *Any Room* football movie) starring Russell Crowe. The usual DVD director's cut bumpf.

With the footlights sliding their light across the cinema floor it's like a city out there, in front of me, and I'm shooting down onto it, strapped to the skids of a Bell helicopter (which is obviously leased just for this purpose), shooting it dark and stylish like Tim Burton shooting *Batman,* my high shot being designed to privilege my audience over my subject, the seats receding toward the front in a neat pattern which is lightly lit with a NO SMOKING sign, grainy on the screen, and now the first takers are slipping into the cinema from somewhere I can't see.

There are some that are coming in because *The Real Blonde* stars Matthew Modine and some who have come because Catherine Keener is in it. Some who consider it might be okay because Daryl Hannah makes an appearance and they have watched *Roxanne* on DVD and haven't quite clicked that it was made over a dozen years ago and things change. Some have read on the boards outside that it's a comedy, and that's got them straight away, and others who perhaps have subscriptions to *Cine Mania,* which gave *The Real Blonde* four stars, describing it as "light but poignant fun," which is a little generous.

I'm thinking that it's time to leave when suddenly I pick up, right of frame, something familiar which doesn't immediately make sense to me but pleases me anyway. Ras is saying something to Goody about passports, about what he might screen at the Festival of the Waters, about Krotow, about Steve Milroy's little death trip.

Meanwhile, I phone track across the window, wishing I was using Panaflex, on the yellow fringed dress that is taking an aisle seat somewhere in the Fs or Gs.

I can see clearly now, and I don't waste any time with introductions but, using the automatic zoom (it is all I have, and that only 18x optical) I zoom in. I follow the line of her forearm on the arm of the chair, not missing one inch, until I am sure that not simply cutting to her close-up is going to kill me, but (very professionally, I might add) I maintain the suspense until I have her face, in profile, in full frame. And then she, with a naturalness bordering on nonchalance, turns towards me.

Knowing her as Leesa Kennedy makes no difference to me at all. Everyone will, by the time she tells the committee she has found a slot for my film when the Festival of the Waters Film Festival opens in a few days, be going absolutely ape because what I have in front of me, as they will see as plain as day, is a perfect Gwyneth Paltrow.

part 2

There are two fundamentals to consider prior to the study of moving pictures. They are: What do we see? How do we see it? There is a big difference between what an audience thinks it sees and what it actually sees.

Roy Thompson, *Grammar of the Shot*

Idealism. *A name given to a group of philosophical theories that have in common the view that what would normally be called "the external world" is somehow created by the mind.*

Antony Flew (ed), *A Dictionary of Philosophy*

one

Donnie Brasco
1997, 127m
Crime/Drama, R/18
Mandalay Entertainment/Baltimore Pictures, (U.S.)

I

One day, I would like to visit Japan, and investigate the cinema of Kurosawa. However, some things about the country concern me. For example, I read the following disturbing information about shoes:

> *Knowing which shoes to wear in a Japanese inn can initially be very confusing, but is a good thing to learn early on. Seeing gaijin take off their shoes as they arrives reassures the inn-keeper that they know what they're doing and will not make some truly awful faux pas like using soap in the bath.*
>
> *When you enter a traditional inn there will be a genkan, a step up from street level, where you remove your shoes and put on slippers. There will usually be a series of pigeonholes where your shoes are stored and a large basket of assorted size slippers for you to select from. In the evening, the slippers will be lined up along the step, waiting for returning guests and new arrivals. In the morning the process is reversed and guests' shoes will be lined up on the street side of the step. The sight of large numbers of waiting slippers is a good clue that an otherwise unidentified (in English at least) building is actually an inn of some type.*

(Library Shelf: Browsing Collection. Taylor. Chris,
Robert Strauss and Tony Wheeler, *Japan: A Lonely
Planet Survival kit*, Lonely Planet: Oakland, 1994)

2

Okay, so here I am in El Monkey with Karen, sitting across the room from the producer of *Honeymoon in Vegas,* Mike Lobell, and David Duchovny who looks as good as ever this evening in a chalk stripe suit with a berry colored twill shirt. Jennifer Jason Leigh and Rupert Everett are here, Joaquin Phoenix and someone who is obviously *A Time to Kill* director, Joel Schumacher, but is trying to remain incognito. Karen is telling me just what a hard time she is having and I am telling her what a hard time I am having making anything out of my film when some people seem so intent on sabotaging it at every opportunity.

"Ciaran," says Karen. "Ciaran," she says, "are you listening?"

Because I have not been listening, because I have other things on my mind such as how I can get the chance to talk to LK about scheduling my film, and what I will have to say to convince her, and whether a show reel would be a good idea and, if so, which section of my film should I use, and should I present it with a treatment plan for the whole film in a neat plastic folder with my name printed boldly in black ink on the top? And whether she is as weird as everyone says?

I am going to shoot this without opting for a wide angle which to me is overused these days in such films as *Deep Impact* and *Godzilla*. But how then am I going to fit in the vast range of stars? And also, what about the cafe which is an ideal place for a murder. In which, if I simply use downlighting, I can suggest a murder will occur. A devious chef, perhaps. Kyle killing customers so that Fynella, his new house surgeon girlfriend, can transplant their body parts into the dead, and bring them back to life. Yes, there are possibilities. Making them both serial poisoners is another option. Everything in a film is open to speculation.

"Ciaran? Ciaran!"

I register now that Karen's voice is raised and I say to myself, privately of course, that I will have to face the fact that what I have here is a considerable problem. To my mind, a problem which is insurmountable because she is not at all engaged with my life, or the possibilities of her own, but only with demands of her degree, the expectations she has, the alternative life she's building beyond my film. And another thing: each day she looks less and less like the real Ingrid Bergman, and seems only able to perform the vague transformational role that all imitative players are forced to perform so that she can leave behind her own ordinary character in order to pick up another, stronger film character. So, the fact is, Karen is literally transforming into a faint ghost of the Ingrid Bergman she once was.

Lighting an MB Light (I wasn't aware she smoked) she picks up her Viennese simultaneously and says:

"I want to talk to you."

"Yes," I say, openly. "What?"

She laughs; not happily I might add. No longer Swedishly. "I don't know."

This seems absolutely pointless and I think for a moment that it might be better to jump cut to the conversation in the corner where Pierce Brosnan and Michele Yeoh are sitting eating a finely sanshoed sashimi from a shared plate, using Japanese black lacquered chopsticks with pearl inserts that click as if they are knitting together international secrets. But then Karen goes on:

"Well, you know, about me."

Now I'm completely thrown. "What are you saying exactly, Ingrid?" I ask, realizing that I have made a mistake, though having no intention of apologizing for it.

"I mean Karen," I say.

"Us," she says, but her voice dissolves into nothing. Sobs. Barely redeemable pieces of dialogue.

Ridiculous as it might sound, I think something from a soundtrack by Randy Edelman might be appropriate at this point. Possibly something like the soundtrack from *Dragonheart* or the haunting melodies of *The Indian in the Cupboard*.

"What?" I ask. "Come on. Tell me, please."

"It's Julian," she says. "I've . . ."

I don't actually direct her to do this, but she has broken down. Weeping. Weeping a weirdly ghostly version of Ingrid Bergman's tears.

3

"Faster will you," I say to the cab driver. "We're paying."

"No matter who's paying," the guy gravels, talentlessly, "I can't exceed the speed limit."

"But you don't understand?" cries Karen.

"Miss?"

"O, nothing," says Karen.

Even though I don't expect anyone, ever, to recognize that the cab driver is De Niro I have advised both Karen and him to play this very straight so I can't help myself when they do it this overblown, unfocused way and I cry out in disgust:

"No! No! No! Cut! . . . Concentration, maybe?

"Let's do it all again."

4

"Faster will you," I say to the cab driver. "We're paying."

"No matter who's paying," he gravels, talentlessly, "I can't exceed the speed limit."

"But you don't understand?" cries Karen.

"Miss?"

"O, nothing," says Karen.

By the time we get to the university it is already seven-thirty and the crowd that is arriving to see The Dandy Warhols is hanging around the Student Union building like a puddle forming around a refrigerator. There are several people I recognize. Students, naturally, and other people from popular TV soaps who are making the move to the big screen and don't mind working cheap. There's a walk on part for Howard Stern, as "The DJ," and Steve Tyler from Aerosmith is playing "Mr Doorman."

"We're probably too late," says Karen. "Who knows. Security, and everything, you know."

"No," I say. "No." I am, voice-off, surprisingly comforting.

As we head up the hill toward the main building with me tilting my phone upwards to get the full gothic effect, I take Karen's hand and stroke it in close up. Her nails are painted Paradise Green. She wears silver rings with aquamarines and amethysts, and one with a turquoise made by the Lakota tribe of Wounded Knee. Her hand is sweating profusely, and the close up I take of it shows that it is uncontrollably twitching. The mysterious other hand (mine, in fact) fills more than two-thirds of the frame and on the index finger there is also a ring (onyx star in 9ct gold, thick-banded) which flickers nicely.

For no explicable reason I think I'll add some history here. Or perhaps because it gives my scene weight and slows it down when, in actual fact, everything is moving so incredibly fast. The main USP building, observable slightly left of frame ahead, was built in 1848 when members of the newly arrived Southport community (fishermen, sea traders, boat-builders, basket weavers and the like) pooled their resources in the interests of higher education. The building is featured as Castle Keep in *Castle Keep* (1969) directed by Sydney Pollack and starring Burt Lancaster. Across its entrance the stone numbers 1.8.4.8 cause shadows which I pick up left of frame and pause on a moment. I tilt towards the top of the tower where, in 1913 (as in *Sergeant York* starring Gary Cooper), a freshman fell to his death after trying what was then called "standing against the sea." I pick up the thick squat wooden door, set just below the ground, where apparently, in the nineteenth century, professors would disappear, making their way to their rooms along secret corridors.

I pause, lift my phone out of my pocket, search through the viewfinder, and set up the shot. In my mind's eye the freshman falls to the pavement beside me, professors in frock coats disappear like dreams through the wooden door.

"Ciaran," says Karen, suddenly pulling me into an alcove of this historical building. "Maybe we shouldn't . . ."

"What?" I say. "What, this time?" I am wondering: did Stuart Rosenberg ever have so much trouble (*Cool Hand Luke*). Did Sam Raimi (*Evil Dead 2: Dead By Dawn*)? Or George Romero (*Monkey Shines: An Experiment in Fear*)?

"We shouldn't go up there," she says. "Maybe, you know . . ."

She bows her head, stepping back into the dark as three black guys pass in the direction of the student union. All three are wearing Orissis wire prescription glasses and collarless four-buttoned jackets.

"No," I say, pulling her into the light which falls down from the floodlights of the Graduates' Lawn. "You have to do this."

Karen begins to weep uncontrollably again.

"My God," I say. "Is this what I get for helping you? Because my ideals are no less high than yours and the sum of our two hearts is no more than the strength of each one. A passionless life is worth nothing. As to your husband . . ." I am, of course, playing the role made famous by Anthony Quinn in *A Walk in the Spring Rain*.

"O, Ciaran!"

"Come," I say, stretching out Anthony Quinn's thick right hand.

As ridiculous as it sounds I am almost happy as we run beneath the portico, beneath the floodlights which light the Graduate's Garden, my garden I guess, our feet in the air, our hearts in our mouths, that type of thing. And in we go into the Griffith Building. Karen as what is left of Ingrid Bergman and me as Anthony Quinn. We go up the stairs at the near end of the English Department, passing History, Modern Languages, Theology and School of Art, its door plastered with stickers of a smiling rat under which it says Vermin (who knows?), until we are on the third floor.

"Shhhhh," says Karen, almost too obviously.

The lights are out but it is not difficult to find Krotow's room whose door is orange and has on it his name in large black lettering and, after all, also has what I think at first is a poster of the creature in *Alien I, II & III* but apparently it has something to do with a conference on Early Modern Martyrs (a meeting of likeminded prize plums, no doubt, sword-swallowers, role-play nasty boys).

Once inside, I reach immediately for the light switch.

This, I've got to tell you, is an absolutely great shot! I'm at the door. Karen, whose sustained and best work in the field of Film Studies has been on women and gender in the later American works of Alfred Hitchcock, is falling back weeping like the Trevi fountain in the corner . . . hard left.

I'm taking very little time with this, though I phone pan slowly enough to reveal that the corner contains also a potted palm and a red pennant from St Hilda's College, Vermont (Let's give a cheer for Ol' S.H.C). Across the room I go. There are several chairs because, as professor, Krotow has been responsible for the supervision of a number of postgraduate theses. Smell the leather (what a pity no one will, the first and last film with Smell-O-Vision being Jack Cardiff's *Scent of Mystery,* released in 1960 and starring Peter Lorre). Observe the copper topped coffee table scattered with copies of the Medieval Studies Review and The Times. By the time I reach his desk I am pleased to find some lighter tones. A blotting desk pad. A computer screen . . . still lit with a screen-saver, lots of little Microsoft signs spinning neatly out into black space. And then—momentarily, briefly, pausing on a reflection in the screen which, between the Microsofts, is indecipherable for the audience but fairly provocative—I zip straight to what is causing it: a stuffed dummy, a kind of scarecrow made of crumpled paper and pillows, dressed in a cheap grey suit, its face drawn on with a thick marker, its hand-less arms stretched out onto the desk, wearing an USP t-shirt stuck with the label:

"The former Professor Krotow."

The effect is very disturbing. Maybe it's the light. Or Karen's sobbing which is turning, I now realize, into a sustained fit of barking laughter.

But I'm not sure I see the joke. The way the arms have been stapled to the white desk blotter, and a paper knife stuck through his chest. He's floating on a puddle of blue ink, which has spilt from the bottle on his desk onto his fine leather chair. The paper knife's handle points toward the foreground; it's weirdly long blade toward the background. Maybe he's being pinned by it to the seat. Regardless, let's just be thankful that the dummy is smiling.

5

Here's a truly excellent cocktail:

Candy Lime Dizzy Dream
Orange-Lime Mint Rum Flavored

1 msr gin
2 msr white rum
4 msr orange juice
2 msr dark rum
1 ½ msr Southern Comfort
2 ½ msr lime juice
50 cl lemonade
2 teaspoons clear honey
6 small sprigs of mint

Making time: 5–7 minutes

Blend in a bowl with a glass full of crushed ice. Mix gently so as not to sink the mint into the drink. Garnish with cherries.

6

I can't seem to stop myself reeling back and forth through the previous scene, pausing to examine portions of it, reeling on, pausing, reeling, until it seems as everyday and ordinary and as un-cliched as my very own life. I even laugh out loud. Maybe from fear, I don't know. Or confusion. Or maybe it's panic. And yet, I can't seem to encourage Ras to put a word in edge ways.

"I have to admit," I say, genuinely rattled, "that I am not sure if it was real or not. If this is real, even," I say.

But to my mind, it would be fair to say that in general terms today's film world has become more real and more empathetic than today's actual world, in my view, on account of fact being stranger than fiction, films being careful to maintain their sense of purpose and logic, life having no real rules, films being wary of alienating their audiences, life getting generally faster and less contemplative, films being faced with fierce competition of non-linear forms such as the net, life likewise being affected by these new forms, films returning to the strength of their inner world, their well-constructed *mise-en-scene,* while life itself . . .

Although I make this speech, and make particular mention of how my work has led me steadily but relentlessly to this conclusion, Ras, for who knows how long now, won't say very much.

He's called Kevin and Alice and Monika and Grace and Cole, tried to raise Karen, but so far can't, and they've been invited to Steve Milroy's place, out of Southport toward the orchards at Roeford, for what he tells me will be a great "mock wake film party" (don't know?), to which I am not, as it turns out, invited. Steve Milroy is coming home now from hospital, apparently.

All I can say, in dazed, hurt return, is: "Ras, it was like in *Dance of the Vampires.*"

I decide that the best way to handle his silence is to refuse to eat my smooth five berry ripple Häagen-Dazs® but as Ras has been working all afternoon at The Roxy he just grabs the pot off the table and, nervously I think, finishes it for me.

"Geez! It was like *Bride of Re-animator?*" I say. "Man, straight through the chest!"

"No," he says eventually, deeply, "that sounds more like *Blue Steel.*"

"*Blue Steel.* Really? Like Jamie Lee Curtis in *Blue Steel?*"

So now I explain how campus security arrived and how they took us "down town," which was actually the security lodge of USP harborside (Oceanography, Marine Science and so forth), the harborside with its corrugated warehouses and cheap toys hanging from cheaper stands, its fun piers aching with arcade machines which crop-haired kids with groovy silver studs in their eyebrows play all night, out over the yellow sea, its stinking fishing boats, and how they forced me to stop filming because they "Didn't want no trouble." and how the whole thing was therefore, he was right, more like *Blue Steel* in which Jamie Lee Curtis plays rookie cop Megan Turner who foils a supermarket robbery, killing the gunman, but whose gun is then taken by Eugene Hunt, an obsessive Wall Street broker, who carves the bullets with Megan's name and sets about on a kill-a-thon while going out with Megan, who thinks she is in love with him. Amir Mokri's cinematography is superb and Kathryn Bigelow, who both directed and wrote the film, has a great sense of style which perhaps her later films, for example Point Break, don't fully show.

"Ciaran, it was just a joke," Ras says. "Karen wanted to prove to you she can still perform, if she wants to. Get it? That she still . . . loves you, I guess, you poke."

"So, do you get it?" I hear Ras ask—rhetorically, as it turns out.

I am in two minds to film him with a shot so long, so weak, that he disappears completely.

"No," I say. "But I get why Barbara Graham did it in *I Want To Live*," I say. "And why Amanda Donoghue does it in *Lair of the White Worm*."

"Yes," he says. "Great."

"Where is he, by the way?" I ask. "Krotow, I mean."

"Don't know." he says. "Getting this exhibition ready, I guess. This Rebane exhibition thing ready, I guess."

"Do you think he's a Roger Corman fan?" I ask, speculating.

"Look," he says, "I don't know. But follow me here."

"Sure," I say.

"What is there to get exactly? It . . . was . . . just . . . a . . . joke."

"Weird that I haven't seen him around lately. Do you think he maybe won a trip to the . . . Maldives or something?"

Because I have no definitive follow up to this and only want to be outside shooting that great scene in which Brandon Lee claws his way out of his own grave one year after he is shot and buried in *The Crow,* which isn't happening except in my imagination but there must be some way I can make it happen. I am thinking: if only I had a tilt plate and a pair of ratchet straps I could mount my phone on that silver grey BMW across the road and take off down university hill shooting every single freshman in sight in a tracking shot that goes right down through the Halfmarket to the beach.

"Or," says Ras, turning a bizarre shade of red, "he's gone because of unfair allegations made against him by the Educational Establishment for violating its principles of order and suppression which oppress the actual opportunities for genuine human interaction which we all aspire to but never actually can hope to reach. Because he is, Ciaran, condemned in his absence of being a threat to the order of a now fatally corrupted notion of a liberal education system which fails to provide for the creative endeavors of each individual regardless of commercial or social worth of those same individuals. So rather than face that, he's . . . gone."

"Maybe," I say.

Ras looks almost serious.

At this point, the scene changes abruptly because Leesa Kennedy walks in through the door.

7

Why do I believe Gwyneth Paltrow is the greatest actress in this world (or any other)? I speculate on the superb possibilities of other worlds, planets, solar systems of giant movie stars.

The answer, or answers, is pretty obvious. For one thing, in the reasonably low-budget rom-com, *Sliding Doors,* she plays Helen, whose life has just taken a turn for the worst because she has lost her job and her boyfriend is behaving like a gimp, when she also manages to miss her train. The film then splits in two. One half follows her life if she had caught the train; and the other half follows her life based on missing the train. Gwyneth plays both roles and absolutely holds the film together with performances which show her ability to make the essential mind-body connection and to keep busy in character despite what I think is Howitt's relatively overbearing direction.

In *Flesh and Bone* she remains totally focused, despite the crazy things that are going on around her. In *Mrs. Parker and the Vicious Circle* she never once over-intellectualizes (this is the story of the Hollywood gossip columnist). In *Moonlight and Valentino* she is, it is agreed, just brilliant. In *The Pallbearer* her ability to adopt mannerisms is absolutely magnificent. In the July 1998 issue (the one with Kim Basinger in that white dress on the cover) *Cine Mania* described her performance as "a small miracle." In *Film On Film* she was listed twice as "the actress most likely to succeed Demi Moore as Hollywood's top female money earner."

And now, acting the role so exactly, perfectly, to all intents and purposes actually becoming the supposed space-cadet Leesa Kennedy. She steps up to the counter and orders: "A Jamaican Blue Mountain."

I waste no time in shooting her head off.

8

The strangest thing happened just now, and I think it is worth rewinding to consider it. Here goes.

Before leaving Plexus because it is getting too boring for words and I have to actually cut three times to a close up of refuse left on the tables—a crumpled packet of LR Brand cigarettes, an Absolut cap, a packet of Fly X rolling papers, a flier for some complementary medicine from a pharmacy that has just opened up around the corner, a used bus ticket, a piece of notepaper with the word "dunno" stamped in big bold letters on it—just to prevent my audience, at this point, from losing interest. Five sublime phone close shots, smash cut together, might just save the sequence. But, just before leaving, Ras suddenly shoots to his feet and, regardless of how ridiculous this makes him look, begins waving across the student union at a bunch of people coming in through the door. They, bizarrely, start waving back. Who are they? I have no idea.

So then Ras is walking over to, well, "greet" them and I'm phone shooting this like something out of a Jimmie Stewart movie (not that I know any by name, thank Christ). But, to be absolutely truthful, it feels like I figure a Jimmie Stewart movie would feel; and Ras fails to see this entirely and just goes on ducking and weaving into this group; until he then decides to bring over to our table. This I cannot believe.

"Hi," says the first one of the group, who turns out, moments later, to be "Diane from Chemistry."

"Gee," says the second, who transforms as we watch into "Dale from Biology."

And so the whole sorry scene pans out, one tedious smiling geekfest after another, until each one of them (order and text of these introductions unimportant) has done their obligatory lines and taken up chairs at our table and are sitting down right in the foreground ordering "a mint ripple, thanks" "a cherry rose meringue," "make mine an *au lait* original," "a cappuccino," "a toffee crisp with raisin/rum" . . .

"So," says Ras, "what's happening?"

At which point Jerome, who is studying Botany, goes on to explain that the "pigmentation test" in which "the full valent growth in each phytochrome" is going fine, particularly the part concerned with "the mesophyll" and, if all runs to plan (he actually says this into his cappuccino!) then by "next week some time, by Rory's calculations"—Rory now smiling dumbly to acknowledge—they will know "where the differentiation lies between the red spectrum in the spongy and red in the palisade parenchyma."

"Wox!" grunts Ras.

"But, you know what?" asks Corey (joking, I think), "there's still no greenstone in the labs."

"You're kiddin' me?" asks Ras.

"I'm not," says Corey.

This exchange striking me as one of the most outrageous I've ever experienced.

At which point, Stowe, who looks a lot like Brendan Fraser, except for his jaw being more heavily defined, and his eyes perhaps a little more narrowly set, says that to his mind if such "morphology studies" work then why shouldn't the university just go ahead and fund a "program in the area."

To which the gathered monkeys all brightly agree; even raise their eyes in my direction to bring me into the conversation.

Only then, and not until then, do they notice that not only do I have no idea, in fact no pooting clue whatsoever, what they are jabbering on about, but that while they have been diving into this great steaming barrel of poke' they're obviously pleased enough to be swimming in I have been building from the remains of a Häagen-Dazs® container, the simply plastic spoon that comes with it, and the three remaining papers I found in the discarded Fly X packet, a kind of cute voodoo doll and I am using the end of the Dazs® spoon, which I have broken into a neat little spear, to impale, and un-pale, my little Dazs® doll on the pile of napkins I've arranged like a bonfire in the middle of the table.

They stare.

Ras laughs, takes a huge slug of his *lait,* and grabs me firmly on my right shoulder.

I whisper close to him: "Who are these people, Ras?"

Only, for some reason, he fails to answer.

9

USP Off-Campus Housing: Tenant Rights and Responsibilities—Some Pertinent Information.

A landlord is obligated to provide the following:

1. Certain protection against the elements (i.e. a roof that does not leak);
2. Plumbing which functions, including sewage disposal;
3. Heating facilities;
4. Well-maintained electrical wiring;
5. Grounds free from rodents, cockroaches, etc.;
6. Garbage receptacles;
7. Stairways and door furniture in good repair;

8. Notice (i.e., 24 hours) to enter the apartment, unless there is an emergency.

The landlord has a certain amount of time to correct any deficiencies. All complaints should be made in writing.

The tenant must:

1. Maintain the premises in a clean state;
2. Dispose of garbage properly;
3. Use electrical and plumbing fixtures responsibly;
4. Keep any person on the premises with permission from wilfully damaging the premises or the facilities;
5. Use the rooms, each for the purpose it was intended;
6. Inform landlord of any changes in the identity of roommates.

> (Library Shelf: University of Southport Student
> Housing, *Off-Campus Housing: Information, 2007*)

10

For over two hours now I have been phone filming LK or Gwyneth Paltrow. For reasons not entirely plain to me I can no longer decide which one. For the moment, it seems not to matter.

I start with Gwyneth, and she ends up Leesa. I start with Leesa and she becomes Gwyneth. And, as the two begin to separate, becoming a kind of blurring Leesa-in-Gwyneth/Gwyneth-in-Leesa which I can barely comprehend except by ignoring whichever of them is momentarily absent from her body and favoring the incumbent, I find myself faced with the weirdest of sensations— like a screen is tearing open in front of me and the world behind it, all its ugly tangled piping, its snaking cabling, the dust and the debris are exposed. What seems to be an entire lifetime of discarded props and moth-eaten costumes, a wardrobe of masks and make-up, acres of plywood facades masquerading as cities, towns, empires, sugar glass windows and rubber walls . . .

For the moment I'd rather not think how to deal with this. More important things are at stake—for example, like tracking to their deep and distant cave the real characters, the private thoughts, the genuine feelings of familiar film stars.

II

She has drunk the following: one Jamaican Blue Mountain espresso; one Kenyan Peaberry caffe latte; one 350 ml Westland Spring carbonated mineral water. And eaten, with that: one vegetarian Sambousek, one freshly made falafel, two genuine Halva. She has called Kyle over twice to ask what the song is playing. In the first instance it was "Sauntry Sly Chic" by Campage Velocet. In the second it was "Crossfader Dominator" by Sniper. She has visited the bathroom once and she has bought a packet of POLO mints. When John Duigan (*Lawn Dogs*) walked in she did not react at all. Nor did she take much notice when Holly Hunter stormed out on what appears to be Jonathan Pryce, though it is difficult to confirm this because he is hiding behind a copy of FHM. She sat through the incident when a guy who I believe works for Eleese Advanced Hair Studio returned his ravigote sauce asking, in a voice too loud and scene-stealing for my liking: "Aren't there are supposed to be boiled artichokes with this?"

The director (that is, to be accurate: me) phone films this with a clear set of commands. First: "Sound!" Then: "Running!" Followed by: "Camera!" After which: "Speed!" Then: "Action!" When the shot is over I say loudly: "Print!"

The cafe freezes. Then, inevitably, I follow her out into the street where, nicely framed by the packed store windows of Argos (several appliances being substantially marked down) and the green glass windows of the Pheasant and Firkin she boards a bus for the city.

Taking a seat at the rear, I shoot her provocatively by manually thumbing each side of the phone lens aperture until the focused area in front of her becomes so absolutely shallow I could paddle in it. An old woman in a seat to the left (bronze haired, skin the color and texture of latex), holding a shopping bag full of pills (Drostanolone, Protripyline, Wintergreen oil, Dexamethasone) leans over and says softly, off-phone, smiling: "My grandson is very interested in telephony." To which I reply, not unfoundedly, and loud enough in case she is hard of hearing:

"Hey, excuse me! What do you think I'm doing here exactly?"

She, pursing her dead blue lips, just stares, her jaw hanging open slackly.

And so I explain: "Well, actually, I'm making a film. If that's alright with you?"

Possibly forcing her bottom lip to jut out as it does over her dentures; she turns back to the window just in time to watch us pass The Roxy, where a poster explains that tonight they are screening a Mario Bava double bill, namely *Dr Goldfoot and the Girl Bombs* and *Knives of the Avenger*. I make a mental note to call Ras.

12

Travelling with the city in front of me and the Halfmarket way behind, the university up on the hill to the right and the beach down below on the left, I am suspiciously pleased, worryingly satisfied. "Had I built this as a set," I say to myself, "I couldn't have built it better."

As I film Leesa, but simply still cannot bring myself to ask if she would even look at my film, that because she is so separate from our group, so independent, she would not even speak to me, never mind schedule my film at the Film Festival, I am imagining what it would be like to actually work with Al Pacino, about how Al Pacino would deal with Karen's little joke.

I am imagining him arriving on the set. He is dressed in a pure black suit. He wears a black polo-neck. His hair is flecked with a silver so hot it swelters. He is wearing the shield of the NYPD.

He says: "Droste. You want I do this . . ." (pulling his hand gun and holding the point of its barrel to Karen's forehead) "Or . . . you want I do like this?" (he re-straps the gun, looks over Karen's head in the direction of his dusty office window and begins, incredibly, to bring tears to his eyes).

I am in two minds to tell him just to "act natural"; but, as Rab-iger says in his book, Directing; this is the worst thing that I could do, so I say instead:

"I appreciate what you're doing for me here, Al. My feelings are that we should go with it."

Al is speaking to Karen. His lips are close to Karen's left ear. Karen begins crying harder. Al is telling her that she is lying. He is saying "You have no rights here, miss. You forwent your rights when you dissed your boyfriend." Though he has left the gun strapped under his arm, it glistens black in the foreground and is noticeably a pearl-handled 45.

"What," he says—dropping down into his worn leather chair which rocks back as he does. He puts his feet up on his desk— "what, Karen, do you want me to do for you? 'cause, you see, now you and me are at that point. I open that door," (indicates frosty glass door to the main PD station) "and I tell that officer outside that you, Karen, are being, let's say, uncooperative, and that, I'm afraid Karen, is it for you. So what can we do about that, Karen?"

He lights a Senator SP Light, draws far deeper than either you or I could ever do and, leaning forward in a blue cloud of his own smoke, offers her one from his packet which, when she shakes her head, he returns happily to his shirt pocket.

Now Karen is pleading. She does this expertly (I guess in a dream anyone can be Ingrid Bergman). She says: "I didn't mean anything by it. I went to see my supervisor. When I got there the door was unlocked. I wanted to talk about my . . . work. About Joan of Arc," she cries." I indicate this with an extreme close up. I give mostly her eyes (noticing, along the way, that they are brown).

"That's all, you know?" she says. "And there he was . . . stuffed!"

She breaks down into the same fit of uncontrollable laughter I left her in outside the USP Security Lodge.

"I thought of playing this great trick on Ciaran," she says, "and everyone said 'why not' because he's just driving everyone in the terrace crazy with this film of is. And so we did but I'm . . . I'm not proud of it."

Al, at the window, stubs his cigarette on the window ledge. Below, in the street, a further complication is arriving. A convertible is pulling up, parking next to a hydrant where three black kids are playing in a rush of water which, because it is so far away, does not register a sound. The car is a Morgan Plus Eight 4.6. In it, unbeknownst to the rest of us until now, is Helena who is either [1] an undercover policewoman [2] somehow reviving her ancient film career [3] dating Al [4] coming to reveal that it really is Julian Krotow who is defrauding the Arts Festival [5] out to buy cigarettes. My film does not give an answer to this; but Al, shaking his head at the city that smokes and browns and vomits outside his window, looks weary when he turns back to my phone.

"Well," he says (making a long, hard sound like a door slamming).

I shoot Al leading Karen to the door. He is more predictable than De Niro but he has more range. Karen is silent, physically and psychologically wasted. She let's herself be cuffed by the officer at the door who reminds me, though it isn't him, of Jack Parlance. Al goes back to his window. The sound of the traffic below can be heard. Horns. Cab drivers shouting. The dull jingle of a '70s busker. I dolly in for a close-up on Al as the door closes, audibly, off camera.

Down in the lock-up the officer who looks like Jack Parlance wants to say something to Karen. He stands at the door of the cell; but, just when it seems he might leave the door open accidently (on purpose) he starts thinking about something in his life (he probably thinks superconsciously that if he doesn't pull off this scene even his sorry career as a two-bit extra will go down the pan). And so he locks the cell door. Bang!

Inside: Karen falls to the stone floor and, lit by the dusty grey light that spins down through the iron grates from the city, grimaces in big close up. And shrieks:

"I didn't mean it, Ciaran!"

DISSOLVE.

13

Things are looking much better when LK gets off the bus. In fact, I would dare to say that I'm confident that what I have so far is not only entertaining but really interesting. She goes down the bus steps and across the road before I follow after her, slightly pissing off the bus driver who must re-open the doors to let me out.

She enters the hospital. I think to myself that the worst thing I could do would be to shoot her through the hospital which will make two full hospital tracking sequences and no one will be interested in that. So instead I follow her quietly, quickly, behind, stopping now and then to compose a disappearing view, over her shoulder, letting her lead me into the elevator where, because I stand behind two pink ladies from the Hospital Auxiliary Association, she doesn't see me.

I swear at one point I pick up in the distance a doctor that looks exactly like Julian Krotow, but as the vision is only momentarily, and does not add a great deal of visual information to what I am after, I ignore it. I have an eye level view of Leesa and record just how strangely attractive she really is. She is absolutely fit. At which point she becomes Gwyneth.

She is wearing a beige textured pile coat, a pair of purple boot-cut jeans, a lilac shirt, and a pair of black Chelsea ankle boots. Her hair is cut to the curve of her shoulders and is, just too perfectly straight. It is blonde (colored that way, perhaps, but fundamentally blonde nevertheless, and dead straight). And yet, it is not only blonde because, with my phone, I pick up the slightest tone of dim auburn. A luminance. Something of a previous color perhaps. And this fact makes her hair, that great hair of hers, even more great.

She gets out on the third floor. Naturally, I follow. I am aware now of two nurses behind me who are wondering what I am doing. Likewise, I realize that if I turn slightly to the left, and tilt slightly downwards, I can film them behind in the glass windows beside me, which are darkened by the night.

They're talking about me. Their conversation goes something along the lines of:

"Hey, maybe he's filming 'Casualty.'"

"Ha! Ha! So where's . . . what's his name again?"

"Who?"

"The one with the eyes, in 'Casualty.'"

When she reaches the plastic swing doors of the Restricted Male Ward I, invariably, CUT. And leave the hospital before the nurses (who turn out, when I quiz them, to be great fans of *Home Improvement,* for poke's sake!) report me to the matron who is, predictably, a one-eyed white-headed Quasimodo.

Down below, in the hospital grounds, the night is made thin by the diffuse yellow lamps of the hospital car park and the queer way I react to it by panning the whole facade with a canted angle. I stretch back on a bench which supports my back and then my elbows and allows me to steady my phone on which I now have, maybe, a 125mm zoom lens. I can make out Steve Milroy in the window of the hospital room above. He is dressed in a white short-sleeved shirt and trousers. Because he uses his hands a lot as he talks it is easy to focus in on the bandages on his wrists which are tight and cream and new. He waves and flaps his way through whatever he is saying. Shouting. Screaming maybe.

Leesa, however, is trying to explain something to him, calmly. Which he, quite obviously, does not understand, or does not wish to understand. And she, sitting on the corner of his hospital bed, her face now and then lowering into her hands, continues. And I'm getting all this.

When she leaves he rushes up to the window and, planting his hands firmly against the glass, screams silently behind it, his mouth wide open, his eyes likewise.

For a second, though it is brief, I'm almost certain he will smash through the glass and, spectacularly audible, jump to his death.

14

How we got here is unimportant. It is morning; but also, it's still night. Through the lens the dark is fading and becoming grey. The grey is spattered with neons and the first whitish rays of something which is not yet the sun. Above, on the promenade, I catch a shot of a milk cart beginning to deliver to the doorways of the stores which are losing their colored night lights to a new inevitable light. In the harbor masts of yachts here for the water festival create a forest of tall thin pine tree shapes which cannot be turned through any angle to a receding composition. I should be cold, but I'm not. The sea is running achingly onto the beach with a soft slapping which I will redouble in post-production. In the background, somewhere back in the Halfmarket, a car goes screeching around a corner playing "No, No, No" by Destiny's Child from its stereo. There are gulls on the rocks of the break-water and on the sand. Fluffing up against the autumn cold which the sea, this morning, seems particularly good at producing, the lower their heads into their feathers and do not seem to notice me. But I am not alone on the beach.

If I could recall the next shot after the crazy crop-duster-chasing-Cary-Grant sequence in *North by Northwest* I would use it. If I had actually seen the film, which I haven't, then maybe there would be something I could use from it; but for the moment my mind has gone absolutely blank and I shoot across the sand by instinct, as the tide going slowly out drags away pebbles to clatter and rattle on the shore and I have a sense that somehow, when we're finished, it will all be alright.

Gwyneth, in perfectly composed medium long shot, stares out to sea. She knows I am here but, like all great actresses, she acts as if there is no camera, as if there is no audience at all. Her face I hold in 3/4 profile. This is classical. Slowly—though not before panning slightly right to reveal her black ankle boots left abandoned on the sand—she begins to wander along the shore-line, her white feet now, firstly, in a slightly lower angle, and now as the camera moves in, padding in the grey water moving in and out over the pebbles which clatter rhythmically. Steadily, out of view, the sun rises and pitches instantly red onto the foreground, and I choose this moment to cut to the promenade above where someone, no more than a shadow beside the bandstand which is old, possibly Victorian, watches her. She begins to walk away along the shore, passing me, gathering the sun around her in a wash of increasing red. The music I hear for this sequence is the haunting "My Heart Will Go On" by Celine Dion.

two

Godzilla
1998, 139m, Color
Science Fiction/Adventure, PG-13
Centropolis Entertainment/Fried Films/Independent
Pictures/Woods Entertainment, (U.S.)

I

Having masturbated pretty solidly for who-knows-how-long this
morning I finally came spectacularly over a scene in which Gwyneth Paltrow sits in El Monkey and, after ordering from the
counter where Kyle is standing in a white food-spattered apron,
begins vigorously eating a vegetarian Sambousek. I am not sure
why this scene made it for me when others, such as the scene in
which she is on the beach without her shoes on, strolling through
the whitewater with her dress tucked up into her sloggis and her
eyes turned dewily up toward the night sky, or the one in which
LK appeared in the dim bookish light of Milroy's office, wearing yellow and carrying what turned out not to be a knife, did
not. But the moment when Gwyneth finishes her Jamaican Blue
Mountain and looks up from the table and, removing her absolutely black Diesel sunglasses, looks hopelessly toward the cafe
counter, and then orders a Halva . . . this really hit right home for
me and I sent a wad flying like a starfighter across the sofa where
it stuck momentarily to the remote's power button before sliding,
neatly, to the carpet.

I then spent the morning comparing shot-by-shot all of the Su-pa-Video sequences, which include one girl who has Neve Camp-bell's eyes, and someone who looks remarkably like Liv Tyler but amateurishly overacts, several guys who are the spitting image of John Cusack I now notice, and Nic, the owner, who I thought was very solid, but somehow fails to convince me on second viewing that he's Nic Cage at all, instead coming over merely as some dour but filthily-monied vid shop proprietor.

I have decided, therefore, that I will reshoot the sequence in which David first appears but this time I will see if I can call around, get Gary Oldman to cameo as the Supa-Video owner, and I will shoot it at night when the prize plums come in looking to rent *The Fisher King* or Bruce Willis in Michael Caton-Jones's lame remake of *The Jackal,* and I'll imagine using a wider lens, maybe 12mm, and move my phone around more, on a curved track.

Now Karen is sitting in the armchair nearest the TV, which is turned off. Sobbing in a fashion which is pretty close to uncon-trollable, she is telling me how has been cautioned by the univer-sity, and must report to the Security Lodge any time she is on campus, until they work out what she was doing in Krotow's of-fice after hours and why she had left there what they are describ-ing as an "effigy."

How ironic!

Though she didn't put it there, but only found it that way, she says, they are saying that she is being included in some kind of overall investigation which the USP Provost is launching into the affairs of "unnamed members" of the College of Arts and Sciences.

The whole nightmare, she says, is unbelievable, and bound to get worse.

As we speak, her parents are flying back from Pyrenees, where they have been . . . err, whitewater rafting. Her mother, who is a production editor at New Idea and traditionally prefers, if the truth be known, to holiday in Prague, is livid. So much for breaking with tradition, I guess. While her father, the Mason in Mason and Hopkins, the wine merchants who have one store in the Half-market and thirty-three more across the country, and apparently once sailed from Portsmouth ME to Reggio on a yawl crewed by Psychology and History undergrads mostly from Menthol College (some tobacco company sponsored frat home no doubt), his old Goober State alma mater, says he plans to take the whole university to court for negligence or neglect or something.

After the Pyrenees they had been planning to drive to Bayonne, where her mother has heard that the frescoes of the fourteen century monasteries are reportedly magnificent. But then Karen's call came and they were forced to abandon their holiday. Luckily her father had not booked a package. But their rental still had three full days free mileage.

Helena, who is dressed in a fashionable caramel suedette suit and looks very focused, lights an MB Light and says these lines: "Get your father to get you some legal representation, Karen. I mean really, you aren't really in any real position to do this yourself."

Sounds real.

I film Karen's reaction in an over-shoulder shot which reveals she is not, needless to say, listening. Regardless, Helena rattles along, an unstoppable, well-dressed train. L&W are passing their findings over tomorrow to "the council," by which I figure she means the local Southport council, who she figures will involve "at least somebody from the police." Police? O, she drops that as casually as she exhales smoke. "Possibly . . ." (?) some flat-footed name I don't catch, perhaps Penrith, "who's scary, you know, but fair." Like a Russian rouletter in a Polanski film no doubt. She rattles on.

The Arts Festival committee is meeting at L&W "on Thursday," except of course that speaking to the Film Festival committee will be impossible. "Did I hear you know Leesa Kennedy, their admin, by the way, Ciaran?" No comment whatsoever on my part.

"Well, anyway, as we can only manage to contact Heather Re-bane, Goodman Ansel, and . . . Steve, and the whole thing in that area," the Film Festival area I guess she means, "seems to revolve around Professor Krotow," and who knows which way things will "fall out" but . . .

She has a great way with words has Helena; I particularly like the bit about how much she considers Bose sound systems combine the best in high performance with elegance and simplicity. Or have I imagined that?

"If you like, Karen" she says, "I can give you a card of someone who is really excellent. A guy I"—exhales—"I know pretty well. I think he'd be great for you. . . ."

But Karen's now genuinely moving sobbing overcomes the soundtrack and I slowly reach out and place my free, left arm around Karen's shoulders, avoiding my phone on my right cheek, but she feels like she's tensing up and I can't make the gesture work, my arm stuck there like a boom gate. Needless to say, I don't believe Helena is thinking of Tom Cruise in *The Firm.*

I would like to light this whole sequence differently but it is mid afternoon and the terrace is slit by a grey light and because Karen called me as soon as she was allowed to I haven't had time to compose anything but have just had to go with no staging and no *mise-en-scene* in a *verite* style which, frankly, I have serious reservations about. I would have much preferred to construct a composite set, with a scrumble-floored laundry, a bathroom wallpapered in a cheap '70s jumbo jet print, a bedroom with a cracked mirror ceiling, but I'm stuck with the flat as it is, and I blame Karen entirely for this, but I can't seem to bring myself to mention it as she sits there will Helena, almost completely inconsolable.

Now below, in the Halfmarket, a parade starts up. Yes, would you believe it? Some crazy parade they've come up with this year for the Festival of the Waters Film Festival in which everyone is dressed up as things to do with the sea. There's a Squidman and a Mermaid, an Octopus, a Seahorse and a Clam and several characters from *Star Trek* including slaphead Stewart, Scotty and

Counselor Deanna Troi, which probably makes no sense, but they are carrying the banner for a new fish place called Voyage, so that explains it. Quite without warning, I remember that today is Saturday and the one o'clock matinee at The Roxy is half price, and even cheaper because they have some pre-festival deal. Today they're showing *Rider On the Rain,* the Charles Bronson vehicle made in France. Tonight it's Cronenberg's *The Fly,* starring Jeff Goldblum and Geena Davis, and I am going to assist in the projection room so I can learn the ropes.

Suddenly Karen, unable to compose herself, sprints, without warning, out of the room and into the bedroom, slamming the door and locking it behind her. Since I have other things on my mind (having resolved in the past few hours to find LK and, if the time seems right, if I can manage to make sense of all this, if my mouth works as it should and my mind matches with some degree of simple but notable explanation, show her some of my film) I don't try and follow her but simply pan over to Helena who's standing by the fish tank, leaning back against the wall, though the fish died who-knows-how long ago, before students started renting in Langford Terrace and the place was a boarding house, before that a custom's house, before that a sand-dune or a primal salt lake or something.

Helena, exhaling smoke into a ring which lassoes her head, says quietly: "I don't think she's going to make it."

"Okay," I say, almost shout actually. "Okay, Helena! This has gone just *toooo* far."

"What?" she asks.

"Well," I say, kind of weirdly hurt on Karen's behalf, "it's obvious you're quoting from *Carrie* and, quite honestly, apart from the inappropriateness of that, I don't think you're doing a very good Piper Laurie."

She seems about to answer my criticism when she changes her mind and, instead, smiles in a way that shows she knows exactly what I'm talking about.

"Ciaran," she says, "if you could name one thing about film—"
she slowly inhales—"one thing that is important to you, what
would it be? . . . One thing."

I pan around the room, think of answering that what I would
want most would be some strong new acting talent, a terrific
new piece of CGI that patches in Elizabeth Hurley's head perfectly onto the body of Kathy Bates, better access to underwater
facilities so that I can reshoot the discovery scene from *The Abyss*
and leave out the poke' floating alien butterflies, an Aimee Mann
music video filmed on set. But the urge subsides and I ask, tentatively: "One thing?"

There's an energy which Helena exudes through the camera
lens which is not unexciting. She reminds me of a young Janet
Leigh. Of Janet Leigh in *Psycho* (the blood in the shower, by the
way, was actually chocolate sauce). She is shorter than average,
being maybe 5'1," and her thinnish bobbed hair is nothing to rave
about, but it catches the dim light at certain times and, in this
way, emphasizes that it is blonde. As it turns out, she doesn't so
much fill a frame as steal it. I'm half convinced I should shoot
her in more green that than this, that she would look better in a
green which has something of yellow in it, a limey green or a tint
of olive. But I don't dare go and find a phone filter and break her
momentum:

"One thing," she says, exhaling.

"I believe lights are important," I say, finally. "Lighting, I guess.
A 650 watt open-faced flood. Maybe the Lowell Tota-Light, 800
watt. . . . The Arriflex BL III. The reasonable pricing of a few
thousand feet of Kodak 500 ASA High Speed color film. The
coolness of a pair of geared head mounts. The doorway dolly."

The list seems long, but practical.

She strides into the laminated kitchenette and, asking me if
I want a Tanzanian Kilmanjaro, which Karen keeps always on
hand, says quietly in my direction: "But one thing," she says.

"No," she says, noticing maybe that I'm not following, not getting this at all, "really. Lights, you said? I think that's great." What

she means by this is not apparent. "But what I was thinking of was . . ."

"One thing?" I ask.

"Yes," she says. "Exactly."

"O, I don't know," I say, letting my mind wander. "The way film is a . . . bridge . . . to other experiences, I guess. Experiences you would not otherwise ever have."

"Yes," she says, her face disappearing in a cloud of smoke, dreamily. "Yes, that's it. That's how I feel too."

"But, hey," I say, checking my watch, "I actually can't do coffee now. I got to be at El Monkey in ten minutes."

She stops what she's doing. "Just a second," she says. "Tell me: what has Karen told you about what Julian Krotow and Heather Rebane have been working on?"

"Sculptures," I say, truthfully.

She exhales rapidly. "Right," she says.

2

Spiced Salmon with Lentil Salad and Sweetcorn Dip

(Serves 4) This recipe speaks, glorifically, for itself.

10oz fillet Salmon
Black pepper
1 tbsp olive oil
1 tbsp butter
1 tbsp olive oil
1 red onion
1 red pepper, chopped
2 tsp coriander seeds
1 tsp turmeric
4 cloves
3 shallots
½ green chilli
1 tbsp raisins
1 tbsp pine nuts
3 tomatoes—medium
14 tbsp lentils
2 tbsp chopped fresh coriander leaves
3 tbsp brown sugar

2 tbsp honey
½ pint water
5oz sweetcorn kernels
4 tbsp yogurt

Cooking Time: 50–60 minutes

1. Season the salmon with black pepper. Heat the olive oil in a frying pan, until bubbling. Then add the fish, and fry for 5–8 minutes, turning occasionally.
2. Heat the olive oil in another frying pan, add the red onion and the lentils and fry for 2–3 minutes. Sprinkle in coriander seeds, turmeric, cloves and shallots.
4. Add the raisins, pine nuts and tomatoes to the lentil spice mix and cook for another 4–5 minutes. .
5. Let the lentils and spice mix sit for 30 minutes in a bowl in a cool place.
6. Mix the brown sugar, honey and water in a pan 10 minutes. Stir in the sweetcorn.
7. To serve, spoon yoghurt onto a plate, place the salmon on top, then the lentil salad mix, and then pour on the sweetcorn dip.

3

Ras thinks I'm crazy, and actually doesn't want to hear about it. He's reached out and taken hold of the sleeve of my jacket and, ignoring the no doubt space cadet overtones of the look I'm giving him, is holding me here against the retaining wall. He says:

"For one thing, Ciaran, someone's probably watching. They got building security or something, I bet."

"For another thing," he says, "the guy is a friend of Goody's, right?"

"For a third thing," he says, "I heard he's a good guy."

I'm watching him watch the balconies of the block like a honeycomb of beach towels and palms above us: "You heard where?" I say. "That's not it."

"It is," he says. "I heard."

"No," I say, arranging my breathing into a slow and steady pattern. "What exactly is your problem, Ras?"

We're standing out in front of Krotow's apartment which is in a block called Seaview right up on the front of the escarpment, overlooking the beach. I have explained to him how before I left the terrace Helena told me her ideas about Krotow, based on her feelings and "some of things she's found out" I explain. That he is, quite frankly, not just a thief but a guy who seduces his female students. "A freaky old letch," I note. And that if Helena knows anything about Karen then she knows that Karen would simply try to bury this because she is under some pressure with her . . . well, research, and so on. "As David from Supa-Video has confirmed," Helena says (!). Karen having now missed three whole days there and is standing, it looks like, to lose her job. And really this is hardly the right way to deal with it, is it? That she suspects, because they work together and Krotow is his superior, that whatever the freak's caught up with Heather Rebane is the reason for Steve Milroy's trouble which, she says, might well be about to ruin a terrific career.

"As a film-maker," she said.

Because I can imagine just exactly what is going through Karen's mind, with her parents flying home now and this crazy medieval literature, and having been completely sucked-in by a freak like this, and as Ras is heading out down to coast for this mock wake film party of Steve Milroy's then it makes sense to at least satisfy my curiosity which, I explain, is in some part surely supported by the facts Helena has presented, or at least to see if any of it makes any sense at all.

"In which case," I say, "he's either home or he's not. And you ask him. Confront him, I mean. And we shoot what he says. And that's it."

"Anyway," I say, "I can always ask about screening my film at the Festival."

4

Julian Krotow's apartment is in an apartment block along a street of similar white apartment blocks and his apartment is on the seventh floor.

I can't exactly see which one is his but, using the phone zoom, I have counted seven stories and I can scan the floor, the general area where he spends his time, wearing black Japanese slip-ons I'd say, a blue silk happy coat patterned with orange blossoms probably, twill shorts, brogues, and listening to . . . Van Morrison! I'm guessing.

"Aren't you wondering about this Arts Festival shit," I ask Ras, focusing on the apartment doors which are between two neat little firs, and unguarded, "just a little?"

"Hey, I can watch it on local TV," he whispers, loudly.

"But, given that the guy is a sleaze-bucket, don't you feel an obligation to do this for Karen?"

He looks into the road where his bike is parked behind a pick-up truck.

"I ain't coming," he heaves. "I don't care what you say, Ciaran. I am *not* coming."

5

Cut to: I am making my way up the fire escape from the sixth to the seventh floor and—you guessed it—Ras is with me.

"Fook-hit!" he is saying, beneath his breath. Whatever he's thinking, he looks great in shallow phone focus against the blue backdrop of the beach and the sea below.

On the seventh floor all is pretty quiet. The corridor is long, dog-legging at half way. A TV somewhere is playing what sounds like a repeat of '80s cop show *Hill Street Blues*. I have no idea which episode and, even though I've seen them all more than once, can't seem to get interested in thinking about it. The carpet being a low pile is allowing me to glide effortlessly and silently over it, while not forgetting to shoot each one of the apartment doors so that the threatening notion that one of them could open at any minute and reveal something (?) is strong in everyone's mind.

When, suddenly, the sound of a door opening is heard I freeze. But hear, simultaneously ahead, the elevator on its way.

Seconds pass, seem like hours. I cut momentarily to Ras who is doing a great: "Wox! What are we doing here?" expression.

The lift arrives. I move forward. But maybe I'm too eager. Maybe I should have waited, because as I come round the corner I shoot a full side profile of a guy with spookily dark hair in the style of Iron Maiden or some '70s heavy metal band and I think I recognize him, bizarrely, as Steve Milroy. Or, at very least, I make this bizarre link myself.

Carrying a Nike duffle bag, he pauses. I count off the beats . . . one . . . at . . . a . . . time.

He steps into the elevator. We hurry on.

I thoroughly intend to jimmy the lock to the freak's apartment, if he's not home. Deftly. Though I haven't told Ras this, and don't intend to. I will "let my Visa card do the talking" as some ad, somewhere, sometime said. I suppose I could put it better, re-write the scenario, come up with something original. But the ol' Visa-card jimmy is basically what I have in mind. The literalness of the business works for me until . . . when, letting my camera phone ride against my right cheek as I lean down with the card in my fingers to do it, I tentatively turn the freak's door handle, and nothing stops me. The thing turns. The professor's door swings silently, smoothly open.

Ras, fearing that someone is at home (Sean Connery, maybe, reading some stolen, secret documents while Q waits in the corner), backs away. But I—shooting now at an upward angle of about 35%—step on in, enquiring, ridiculously, if anyone is home.

"Hello?" Pure sweet corn.

You'd be right to say I don't actually want to invade the freak's privacy, particularly as Ras could be on the money about this building's security, but I'm calling out and not getting any answer and I know this is not coming over at all well because I need some reason for going further into the place, some obvious motivation from the world around me. And it isn't coming.

It strikes me suddenly that, despite the ideal set-up here, the preternatural filmic qualities of the thing, I have not acted in any way like Detective Frank Sinatra. I haven't acted like Lieutenant Gene Hackman either. Not like Bruce Willis or even Chow Yun-Fat. No voice-over has announced my intentions, no close-up has caught me cocking my gun, and no change has occurred in the quiet, ticking soundtrack accompanying me.

I am, therefore, seemingly without any identifiable point of reference as I step into the apartment and I don't recall, in recent times, feeling like this. It is an odd sensation, this free-falling thing, my head kind of light, my eyes weirdly shifting back and forth, my limbs kind of following their beams of sight, loosely attached to whatever body is mine in this strange half-light. I want to cry out, all of a sudden, let loose some bark or squeal and, in doing so, fill the room with a team of activity, with light and with sound. A film set of movement and industry. But the urge, once arriving, is just as soon departing and I simply stand there, drift there, wondering what to do next, how to act. No doubt, I could shoot a view of the ocean from the windows if I could see it beyond the closed slim-line venetians, the place being lit with lamps that seem to have been burning all night . . . except that now I begin to pick up the state of the place.

"Man!" I hear Ras say, somewhere behind me. "What a hoot."

Furniture's upturned. Doeskin lounge chairs. Ceramic coffee tables. The lot. Stereo's on its side. CDs and DVDs scattered all over the place. There's one lamp tipped into a potted palm and the kitchen cupboards, French mustard, Ketchup, Rice Krispies, Marmite, Chicken seasoning, you name it, have been emptied onto the parquetry floor. Even the bathroom's been trashed: diet pills, Zantac, shaving foam, Joop! smashed out into the tub which is deep and has a fitted opaque glass shower screen with etched tropical fish. There's worse, though. The bedroom's upside down and the result reveals the professor's no lover of Lycra or pure new wool. His taste in shoes runs to hiking boots and sneakers, brogues in black. Panning left across the hall where inscriptions of poetry in silver frames adorn the walls, I zoom into what must have been his den and shoot there, what might have been the fall of *The Last Emperor,* several scenes from *Ben Hur,* a section of *Starship Troopers,* a bit of *Titanic,* but somehow isn't, the walls having absolutely spewed forth their books and left them like an Everest of yellowed pages and ancient leather covers, torn and trashed and junked them together with papers bills letters, letters I move in on and phone shoot in big close-up, letters, personal stuff, strewn from the roll-top desk which is still upright but broken open at its lock until the best I can do is to fade, fade, fade . . .

"You don't suppose," Ras says, absolutely deadpan, "the guy really is a full-on party machine?"

6

You might recognize the previous scene as being swiped directly from *Heat.* Or decide that it comes from *The Untouchables* and that, however unlikely it is that I would cast him, Kevin Costner was somewhere in it. Maybe you figure it's the third sequence in *Sharkey's Machine* where Burt Reynolds tries to make a point about his excellent cop status but ends up running downtown vice with a bunch of two-bit losers. Well, let me tell you, it was not like that at all. No, it was different. Freer. Less structured. I have no sense of where it came from or why it was there, and only a vague understanding of how it might be understood—as a part of the film I'm making, or just a part of my life, Karen's life, our lives here in Southport.

Now I'm following Ras up into the Roxy's projection room but I'm not thinking of us showing *The Fly,* though it's a truly great film, maybe Cronenberg's best, and certainly better than *Naked Lunch* which suffers from trying to be too much like the book, which Karen has actually read cover-to-cover. On a par then with *Shivers.* But I'm following Ras up the fire escape stairs, the sun just slipping down now below a slight grid of grey cloud which sliced in from the sea, and I am not thinking of the projection room at all, or of learning the ropes. . . because I have noticed, on reviewing the footage I got in the professor's apartment, something disturbing.

While Ras is explaining how some cinema projectionists, such as those in most modern multiplexes, just never change their aperture plates so that actors in quite well known productions get the tops of their heads cut off and prints go out of focus, I'm only half listening. This is important to know, but I can't help just staring at him, his black hair tied hard back and him wearing what appears to be a bottle green Tommy Hilger sweatshirt and a pair of leather bike jeans, and remembering the footage I shot this afternoon at Professor Krotow's apartment because, on reviewing it, I noticed the scene where I saw poking upward from the papers which were strewn over the den floor, something that looked like a copy of Steve Milroy's book *The Film Revolution,* so I watched myself dip down, my hand in the foreground, the papers and then the book growing larger and larger, in and then right out of the background. My hand reached the book, and I opened it and there I found this inscription:

"For Julian—'Conscience is the Internal Perception of the Rejection of a Particular Wish Operating Within Us.'"

No matter how many times I review this section of my film I cannot make out what this inscription might mean, how I should interpret it, whether I should report it to Helena, and she can take it to who?. Detective "Penrith"? Richare Gere? Will Smith? Whether, in fact, it means anything at all. Only that it is there, in my phone, in that book, recorded, saying something which seems to me to be . . . well, passionate.

To make matters worse, on top of this I'm having these flashbacks in which I'm entering Steve Milroy's office and, just to the left of frame, Leesa is standing there in the half light and she's holding a knife, a knife that is in fact her right hand but as I recall the scene my camera phone constantly turns that hand of hers into a knife, against my better judgment, and I simply can't tell you how disturbing that is. The hand, the knife: it just goes on like this. And I can't help feeling that this comes about because everyone is saying she's a bizarro chip off the old block, her mother's fruity *arteestic* daughter. And that this is prejudicing how I feel.

It's like an epiphany. Her behind the desk in the half light, barely light at all, but what light there is glinting so wonderfully off a knife, and all the reason I can muster cannot stop it changing into the hand I know it is. I should be concentrating on how great this looks but now I'm feeling kind of done about the whole sequence. For one thing, I'm suffering these crazy broken connections that I don't want to think about, having these flashbacks which include that weird inscription in the professor's book, and I can't do a thing about it.

Suddenly Goody Ansel comes in from the fire escape. Looking exactly like Dennis Hopper, and dying of cancer, he says:

"Been waiting long?"

Then he drops down into his deluxe high-back operator's chair, coughing once only and putting both feet on an oak and ebony laminate work center.

"A while," I say, trying for no reason to get a reaction. "Maybe a half hour."

"Yeah," says Goody, sneakers crossing. "That's too bad." He smiles with teeth which cannot be real and drops his hands way back behind his head. "You spoke to Leesa yet?"

"No," I say, torn between wanting to admit that I haven't and wanting, actually, to admit that the reason I haven't is that she reminds me, in many ways, of Gwyneth Paltrow and this slipping in and out of Paltrow-ville, Paltrowism that she does, disturbs me in ways I can't quite grasp. "No I . . . haven't."

He lights some kind of volatile rat dung, draws on it heavily, lets those spidery eyes weave a while on me, and then spurts the smoke under the desk because the ceiling is full of fire sprinklers and he doesn't want to set any of them off. Then he offers the same ratbus to me which, naturally, I refuse.

Ras, however, takes it. He grips it between his thumb and index finger in his right hand. "No," he says, drawing. "It wasn't that long, Ciaran. Maybe ten minutes."

"Well," I say.

"So we're loaded then?" says Goody.

"You are," I say quietly, kind of in his direction. "I guess."

"Ho!" coughs Goody in Ras's direction. "Ho! Man, what's wrong today with Mr. Speilberger, huh?" He opens the projector. Like an oven, the thing gapes, warm, deep, waiting. "Problems with your CGI? Can't get Tom Cruise to do it for under fifteen mil? Got rat in your sausage?"

"No" says Ras, nervously. "He hasn't got a problem. Have you, Ciaran? You don't have a problem, right?"

"Had a visit this afternoon from Helena," Goody says, sliding "Helena" across his tongue like a wad of gum.

"O," I say, unable to control my intrigue.

"Smart chick," he says, opening the can and, hawking forward, checking the print. "Looking for a tape, apparently. You been sending people tapes, kid?"

"No," I say.

"Well . . ." He clicks the reel onto the projector, back to me now, and thus indecipherable.

I struggle to bring myself back from my phone film and into the projection room and smile weakly at the two of them. Shooting in two shot I imagine these two as father and son and the thought of it calms me down and I soften a little.

"It really gets me," I say, raving with minor relief, "the things people pay to watch. You'd think they'd be a bit more discerning, you know. You'd think they'd at least know something about what they're paying for." But none of this makes any sense.

Goody clamps down the print, holding his weed in reverse in his mouth like they do in all the war movies so that glowing tip doesn't show. "Wow Speilberger," he says, pulling out this weed of his and blowing smoke through his nose. "Maybe you should be like Bergendahl here and just chill. You know, chill?"

"Maybe," I say, stepping over to the projection window. "Maybe."

The cinema is lit. Leesa floats in through the door, right, wearing a brown leather swing coat with a grey fake fur collar. There is no one else in the cinema. None inhabiting the crimson seats which are faded even in the dimness of the pre-show and their backs stuck with brass numbers and the low lamps which spin webs over the aisles in front of her. But which she avoids. Instead, she glides down toward the front. And I am filming her gliding, shooting her from behind as she moves away from my phone but does not become less prominent. I have no idea how this is happening. All I know is that, although I cannot zoom in any further, although I am technically too far away to record the things I am seeing, I am certainly able to make out her slim figure as she glides down the aisle and the light, which is so low and tinted this firelight yellow, just as it catches the brushed checked shirt beneath her coat, in a camel and cream color, and alights on her hair which, as you'd expect if you've seen any of Gwyneth Paltrow's films, she has pulled back and pinned up on her head, and when she turns, as she does, momentarily, just a single concerned expression wondering where in this vast old cinema with its low worn velvet seats and its grandly plastered ceiling, rosetted and rose petalled and fretted, and its truly vastly curtained screen along which you can still see the thick golden curtain ropes, she should sit, I make out, briefly, her eyes which, literally, glitter. The trailers start rolling. The first is for *Confidentially Yours*. Meanwhile, Goody is loading in the main projector: *The Fly*.

7

The Fly succeeds on many levels. Cronenberg has never elicited better performances from his players. Goldblum is superb in a rare leading role. Davis is also on top form. As a couple, they are so convincing and appealing that one regrets knowing that their love story will soon become a tragic horror movie. As a remake, The Fly *transcends the original, taking it in new directions, and exploring its underutilized potential. Whereas the original degenerated into a campy fly hunt, the remake opts for a slow metamorphosis from man to fly that develops as a disease might. This gives Cronenberg time to examine the implications of such a process, mediating upon our fear of disease, death and change.*

(Library Shelf: Professor's notes. Steven
Milroy. "The Fly" in *The Seventh Virgin Film
Guide,* Ed. Ken Fox et al. London: 1998)

8

At which point, completely unpredictably, Ras walks over and, with his face at the projection window and his back to me, announces that tomorrow—when I will be shooting the important final sequence of my film: which I once thought would be a whole tracking sequence on the beach with whales dancing on their tails in the background (if I had my way), and maybe a blood bath on *The Corso* with samurais and chainsaws and a deep meditative ride down a monstrous fun fair rollercoaster, but maybe it won't be—he cannot come with me.

Will not come with me, to be accurate.

I don't react immediately. Instead, I focus in on his face; producing a series of extreme close-ups so that, if some great filmmaker in the future, some fantastic Kevin Smith or mighty Paul Verhoeven, goes ahead in his student days and looks deeply into my film, he will see that this whole sequence is composed of a kind of facial poetry, with Ras's features joined together by an invisible line, the very same famous line you read about in books: *The Bible of Cinematography* by Herbert S. Walton and *Being a Great Film Maker* by N.T.Walsh.

"Really," I say, "how come?"

"Oh," he says, but before he has finished I fill in the gaps for him, the simple picture I have of Kevin and Cole and Monika and Alice and Grace and Karen, all together on a set that looks just like the terrace, comparing script notes for some USP sitcom.

If anyone did follow my invisible poetic line—the three-quarter profile of Ras's cracked lips, the slow pan across his right cheek

155

to his now reddening right ear, the whip to his forehead which creases, on cue, the crane down to his eyes, the eyes speaking volumes—if they followed the line through these shots, one after another, one connected intimately to another, then would they find that he is not telling me the whole story?

Possibly. Probably.

"Well, I guess," I say, "in that case, groovy then."

He tries to crack into some kind of smile, but his lips quiver and his eyes flicker and he ends up looking like someone catching the scent of some of El Monkey's excellent *crabes farcies,* but not knowing whether to head straight toward it or take off immediately in the opposite direction.

"Anyway," I say, "you probably won't like what I've decided to do with it." I pause purposefully. "I've changed my mind."

"O?" he asks, and I can see in the way he is faking checking the projector mechanism (for what exactly?) that I have found the nerve I was looking for.

"Sure," I say. "For one thing I'm going to use a pale pink filter—a Wratten or a Zone more than likely—and take the blue right out with it. For another, it's going to be an aerial shot."

"An aerial shot!" He huffs loudly, down behind the projector and, over by the main projector, I notice, old Goody coughs in support.

"Right," says Ras.

"A crowd shot," I say. "With nothing but sea behind it, and the whole of Southport kind of out in front."

"You know, Ras," I say, "Goody," I say, wandering toward the door to peer down the steels stairs to the darkening car park below, "I have this real problem with Hitchcock films, don't you?"

Silence.

"I mean," I say, into the new night, "I just can't see how anyone can watch a movie where everyone either lies or dies. You know what I mean?"

Ras just stares.

"Really!" I say. "How do they do it?"

I get the feeling that Ras doesn't know what I'm talking about.

9

I'm sitting in the row plated 7C while LK watches Jeff Goldblum in the lab in which he is trying to "change life as we know it." She sits with her head back slightly, slid down in the seat, her knees tucked up in front of her against the back of the seat in front. She has sat, without taking her eyes off the screen, through the trailers, the final one being for *Communion,* starring Mark Wahlberg, Elizabeth Lindsey, Bryon Mann and Chow Yun-Fat, directed by James Healey and produced by Terence Chang and Oliver Stone. While the lights were up before the feature she went out to the Snak Bar and bought a small Diet Coke, a Flight bar and a second Flight bar which she slipped into the top pocket of her brushed checked shirt. She then returned to her seat, pausing half way down the aisle try and re-focus her eyes so that she could see where she was going. Then she found where she'd been and, smiling at the guy on the aisle who is a fairly stinking looking prize plum, she slipped on through and sat back down, forgetting her Flight bar and taking a lengthy sip from her Coke. When the film began she slid down in her seat and placed her Coke in her lap, which she had created by drawing her knees up. She did not open her Flight bar, nor has she even acknowledged that she has another one in her pocket, which makes me wonder now if she has simply forgotten that she bought them. She watches Goldblum cross the lab, doing his work on teleportation while thinking about the science-magazine reporter Veronica Quaife, played by Geena Davies.

I'm wondering if Leesa knows what happens next. As she watches the awkward scientist Seth Brundle (Goldblum) I'm wondering if she realizes that his relationship with Geena Davis is not the only thing that this film is about. I'm wondering as she watches him being intellectually brilliant, but absolutely clumsy, what is about to happen. . . . Because Karen always did.

"It's a story about methods," she said, the first time I showed her the film, repeated this in a similar fashion the second time, adding "and fear." Followed this with a knowing pout at the screen on the third. And will watch it any time at all as long as I fast forward through the scene in which Brundle unsuccessfully tries to transport a monkey, which she finds "both gross and irrelevant."

The fact is, they are about to, of course, fall in love. As the film progresses they will become a heart-warming couple, him trying to impress his prom-queen girlfriend with his new science project. I'm thinking that Leesa has probably worked this much out. She is probably falling this line of the story which has a certain significance (certainly for me). There have been, after all, a number of fairly heavy hints . . . such as the way in which Davis is so impressed with his project and the endearing quality of Goldblum's clumsiness. Likewise she must see that this, Cronenberg's most mature, controlled and insightful film, is leading us to consider the implications of love and death occurring together. But I get the feeling that as she watches Brundle/Goldblum working on his teleporter that she is unaware that he will, ultimately be successful. Likewise, that the arrival of this success will, simultaneously, be the sowing of the seeds of his failure. I'm convinced that she doesn't realize that when Brundle/Goldblum grows bored with transporting objects he will move on to transporting living beings. This will be fine for a while. But when he decides that he must finally transport a human being and, naturally, nominates himself, it seems inevitable that something bad will happen, something awful to disrupt the rom-com situation that has by then developed. Wishing I could shoot her as she unknowingly waits for this happen, I wish I could capture on film her reaction when Goldblum steps into the teleporter but does not notice the little fly that has joined him. I wonder, at the same time, whether she sees me, here in the dark, eyes half glued on the screen and half on her, wearing a navy Replay sweatshirt and stone colored Jeep jeans, my phone tucked down firmly on the seat beside me while I'm sipping sometimes on a medium Coke, no ice, and thinking I should probably have also bought a packet of Maltesers, but no matter.

And I wonder what would it be like to record her feelings as Goldblum, his genes irrevocably entangled with those of the fly, his life shattered completely by an accident which, had he been more observant, he could have prevented, begins slowly to transform?

I would love to record that, to capture her reaction, like a real old-fashioned confession.

10

As the film ends, the lights naturally go up. What people there are in the place leave quickly. The lights then go down to a dim glow again. Through the projection window I can see Ras moving about through the projection room. He seems to be waving to me about something, trying to mouth words and, when I raise my phone up and zoom in on him I swear he is mouthing:

"Attack! . . .

"Ciaran, attack! Attack!"

Or maybe I am still reeling from his refusal to come with me tomorrow, and this is something brand new in my film oeuvre: a kind of symbol of how I feel at this moment about Ras and the others. Their absence. My current contempt for them and their ways, their stupid plans, their ideals. Or maybe it is entirely for Karen that I seem to see these words forming in Ras's mouth, knowing that when her parents arrive from the Pyrenees every-thing will change. Not least, because my feeling is they will con-vince her to transfer somewhere, most likely back to Roeford, and continue her study there. And then the chance that this whole business will blow over will be wasted, because the reason to even care about it will be gone.

Either way, trying to work out what Ras is saying, and still in the dark facing the screen, I find myself distracted when into the cinema runs someone who, for the moment, I can't at all recognize.

He—I can just see it's a male—he bursts in through the fire doors to my right, and sprints swiftly toward the left. But before I've had time to get him in frame, he's turned toward the front, through the center of the cinema, and no matter how fast I apply the line and pan pan *pan* after him I am unable to keep up.

I'm getting nothing but half-shots, the back of his head, his weirdly flapping arms, and I want to scream. I want to shout out:

"Give me a break, will you, buddy?"

Or just stop. Turn off the camera. Slide the covers over that take its lens into my phone again. Let the whole thing happen in front of me and leave it un-filmed, unrecognized, ignored. But, to make matters worse, he now starts jumping over the seats, forcing himself into the frame, thus making me keep going.

He scrambles toward me, a silhouette, literally floating over the seats, like he's out of his tree, has just dropped 300 mg of Papaverine and followed it with 500 mg of Imipraminine or something, and there's no stopping him. When he seems almost on me, he turns and decides instead to run up the aisle way way toward the front, lit by the eerie sallow glow of the cinema which, to be frank, is making me feel pretty sad just to look at it.

By now the three service assistants from the Snak Bar have come in, two down the right side and the larger one down the left, and the larger is crying out "Hey! Hey!" which only manages to drive the guy even crazier as he runs headlong toward the couple getting up out of 6D who have spent the entire film absolutely down each other's throats, and they only manage to scramble out of his way at the last moment.

I'm trying to think what this reminds me of. I'm undecided whether it is the Tuesday Weld at the lumberyard sequence in *Pretty Poison*, also starring Anthony Hopkins, or the "Hedra Carlson is a psycho" sequence in *Single White Female*. When the guy starts screaming "Don't try and stop me!" I'm thinking maybe it's neither of these and is actually the "Isabella Rosselini in the Nightclub" (Part 1) sequence in *Blue Velvet*. But as the whole of *Blue Velvet* is not supposed to make sense I come to the conclusion that I'm losing my bearings and shoot as wide as possible, though the light is too low to do any shot justice.

Annoyingly, I now lose sight of LK in all the ruckus, but can't yet deal with this.

The tallest of the service assistants—an African American guy in a black Nehru suit and tangerine shirt, on evidence possibly a Will Smith fan—pulls out what looks like a hammerless .38 caliber revolver by Iver Johnson, but could be (I guess) a Walther PPK and points it straight at the guy. Two hands clasping the gun out in front and spreading his legs wide, he says:

"You're either going to stop or I'm going to stop you."

But it's as obvious to the other service assistants as it is to me that this line comes from the mouth of Gene Hackman in *Unforgiven*. They (and I) groan audibly.

Seconds later, nevertheless, the three of them rush forward. There's a tussle, but the African American guy is unbelievably quick and pistol whips the runner to Hell and he drops, on cue, to floor at Aisle 4 or 3, flat out on the worn red carpet. Holding his arms between them the assistants drag him, unconscious, toward the Fire Exit.

It is then that it dawns on me, as the red Fire Exit sign comes gradually into focus, the screen now white and blank, that the whole event, from Ras at the projection window to now slumped down here in my seat, has been some sort of little dream of mine. Awake now, I realize the cinema is empty.

11

For interest:

The camera phone, like many complex systems, is the result of converging and enabling technologies. There are dozens of relevant patents dating back as far as the 1960s. Compared to digital cameras of the 90s, a consumer-viable camera in a mobile phone would require far less power and a higher level of camera electronics integration to permit the miniaturization. The CMOS active pixel image sensor "camera-on-a-chip" developed by Dr. Eric Fossum and his team in the early 1990s achieved the first step of realizing the modern camera phone as described in a March 1995 Business Week article. While the first camera phones, as successfully marketed by J-Phone in Japan, used CCD sensors and not CMOS sensors, more than 90% of camera phones sold today use CMOS image sensor technology.

notable events involving camera phones

The Boxing Day Tsunami of 2005 was the first global news event, where the majority of the first day news footage was no longer provided by professional news crews, but rather by citizen journalists, using primarily cameraphones.

On December 30, 2006, the execution of former Iraqi dictator Saddam Hussein was filmed by a video camera phone, and made widely available on the Internet. A guard was arrested a few days later.

Camera phone video and photographs taken in the immediate aftermath of the 7 July 2005 London bombings were featured worldwide. CNN executive Jonathan Klein predicts camera phone footage will be increasingly used by news organizations. (http://en.wikipedia.org/wiki/Camera_phone. Last accessed 1 February 2009)

12

When I make my way out in front of the Roxy, Ras is leaving on his bike following, would anyone believe, an ambulance whose blue lights spin and glare and whose siren wails right over the conversations of two geriatric Cher-lookalikes who are discussing *The Wedding Singer,* and saying how much they hate it. Half awake, it could all too easily be part of the proceeding dream.

"That Drew Barrymore is just *tooo* cute, you know." That kind of thing.

Before I've had chance to digest any of this, LK comes out of the glass swing doors and, driven on absolutely and only by instinct, I shoot her directly in the face and shoulders and, just as I do, she raises her eyes and looks me straight in the lens.

"Hey," she calls, striding Gwynethly towards me. "Hey, don't I know you?"

Wearing a brown leather swing coat, she passes posters for the forthcoming screening of *Something Wicked* which I will not miss in a million years and plan to see at the premiere, and perhaps a few times after that, mainly because I like the tag: "What's in the woodshed doesn't compare to this!"

"I know you," she repeats, getting closer, wearing a version of something Goth on her lips (some dark lip gloss, or something).

Recovering my composure, I back away, but only so that I can get her in medium shot which highlights the patterning of glass doors behind her, all falling away with a clapping sound as a family of poke's makes their way out to their ranch wagon, to go looking for a Burger King, no doubt, buy a tray of Cokes, fries, talk about the relative short life of kids' shoes. The fact that LK is standing under the main archway of The Roxy with its long independent history of film exhibition doesn't escape me.

Finally she says: "Oh, but I can't place you."

Helping her out, I string along neatly: "Well, maybe I'm that crazy bastard who abducted the Minatone sisters from K-Mart and was caught on the security camera."

"No," she says, looking suddenly pleased. "No. I . . . I . . . I . . ."

"Okay, what about . . . I'm the guy in the Nescafe ad who does not want his friends to leave without trying a cup."

"Excellent!" She looks genuinely pleased. Fingers the lapels of her swing coat. I have a strong urge to reach out and touch that pleased look of hers. The weird glow it gives off around her eyes. The cruel twist it puts on her lips.

"Hey, you show me a crime and I'll show you a movie that might have caused it."

"What?" . . ." She shrieks with joy and looks around, noticing with the sound of engines starting that the car park is clearing.

"This is probably a stupid question," she says, stepping onto the road, "but do you know Steve Milroy."

I, naturally, confirm this.

"Talk about art imitating life," I'm thinking. And because this kind of imitation seems so life-affirming, lively but safe, I think for a moment what this film might include, some of its highlights and lowlights, I guess, the leading lady confused but beautiful, her boyfriend, a film-maker, the wrist-slashed auteur, the crazy old freak, the dying cancerous hippy, the friends huddled around the body of the friend they have killed, the whirring sirens, the accusing detective, the final scene with the dying whale, the fatally injured pup.

"Well," she says, finally. "I liked . . .

"*The Fly?*" I say, picking up her thread. "Sure. What's not to like?"

"I liked Geena Davis. She was . . . excellent."

"Sure," I say, "but wasn't she better in *Earth Girls Are Easy?* Funnier, at least."

She then precedes (Can you believe this?) to explain to me absolutely the entire plot of *eXistenZ,* making a great deal out of the nostalgic singalongs, the Motown, the wedding rehearsal, the flares, the haircuts—all of which are not even in the film! Is this innocence or some other thing, some habit of hers? Some other habit I think. She seemed to know what she was doing.

I want to tell her that if we go back inside we can probably buy tickets for the Festival showing of *Groundhog Day,* starring Bill Murray and Andie MacDowell, which is, let's be honest, a very very funny film (the bit where Murray first realizes he is cursed to live the same day over and over again is truly fit!); but I don't know how to get around to it because she believes I am just this great fan of the ditsy rom-com *Up on the Roof* and therefore she will not expect that I would be interested in a film as funny, as uproarious, as downright sorted as Harold Ramis's *Groundhog Day.*

What happens next is in slow mo, with no sound, in black and white. The wind, which was not there a second ago, is rising over the car park of The Roxy which stands behind us like the Taj Mahal while this mysterious wind teases empty packets of Twisties and Scooters, wrappings of Flights and Peebles, the silently clattering empty cans of Diet Coke and Sprite. The car park clears and we're standing there as the lights of The Roxy flicker, one, it seems, at a time, downlights along the front wall which pick up the posters for *Something Wicked* and also for *Total Recall 2*, which I have not considered until now but which I will probably also see, just to find out whether Doug Quaid, played by Arnie Schwarzenegger, comes back as a construction worker or a super-agent.

One of the service attendants comes out to see if there are any takers for *Logan's Run,* and then slips back inside, and we are alone on the front steps, which are not marble but cement, though what the Hell, and the sky is clear and starry and the streetlights glitter as if through a star-filter, though I am not using one. There is a slight yellowish glow from the highway beyond the glade of trees and the office towers and maybe mist or something from the docks nearby where yachts are moored and a number of cruisers and broken shapes of old apartment blocks which are being re-developed as a leisure center and before I have even determined phone placement, checked the battery or announced "Going for a take" we are driving out along the open road in her car, I mean convertible, through the city where stop lights fall away to green and the sidewalks, drunks, Burger Kings, gradually peter out and become uninhabited verges and pretty soon we're out beyond even the worst suburbs, even the suburbs with Superstores, and the country opens out into forests and fields.

The music playing now is "All My Life" by K-Ci and Jojo; but it is impossible that this playing on the CD player because the top is down and the sea wind caught in our speed-stream is raising quite a ruckus. So the music seems actually like a soundtrack, in my head, and mixes with the rush of the scenery as we spin along down the coast, through villages thick stoned and thicketed and definitely nineteenth century or something impressively earlier, and the overhang of trees which are growing spindly and creepy in the unusually mild autumn and the constant glitter of the sky through the canopy picked up through a 25 mm lens stopped to f/2 and nothing ahead but darkness which the lights of the convertible—which is, hardly incidentally, a BMW, a completely groovy ancient little Beemer in silver—picks up in long white steaming beams.

Soon—to be accurate after no more than five minutes in which I switch periodically between watching the road ahead and watching her driving in the shadows of the cars lights, dappled by the trees, smiling Gwynethly, through who knows how many villages so quaint they weirdly make my gut ache—soon we pull into a drive which begins by winding down between two half fallen gateposts. A collapsed gate. Over a wooden bridge under which a small stream flows. At which point the track ahead, its hard dirt and ragged stone, begins to widen and from somewhere—"Can you believe this?" I'm thinking—chickens, unbelievably chickens (!), scatter.

A black dog, possibly a Labrador or a wolfhound or something, comes loping up toward the car, as we pull up.

"There's Newman," she calls toward the dog. Then dewy and bright, unbuckling, to me: "He's alright."

The cottage is stone with latticed casements and a high slate roof. I get out and stand beside an axe and block where wood has been chopped. What looks like an old sports car, perhaps a Bugatti or Berlinetti or something, something European, is parked in a rough lean-to, its wheels missing, a clown's patchwork of a paint job. There's a 4x4, a canvas-top, by the creek. And there is one of those machines over by the forest, bricks around it, those cement machines that you crank around to create cement which you use to repair your old cottage, form-up paths, build retaining walls, a firm drive, a nice bright patio. A man's lumbercoat hangs on a low branch in a nearby tree.

"Have you seen *Fried Green Tomatoes at the Whistlestop Cafe?*" I ask her.

She laughs out loud, lightly, streamily, and notices the dog has taken to nosing my crotch.

"Hi, Newman," I'm saying. "Good boy."

While I'm patting Newman's hard grey head, keeping him at bay, she's now over at the front door. The place is unlit; but, once she has unlocked it and reached in, lights come on along on the porch and the rose, which grows thickly around it, lights up and its flowers are butter yellow.

She calls me from inside.

If my eyes were a camera they might zoom now on the dark canopy of the forest over yonder, enter the great leafy overhang, find a bat there and visit its musty den. But I am not singularly able to shift away from the glow of the house and I step up on the porch and then, smoothly, not breaking the movement, in through the door.

"Hey," she calls from somewhere indistinguishable, "can you hit the flood switch for the patio."

When I fail to answer, she appears from a back room, her swing coat now removed, wearing a brown checked blouse, jeans.

"What?" she says. How I look goes unrecorded, stiff in the open doorway, some kind of insect clicking its gossamer legs together in the night behind me. "Are you okay?" Again, how I look is unrecorded. Finally she says, in a thin, soft voice. "You haven't been here before?" I would like to answer but fail to. "Oh," she says, more loudly and confidently. "This is Steve's place."

"Milroy?"

"Bingo!" She hits a switch on the wall beside which lights up the rear of the house and the forest and, leaving me to gather what remains of my pride, goes about feeding the dog on the patio.

The immediate effect of her revelation is to unbalance my sense of light, raising the low orange glow from a tall shade in the corner and dislodging my sense of shape or space or depth until I shuffle slightly rightwards and the walls spread back and books in cases and then films, video films, on thick wooden shelving, thousands of them, and posters for *The Prisoner of Zenda* with Mary

Astor and *The Goodbye Girl* with Richard Dreyfuss and Marsha Mason and *Agnes of God* with Jane Fonda and Anne Bancroft, models from *Star Trek*, mugs, *Field of Dreams* trading cards, framed autograph pictures, caps, coin banks (Godzilla the money-box), a full-size cardboard figure of Harrison Ford as Indiana Jones.

I pick up each portion of the room in a slow rightward movement, passing over Sigourney Weaver in three separate poses, shave-headed, face-blackened, determined, and Sean Connery with thick silver hair, a poster of Branden Lee in *The Crow*, before he shot himself in that bizarre accident which maybe was planned anyway, which maybe was a suicide, a cry for help, past an animated outtake from *Antz*, a *Desperado* still of Antonio Banderas, a picture of Russ Meyer, until I feel a hand on my shoulder and, turning swiftly, find her there, close. Then closer.

Somewhere, in another world, a film world, a door begins to open.

three

A Life Less Ordinary
1997, 103m, Color
Rom-Com, /15
20th Century Fox, (U.S.)

I

Vanilla-scented couscous with Potatoes, Carrots and Turnips

(Serves 8) This is a good end-of-week recipe, when no one has been to the store. I have included instructions here for vanilla-scented, but you could have any scent, depending on what people have been using in the house—peppermint essence probably would be too much, but almond or orange or anise or ginger or kewra water would be fine.

20oz couscous
Boiling water
4 smoked jalapeño chillies
I lb carrots, chopped
8 turnips
I tbsp vanilla essence
Black pepper

Cooking Time: 30–35 minutes
1. Place the couscous in a bowl and pour in boiling water and vanilla essence. Leave to soak under a tea towel for about 10 minutes.
2. Break up the couscous with an egg beater or knife.
3. Chop chillies, and mix chillies into couscous. Allow to sit to that the flavour can seep.
4. Chop carrots and turnips and place in pan of boiling water for 20 minutes.

5. Add carrots and turnips to chilli couscous.
6. Season with black pepper and serve on plates.

2

Chargrilled Tofu with Green Vegetables, Lemons and Bananas

(Serves 3) A vegetarian or vegan diet can be very cost-effective, and shared houses can even have shared vegetable gardens. With that in mind, this recipe starts with tofu (which, incidentally, is made from the extract of soya beans) and adds to it items that are often discounted at supermarkets and other stores. You can substitute any of these, taking care to ensure the flavours do not clash.

2 packets of tofu
3 tbsp olive oil
5fl oz pot of double cream
2oz breadcrumbs
2 tbsp chopped fresh coriander
6 lemons
I lime
I clove of garlic
2 onions
I green chilli, finely chopped
I tbsp soy sauce
6 shallots
4 large bananas
10 oz broccoli florets
I leek
14oz pak choi
I fennel bulb
2 tsp cornflour
Black pepper

Cooking Time: 17–22 minutes

1. Preheat the oven to 450F
2. Soak tofu in olive oil and place in a griddle pan. Turn the tofu slices continuously, and remove from pan when charred.
4. Heat the cream in microwave oven.
5. In a bowl, mix together the breadcrumbs, lemons, lime—all chopped, with skin removed—garlic, onions, chilli and shallots
6. Mix together the bananas, broccoli, leek, pak choi and fennel. Place into the oven, to cook, for 15 minutes.

7. To serve, tofu slices on side of a plate and the banana mix on
   the other side. Sprinkle the breadcrumb mix over the top of
   both.

3

"I accept," says Helena in a manner which I can only describe at
the moment as clinical and horribly abrupt.

I have just agreed to bring her what I have in the can from the
professor's apartment if she will find Karen for me. Find her immediately. Find her today. And I will bring her everything.

I will give her, I said: "My whole film, if you want, Helena."

To which she sat dumbfounded, inhaling, then exhaling
smoke.

"Really," I said. "Take it."

But she's declined the offer, just wants me to find the Krotow
sequence and bring it to her, and agrees that she will mention
nothing I have said to her, nothing I have discovered, until she can
find Karen, drag her away if she must from her parents who are
probably trying to convince her as we speak to pack immediately
and return to Roeford, and bring her along here to Candia the
minute she's found.

My head is pounding. I am unable to focus properly on anything and admit that, in that weird, hallucinatory fashion that in-
vades real life at times like this I've considered this morning just
walking out across the Promenade, across the beach and into the
sea and, like in . . . like in some movie which escape me, some
un-recallable scene, just continuing, letting the water rise up,
right up over my head until I am walking under the water somewhere out past the marina with my clothes gone all angelic, floating detached from the dying guy within, but my eyes still fixed
determinedly on that distant spot on the horizon, that warm glow
out through the filthy water.

So take the sequence, Helena. See there beneath the books
and papers and old copies of *Rolling Stone!*, trashed in the freaky
professor's apartment that weird inscription in The Film Revolu-

tion, "'Conscience is the Internal Perception of the Rejection of a Particular Wish Operating Within Us.'" Interpret this any way you want. If it matters. If any of it matters now. Take the whole thing to the police. to your Detective "Penrith" if you want. Enlist the help of Harrison Ford, Sean Connery, Brad Pitt, Jodie poking Foster, but not before you find Karen.

If I love Karen then I am now a complete fraud. And if I don't love her, then the great sense of purpose that drives on real artists crumbles right here, because why did I start filming her in the first place?

I am sitting in Candia with Helena. It is 8.45 in the morning and yet the place is strangely full with public, ordinary NEXT, Body Shop, Sainsburys, Virgin Megastore public, and she has finished, up to the minute, two Mexican Margogipes, one of which was Turkish and the other *au lait,* one Pearl Spring water and three MB Lights. She just finished telling me that she is seriously considering leaving Lystead and Wishhart and I have tried to look interested, to appear like I'm listening, but probably I have not appeared that way at all because I am looking for Karen in the crowd, perhaps out with her parents, or hiding here in Candia which is more brightly lit than El Monkey and opens earlier than Plexus.

Helena seems smaller at this moment somehow and her suit, which is deep red and pin-striped and the trousers zip fastened, is a little too loose on her not unattractive body. I have noticed in her eyes this morning some kind of yellow wash which makes me think she might be suffering from Hepatitis B or something. I wonder if David is aware of this?

I am undecided whether I can be bothered ordering a plate of hash browns or the thing which Kyle has just chalked on the blackboard; namely: Chuoi Dua which is, essentially, bananas in coconut milk, to which they add cinnamon and a sprig of lemon grass.

Someone says, after a while, "I'll take the Chuoi Dua." maybe it's me, but I can't recall telling myself to say this and so can't be sure.

Given that I am not very hungry, my mind racing back and forth across the cafe so fast that the whole atmosphere seems spiky and staccato, I may not have anything else but just sit and stare out into the street where I can try pick up a sense of scale in the hurried cramped people passing, their heads down like monks and nuns in their coats. There is a light rain falling.

"I think there's something you've worked out already, Ciaran," Helena says suddenly, methodically, addressing (maybe) her cigarette which she is holding between thumb and forefinger in front of her tiny mouth. "But I want to say it anyway."

She says this while I am still trying to shut everything around me out by wondering if some guy, some real guy like Spike Jonze or Kevin Smith or P.T.Anderson, a talented new-blood gungho director with a good sense of the pace and focus of modern life, using a long shot of the Woolworths store opposite with its windows stacked with rainbow colored kitchenware, PC bargains, and Big Blue Talking Robots, would in any sense capture my mood. I doubt it.

"There . . . is . . . something . . . you . . . should . . . know," Helena says again, pacing the words out through the soundtrack in my head like she thinks she's shooting silver bullets from a large handgun. "Steve . . . Milroy," she says, over the rain, "is . . . . my . . "

"Your what?" I say. "Lover?" I say. "Screw-bunny? Lover," I say again, confirming.

I stare blankly at her, her lips glossed in Frost White, the rain framing her in backdrop through the window.

"Is?" I say. "Was?" I say. "Whatever."

"Yes," I say (side-glancing to confirm it). "I've realized that." Which I just did.

Though I want simply to dwell here, between Helena's half-understanding, largely stupid smile and my own complete feeling of disaster, I find I'm also thinking simultaneously that the Festival of the Waters is about to start and I have not one sense of what it will be like, what is showing, who will be there, whether they have got Cruise or Lopez or Wahlberg or just Jeff poking Goldblum for that matter. . . though outside, even in the now quite heavy rain, the Arts Festival is already up and running, and has managed to stretch its art toward (now momentarily postponed) jet ski races on the beach, and an exhibition of recommended warm water tour locations in the Solomons, the Antilles and the Leewards, a Toastmakers event featuring International Yachting Stars at the marina-side Southport Yacht Club, an exhibition in the Town Hall by the Southport Amateur Underwater Photographers club. All of which adds substantially to my sudden feeling of doom. So even when a guy who is the spitting image of Renny Harlin strolls into Candia I decide immediately to ignore him, figuring that his own foray into water (that is: the career-busting *Deep Blue Sea,* which he also produced) is just where I'm not going.

"Can you repeat that please?" I say to Helena. "Repeat, please, what you just said."

"If this was the movies," I'm telling myself, "and Karen was a younger Ingrid Bergman, and Leesa Kennedy was Gwyneth Paltrow, and I was Ben Affleck, Brad Pitt or . . . another one, any one, of her lovers, then who or what she is, or was, would be common knowledge and how I approached her would be set firmly by this knowledge and though I would have the option to go out with others, with Renee Zellweger if I wanted, with Christina Ricci, to screw other stars, be seen and photographed with other stars, I could still return at any point to Karen, and nothing would have changed."

"I said," she says, "Today then . . . I'll find Karen today."

"Yes," I say. "Oh, yes. But after ten remember," I remind her, "I won't be here. Call my phone, before you bring her. My phone," I repeat, as a kind of safe, reassuring mantra. "I have . . . things to sort out."

"Sure," she says, and stands up. Inexplicably she reaches out and, taking my hand between her two smaller hands, nods her head. Behind her Classic Polo sunglasses (grey tint) her eyes flicker across me.

"Right," I say, unable to comprehend what this hand-holding thing of hers is about, drawing my hand back.

When she is gone I order a coarse grind Brazilian Santos continental roast Viennese and sit back in the white hard plastic and, turning my phone inward into Candia which is filling now with USP students, feel the whole awkward scene clouding over, becoming blurred, and the whole thing turning kind of . . . nightmarish.

DISSOLVE.

4

The fact is, I woke this morning (as a cheap flash cut would show) alone in a double futon, under a floral duvet, in a stone cottage, somewhere out in the country.

A scent, which I now know to be Dolce & Gabbana because, like some kind of lost but over alert sleepwalker, I have been to the Southport Beachside Pharmacy to check it out and, after cautiously insisting on trying each of the perfumes they had on display in turn, I discovered what I smelt this morning was Dolce & Gabbana, that same sweet but wooden aroma infused in the air.

Because circumstances seemed to have changed, moved strongly and swiftly to the positive, and the battery was charged in the socket nearby the futon, I let my phone roll again, felt pleased to be back on track after my lapse, that sense of frustration and despair that all film-makers at some point feel, began to think of what the final sequences of my film might look light, whether I should call Ras immediately and invite him down onto the Halfmarket, try a shot with crane over the beach, a close-up of sand swirling on the Promenade, a shot of USP lit like a cathedral at night, use some of those labs of Ras's to do some kind of bubbling, glass-tubed sequence, a great little Sci Fi ending with a chase through great elephant-eared palms, slap, slap, slapping through a panting urgent soundtrack toward a piercing scream.

My first long phone shot slid through the air like a boat hook and, striking the wall near a picture of Bart Simpson (?), caught the light coming in through the latticed window, nicely splitting that over tapestries that hung on the wall there. Yet, for a while, I was unable to properly focus and, for what seemed like several long and not unwelcome beats, instead allowed myself to slip in and out of the previous night. Leesa standing near the fireplace, and me seated on the sofa, as the conversation turned to film-making and, made brave by the bottle of Los Camachos Cabernet Blanc, or whatever, we'd already drunk, I asked her outright if there was any chance she might be able to get my film screened at the Festival and she replied that she couldn't see why not, that it would be, as far as she could see, "absolutely possible" . . .

"Why not?" she said, in that voice she has which, perhaps because her mother is an artist, an art animator, seems so animated itself, kind of high and airy like a . . . bird's voice, I guess. The voice of some spectacular animated bird.

And me: "You're kiddin' me?"

"No," she said, sliding across the polished wooden floor toward me as if on a waxed pair of blades. "Bring me a print."

I was on my way with that print (in my mind, at least) when I half-woke the next morning. When I came-to properly, maybe ten minutes later, the light had shifted and reminded me of a summer afternoon in Vermont (via *The Bridges of Madison County*). I lay still a while, expecting my waking was the cue for noise-off; but nothing was immediately apparent and my first furtive response was to call out:

"Everything all right out there?"

Then: "Mmmm that smells good." though nothing was cooking and chances are I might have been indiscreet enough to have taken these words straight from The Brady Bunch Movie.

I fell out of bed, not literally but certainly my phone followed me and, by the time I was tracking down the stairs the effect was dynamic and a canary nearby, which I hadn't noticed the night before despite the fact that it was a strangely pied yellow/orange, was singing cheerily along with me in its tall canewood cage.

As it turned out, the kitchen was empty. There was, however, an open packet of Amatil on the draining board which suggested, though I still have not indicated it personally, that together we'd finished the three bottles of the Lost Camels (?) we'd opened the night before and that perhaps, given the evidence, that the hazy memory I had of considering and then rejecting the idea of taking two Tytermil capsules which Ras had suggested some time ago truly hit you where it helps, might be real enough after all.

Newman, who appeared to be a dead old wolf on the hearth in front of a fire that was still lit but only dimly glowing, raised his tail once when he saw me.

"Hey, Newman," I said. "Hey old boy. There's an old boy."

I didn't want to make too much of it, but shot for shot I was wondering if this wasn't my very best work so far. The pan across the hearth at a pace hangs on every brown stone. The prolonged tight shot of the photo of Leesa standing close to Steve Milroy in front of what appeared to be the piss-elegant offices of some obviously important but unmemorable casting agency. The photo had obviously been taken with one of those multi-format still cameras set to "panorama" and, the realization that someone has thought about this, has spent time thinking through whether "portrait" or "panorama" would be the most suitable aspect, makes me laugh out loud and it is this laughter, this sudden outburst of pent-up nervousness captured on film, which helps me cut to the next room.

All around the living room the walls are stuffed with films and I'm shocked. I am not able to focus my phone. I cannot decide whether to dolly in or zoom. I reach ridiculously for a script, a storyboard, a schedule, none of which are available. Maybe this is still the residual alcohol talking. I call for "Continuity!" and then "Camera! Camera!" Not that there are films. Films and more films. This is fine, perfect, acceptable. But there are many films which I have never heard of. There are many foreign films with actors I have not ever seen. There are old films by directors I know nothing about. And what I want to do, jump cutting from one unfamiliar DVD box to another, is watch them all now. I want to sit down in front of the TV and run the DVD all day and night. I want to play them back to back, one after the other, continuously. I want to freeze frame them, sequence by sequence, shot after shot, so that I know them intimately. I am aware of what they are about. I want to memorize songs, crew, lines. Play them again and again. I want to know these films. Know them absolutely.

I call out, loudly: "Leesa" but there is no answer.

I say, fairly innocuously I think: "Well, is there anyone here?"

Getting no answer, I take a video tape from the shelf. It is called *Golden Eighties* and is directed by (quote) "exciting minimalist Belgian director, Chantal Akerman." I slip the tape, described as "a musical whose setting in a shopping mall triggers a true spectacle" into what must be at least a 48 or 50 inch TV, a Sony it appears. The film starts. The picture quality is excellent and, because the TV has a Hexacone dome sound system the sound is superb.

There is, in the opening sequence, several wide shots in which the city disappears and the countryside gathers to the surprise of a small quaint town. The town is tucked up against the sea. The sea laps against a small beach. There are fishing boats. Two kids play amongst crab pots woven from cane. There are several shots inside a car, a Chevrolet maybe, possibly two-tone, blue, which is travelling along the country roads at considerable speed. All real high production values—this film must have had *sooome* budget!

Five persons are inside the car, two guys and three fit girls. At this point, their faces are not on camera, everything being shot at chest height. No words are spoken and, darkly lit, it is not possible to make out exact profiles, hair color, distinguishing mouth shapes. There is music playing over everything. I recognize something by Nirvana, something from maybe seven or eight years ago, Union of the Snake by, I think, Robert Palmer, something from the '70s, Metal, one song finishes and the others starts. The car enters the small coastal town. There is a house overlooking the beach. It is a mansion, large, white once, but the grass that grows around it is long like wheat. The five laugh as they get out of the car and tramp up to the house.

One guy's voice says: "Just like the Addams Family!" which makes the others laugh.

"My mom would love this place," says one of the girls, still unrecognizable but the medium shot below the shoulder showing her to be even more sound than she first appeared, wearing a black half-sleeved KH Denim zip up dress. The effect is quite spectacular.

The others follow the Addams guy into the house. The place is shot with dust which the light turns into yellow beams and the background is really very grainy. Lots of whites, browns, beiges, stonewash. Things, tables, a sculpture of perhaps a horse, a leather suite, are covered with white sheets. There's a Wurlitzer dome top jukebox which is definitely not a restoration and it starts to play, inexplicably, One Night in Heaven by M-People from what? ten years ago.

"Oooo," say the girls, now beginning to dance. "Remember this?"

I'm not exactly following. They dance woodenly. I'm thinking: "This looks more like it's going to be *The Shining* than something to do with a shopping mall." Also I'm thinking; "If this is Belgian shouldn't the voices be dubbed or something? Shouldn't there be sub-titles? But there's no time to consider this because the film is moving really fast now. Fast and expensive. The three girls, one in a beige colored textured pile coat, the other in a mesh top with flock print design, and the first in her black half-sleeved denim dress, two blondes and a hennaed brunette (them shot from behind), discuss something Earthshattering in the corner by the stairs. Then the blonde in the mesh top with flock print says, quietly, maybe a little woodenly:

"Hey Kevin, come here for a minute."

There is a CUT and, the next thing, Kevin Lewin is in full frame and his face is squeezed up in what I take, momentarily, to be pain. But then the shot widens and reveals something . . . else. Flat on his back on a futon which is not an unfamiliar to me, his cock is being strummed by Grace, the blonde in the mesh top, with a steady eager rhythm. She, meanwhile and simultaneously, is hissing something which sounds unmistakably like "Keep going." in the direction of the ceiling while the track playing is now China Girl by David Bowie. The camera tilts. Who's going where is not, well, indicated; but the camera now finds the beige textured coat, the girl in the beige textured coat (that is: Alice!), and she is stripped and, down on her knees, is lapping slowly at the club wear Grace has on, the lace thong worn by Grace, who grinds herself downwards in response. After a while Grace has obviously had enough of this and, turning herself around positions herself over Kevin's cock which points, stupendously, upward. But she does not lower herself; instead she leans forward and encouraging Alice to turn herself around begins fingering her asshole with studied interest until the camera moves up for an extreme close up and, parting the hole with her index fingers, Grace disappears and only her tongue occupies the frame, narrowing, twitching, drooling, until it contacts spectacularly with the now spread, bulging hole. The song now is I Owe You Nothing by Bros.

Meanwhile, following a connecting shot of two doves (who knows?) the sequence slips down stairs, along the banister, pauses half way, zooms in on Colleen in a denim dress who is now stretched out over the Wurlitzer with her dress up over her head. The Wurlitzer sparkles and glows in red green and blue while she is willing herself to be screwed from behind by the Addams guy (that is: Cole!) whose cock proves to be larger than normal and has trouble at first going in so that Colleen responds by reaching behind her able to clasp both her cheeks, lifts herself up until her cunt stands on top of the jukebox like a red light and blinks some sort of emergency code. He, maybe having a plan or, alternatively, not knowing what the Hell to do, begins rubbing his cock against the Wurlitzer itself which is chrome and smooth and has, he suddenly realizes, a coin return slot. Screwing the jukebox, checking for change, he tongues her cunt which blinks redly in distress while she, reaching around, finds her clit and begins, stroking the lobe. The song that starts playing is "I Guess That's Why They Call It The Blues" by Elton John.

Back in the bedroom, where the shot is now high and softly lit, Grace is coming as Kevin slides a Butt Plug non-electric dildo in and out of her cunt clumsily but relentlessly, the box is on the bed nearby another box labeled 9" Jelly Cactus. Monika, whose job at Pencils is maybe not such a long distant memory, is busily sucking Kevin's cock, rounding the head like it's Cape Horn as she sits and re-sits on a lime green Angels Delight Love Egg which disappears into her cunt, over and over again, growing more glistening as it does and, I swear, changing color every time. Green, Amber, Red: she doesn't know if she's coming or going! While Grace starts to come, shouting the words "Armageddon!" as Kevin sucks readily on her tits, turning them into two picture postcard peaks of the Swiss Alps, and he can't hold himself back any longer either, grabbing Monika's ears as she's sucking his cock, grabbing them like she's a bucket, and hollering, suddenly:

"Timberrrr!"

At which point the film ends.

Then I notice something: the film is directed by Roy Milhouse. I wonder?

5

Traveling matte is a general term for any process in which the background and the foreground are photographed separately and combined after the fact, either optically or electronically. The most basic of these processes is chroma key, which works in both film and video. The foreground subject is photographed in front of an evenly illuminated blue screen. The blue is then subtracted from the scene, leaving empty space around the subject. This space then receives a background scene. It is not essential that the backing be blue; the only requirement is that none of the color appears in the foreground subject.

(Library Shelf: T055589, Blain Brown, *The Filmmaker's Pocket Reference*, Focal Press: Boston, 1994, 177)

This is an explanation of why some things in film do not appear logical or, you might say, in the manner associated with reality or, *poke-alert!*, like some folks might like them. Film captures, film creates.

6

In the past hour I have watched the greater part of several high-budget films, all bearing those Roy Mil, that is Milroy, traits and many of which, alarmingly, star Leesa Kennedy.

I have watched some notable works supposedly by director's whose work I have not previously seen. For instance, Jean Luc Godard, namely Le Mepris in which a guy who I think is a USP performance major is screwed to distraction with an Orgasmo-tronic Delight Giant Vibrator by Leesa who is wearing a University Canoe Club sweatshirt. I have seen *Prenom Carmen* which features a sequence with several girls in red Lycra miniskirts, dancing out of a club (or so it seems) and being led into an ice-cream van by a guy in a white Stetson hat. Needless to say, children are warned to be wary of crossing the road behind something like that. I have seen *Sympathy for the Devil* which does not feature, as I was told it did, a Devil, but three guys screwing Colleen Donnelly on a sheepskin under a 500 watt fresnel. Films by Herzog, Eisenstein, Wenders, Fassbinder, Renoir, Greenaway, Bertolucci, Ingmar Bergman, John Cassavetes, Robert Altman, Stanley Kubrick reprise the earlier roles. The guy in the Stetson, his face always covered, delivers several flavors, cones, hot doggies, muesli bars, never leaving them where you'd expect. Sometimes the action takes place in the house by the sea. At other times it happens in places I think I recognize, but then can't always be, in one of the laboratories in the Biology Department, in the Library (from Short Loans to Browsing Collection to Shelves T055589 through Professor's Notes P044448), in the little square beside the Founders' Green, in the dark. I see guys who I know work in the Student Union and one guy who, at the Orientation Week, was so shy he didn't want to provide a photo for his student card. He's in something called *The Reckless Moment*, directed by Max Ophuls. In it his whole face is swallowed by the cunt of a woman in stretch velvet corselette and high heels who must weight fifteen stone if she's an ounce.

I see fit girls from Sociology, Psychology and Nursing, and then, in one scene, in Pedro Almodovar's *The Flower of My Secret*, hidden a little behind a guy from the USP Swimming Pool, that is, from the Sports Hall, who seems to be hamming it up too much with a full-size doll he calls Sue, I recognize Leesa.

Now there's a knock at the door.

7

Suddenly, there's a knock at the door. A guy enters. Balding. Maybe 45; maybe 5 10. He sees me in the chair in front of the video machine and doesn't say a word, heading out back to the kitchen. He's only gone a minute and comes back smiling.

"Where's Steve?" he says.

"Steve?" I ask, but my mind is racing and I'm not focusing quickly enough. "Isn't he . . . with you?"

He looks me over suspiciously.

It is then that I notice, out through the curtained window, the 4x4 moving off. I rush to the door but I cannot get there fast enough, shouldering my phone and trying to get the shot, fumbling stupidly, unprofessionally, with the door handle, until I have lost the opportunity and the 4x4 can be seen, not very well but certainly obviously, as a brown swing coat flash moving down along the road through the forest.

"Shit!" I cry. "Shit! Shit! Shit!" but it is superfluous, unnecessary dialogue and I will no doubt choose to cut it.

The 4x4, meanwhile, is disappearing from the frame.

The guy, who turns out to be "a cinematographer," Pete the cinematographer (who has he worked with, I ask. Jess Franco, he says!), Pete says: "We're going to have to watch that one."

"No," I scream. "This is the end of it!"

8

A sexuality defined as transgression or eroticism cannot be described in terms of liberation. The mise en jeu, as Foucault states, cannot be thematized as an abolition of limits. It must rather be conceived as a limit-case of an im-possible closure whose modality is not only constraint but also "tremblement." Against this background, the relative sexual abandon of animality is correctly perceived by Foucault in Bataillian terms as "happy" but indifferent profanity that has neither a positive or a negative relation to the basic dilemma of subjectivity. "Humanity" is no more an originary animality upon which a prohibition would be imposed than it is an originary receptivity upon which a contingent, contaminating motivation would be imposed. It is rather the imposition of such a problematic closure or the process of such a closure in its very being.

A second basic elaboration of the concept of transgression in Bataille's text is the description of the sacrifice. Within this context, Bataille interprets the ritual destruction of goods, animals or human beings through his terminology of the mise en jeu, the glissement, etc, and therefore develops as most basic ontological meaning for the term "sacrifice."

(Library Shelf: Professor's notes. Steven Milroy. Reading: Film, Culture and Society: 37070. "Excess and Imminence: Transgression in Bataille," Joseph Libertson, *MLN*, Vol. 92, No. 5, Comparative Literature, Dec., 1977, pp. 1001–1023)

9

? . . . I don't know.

I am driving in a little old silver Beemer, the rear seat now stacked with old video tapes which I am taking (or so I told Pete) "to sell." I feel slick but foul, my head is dancing in a strange red and silver light and I'm wondering if I really did take those Tyt-meril sometime this morning after all, if I took them both my-self, or if that was in some other folklorish film, some other older guy's missive. I'm shaking with fear or rage or fear or something and my top lip is sweating profusely and my gut is turning over and over itself, but things are improving. The seat hugs my hips. There's a calming pulse in the wheel, which is made of soft leath-er, and the gear shift is disconcertingly smooth. I shift up into fifth and the countryside passes as if it's rolling past on a carousel. I'm only mildly aware of the light rain which has begun falling but the top is up and the wind noise is low and there's a light in the cabin which is keyed and leafy and soft. I press my foot downward determinedly, and I watch the instruments which are perfectly laid on a binnacle highlighted with chrome. They slide, temper and needle the action. 70 . . . 75 . . . 80. The camera tilted slight-ly downward, the roadway is passing blurringly, flashing, beneath and, pressing on the CD joystick which automatically selects a CD from the 10 stack the player holds, the song that starts play-ing is Big Mistake by Natalie Inbruglia.

"I'm going to find Ras," I tell myself.

"Karen," I say loudly, maybe even cry out.

"Karen. . . . !"

10

It is the strangest thing, the weirdest thing, to just wander around the USP campus thinking about this, to look into faces and won-der if they too have been in *Dennis's Devilish Donut* or *Claudia's Clit*. If they have been to the house on the hill where doors open into impossibly red rooms, green-lit rooms, and to wonder what I should do about it. If I should do anything about it, in fact, phone Helena, find Milroy, phone USP Security, phone the police.

The speculation is intense. A girl I'm sure once served me a *quesadilla fritas* in a sandwich place way to the east of the Half-market, that used to be called Naples but now is apparently called Lamonts—which once had great faux Mexican but took blend food too far and so its mix of Indonesian and Caribbean just didn't work because peanut sauce simply does not enhance the taste of conch nor callaloo leaves go well whatsoever with bean curd—this girl I think was in several poorly lit scenes with a guy in leotards (a standout electric blue color, in fact), with another girl who reminded me vaguely of Melissa Joan Hart, but not enough to make me sure it was her, and in a room decorated almost entirely in Ekirna Swedish Futons, and the whole thing just throws me back on gut instinct and I can't quite decide if everyone should be allowed to choose how they live their lives and just let those lives be lived, or if I hate what Steve Milroy has done because it so incredibly cheap, or if . . . or if I want to know why they did it, and suspect it is for money, to finance their degrees maybe, and if this is in some way much worse.

I guess this is what Matt Damon calls in *Dogma,* a "genuine moral dilemma of modern times." And, having said that, what the Hell does Matt Damon know?

I'm entering the Student Union even without making the decision to do so and I'm ordering a Kenyan peaberry pale roast espresso and I'm taking up a chair near the window that looks out on the Arts and Sciences Quad, its flower and trees and fountain gushing water from the bronze arms of Apollo or Zeus or someone, and angels and imps, and I'm drinking the Kenyan and I'm unable to dislodge from my head a new song by Trapp, which is a remix of the same song by Ghostface Vadim, but more driving somehow, more alive, and. . .

Over at a table about fifteen yards away, beside the Clubs & Societies Noticeboard with posters like "Mountaineering Club Wall Crawl This Week" and "Are You a Registered Chairperson" and announcements like "School of Arts Block PC Terminals are not for Personal Email" I notice one of the prize pups that Ras introduced me to the other night, one of the people he brought to our table but, for a moment, his name escapes me. Then, just as momentarily, it falls into place.

It is Dale. And that there is Diane from Chemistry. Dale is from Biology. There is Jerome and Rory and Corey and Stowe.

All the science MS's, whom I watch for a moment, subtly from the height of the table so they rise up from an interior landscape of Laminex and salt shakers and Pago Juice ad cards until Corey, at least I think it's Corey, calls out:

"Hey, Ciaran, why don't you join us?"

He's actually standing right up on his seat.

Though I try to make it clear that I have no interest in doing this, shaking my head pretty vigorously, not moving out from behind my table, now another of their group is calling out and maybe this time it is Stowe, and he is saying:

"Yeah, come on. Check this out, Ciaran!"

So absolutely everyone in the Union is now turning to face me and the effect, the ambience, completely disintegrates and the choice passes out of my hands and into theirs and so I inch over reluctantly, just hoping that somewhere between here and there a portal might open up in the floor and I will fall through into another dimension where everyone is issued with Stormtek outer garments as a matter of course, and it is possible on Global Mail Order to order in anything you want with just a PC and a credit card, and the thousands of celebrity addresses which are regularly advertised actually do get personal replies, and the Lyricist Lounge is just one of a hundred venues which never ever stop, and nobody, not one person, ever thought about making another movie about impossible missions or alien invasions, nobody . . . ever.

A whole raft of what seems to be travel magazines have fallen into the prize pups' hands and they are passing them around and Diane is saying that, as happens, all the USP MSs have just been contacted by the owners of some plantation in Columbia who want them all to fly down there, tomorrow or the next day at the latest, and start a mink farm and raise otters and live on fortune left by a famous Hispanic opera singer and use his yacht and raise his children, who are all beautiful, and by this point they are all laughing and their laughter is attracting even more attention and I pan around the room and there is no one, nowhere, who is not watching this table, or making it the center of the entire universe, and at its core, getting louder and cooler are, by the minute, these prize pups.

Incredible.

| |

Barely an hour later and I'm on the verge of insisting that the police explain themselves further, but the phone goes dead.

The phone goes dead and I'm alone in the terrace because Karen is not here and I cannot raise anyone on the Supa-Video number, or Helena's or Ras's or even Kyle's number . . . because, in desperation, I have called both Candia and El Monkey and asked if Karen is there and all Kyle will tell me is that Eva who is studying social work, Pippa who skis, Susan who is a sandwich shop slinger and also doing a degree in History, Sophie who drives a beach cab, Vern who is apparently a tutor but I don't know what in, Helen who's on work experience at a stock broking firm, Fynella who is a new house officer in general surgery and Tony who is a flight attendant for Midland and can get cheap flights, though I've never asked him for one, are all there but Karen is not.

And now the police are calling and asking if I will come down to "assist them" a moment, though this seems far too *Hill Street Blues* to be real at all. Because of the "delicacy of the situation" they will not tell me what it is that they want me to assist them with, and I am reeling through everything that has happened and can't decide if they want me to help them regarding the USP students and pornography, or if something has finally developed regarding fraud at Arts festivals, or if it is to do with . . .

LK standing dimly in Steve Milroy's office, her hand like a knife. LK at the hospital, high in the window. LK in the cinema watching The Fly with her knees tucked up in front of her, her eyes fixed on the screen as, with a shotgun, Jeff Goldblum is blasted into tiny fly-like portions by Geena Davis, his girlfriend. LK screwing the guy from the campus sports center while the camera closes up on her intense expression, the red Gwyneth Paltrow of her lips, the absolute Gwyneth Paltrow of her eyes which are, well, absolutely searching, the Gywneth Paltrow of her . . .

Of her imitation porn-queen Gwyneth Paltrow profile, I guess, her slender jawline as familiar to the world as none other, her famous, yes I believe I can say imitation famous, nose, her slender but suggestively prim body, all intact while the meathead taps something military on the very Gywneth of her prim porn-queen tits and tries to screw her with something like the tenderness of Woody Allen as the camera zooms into her golden eyes and captures superbly the actual Gwyneth disgust she is feeling.

All these things are reeling backwards through my mind, as if at this very moment I am viewing them on a Steenbeck flatbed editing machine and, surrounded by Ecco film cleaner and mylar tape and grease pencils and split reels, and someone is saying to me—it's Joel Cox who edited both *The Rookie* and *Sudden Impact* and is probably my favorite editor, that is, if I discount Freeman Davies whose work on Trespass was absolutely phenomenal—that I should choose one thing or another and go largely for relational cutting, for identifying how one thing relates to another.

But I cannot choose. I have no idea how I will tie things up and I'm saying to myself:

"I used to have a thing about Gwyneth Paltrow. . .But now . . ."

The bus is packed and I wish I hadn't taken a seat because I want to watch the driver going about his everyday business. I want to watch him driving me onward to who knows what, his slaphead like a small desert landscape.

Toward the back of the bus, several Sports and Leisure undergrads are arguing about their scores on Toonstruck, in which all the toons, the characters on two absolutely action-packed value-for-money CDs, speak to you in the voices of Tim Curry and Christopher Lloyd.

12

When I arrive at the station, which is on the corner of the Promenade and East, a middle aged policewoman shows me to a small room which is labeled K4, a sign which gives nothing whatsoever away. I anticipate she is going to ask if I want to make my single phone call, that one that is to my "lawyer," and so I say:

"I'm afraid I haven't appointed a representative."

But she says, smiling horribly, "We don't do that here." And that cuts that.

I'm sitting maybe fifteen minutes, folding and unfolding my legs while I simultaneously bite my right thumbnail to the quick wondering if the mirror opposite allows for two-way viewing and deciding that naturally it does, when the door opens and an arm, at first seemingly clad in the light blue twill cotton of a police department uniform, comes into shot, holding the door half open, and next thing Ras steps in.

"Man!" he cries, "am I glad to see you."

But I'm not happy with this and we each cry, literally in unison, for different reasons perhaps:

"CUT.

"CUT

"CUT."

13

Lowering my face, I take a moment to reflect. You would think that as you learn to do something you would learn to do it better. Film-making. Life. Whatever. More is better, kind of thing, with some attention being given to technical ability and, let's be honest, a degree of talent and creativity which money can't buy. In that sense film has considerable advantages over life. If it were it possible to . . . well, storyboard life, what would mine look like? How would I shoot it? Who would star? On the other hand, would I really want to know?

I urge Ras to start again, to just slow down:

"So tell me," I say, "what is going on?"

This time with Ras speaking more tentatively, hand rising simultaneously to his eyes, rubbing distractedly at his cheek, the scene gets instantly better and, pulling back to sit in the hard chair behind the equally hard little table in the far corner, I say:

"At least I found you."

Once I'm sat, Ras drifts over to the window, which is dusty and barred, and he lights an Embassy Light.

I'm still not sure what on Earth I'm doing here, and the feeling that I may have lost control of . . . every part of my life, from Karen to Milroy, to my film to . . . everything! This feeling is starting to weigh on my mind so much that I stare dumbly at the top of the table on which someone has carved deeply in rough hewn letters:

The Backstreet Boys Are a Bunch of Fag Hags.

At the moment Ras's relative silence is not helping and I keep drifting back to the scene in which Leesa Kennedy is being screwed, just out of sight, in and out of frame, that I can visualize relentlessly and, the worst thing, or not the worst but certainly a disturbing thing that strikes me, is that the unnamed and largely unseen guy, the awkward, humping shape that teeters over the floral futon, is me . . . could actually be me.

Ras, dressed in a yellow Crestone parker and a pair of stonewash combat pants, his hair hanging loosely out over his shoulders but tucked firmly behind his ears, stands staring out the window with his Embassy swirling its white smoke snakes right up through the light. Suddenly, he turns to me, his eyes glaring like 1000w frensel lights, his lips inexplicably quivering, and he comes rushing over and puts his Embassy out firmly in the foil ashtray on the table beside me.

He says something which I am unable to pick up, and so don't answer. Instead, I begin to explain what I have seen at Milroy's house, to take him through each part of the discovery, list the residents of the terrace who appear to be involved, "porn," I say, with a kind of intensity that builds from my film-maker's contempt for this cheap crap to something else, something larger, more awful, yet Ras seems detached, barely registering what I'm saying.

All of a sudden he starts shouting:

"Why didn't you come when I called you, Ciaran? Fook-hit! What were you doing? Why didn't you fucking well *come*?"

I have no real answer to this and, trying to make up for this, simply repeat what I have been saying, staring intently at the light streaming in from alleyway outside, dancing wildly, insanely, through the barred police station windows.

"Listen . . ." I say, wanting to discover why I'm here and to calm Ras down before the balance of things is thrown over with his histrionics. But he stops me before I start and, waving his thin arms about, clamping his eyes with his two fists, says:

"They say Goody's . . ."

"What?" I say.

He shakes his head.

Suddenly, he begins to lose it completely, not forcing it or anything but just standing there, slightly back against the wall beside me, and the tears, which are not like my own I'm sure being much smaller, more rapidly flowing and coming from a totally different place in his eyes, slide so swiftly over his unshaven jaw that they dribble immediately down his neck.

He tries to mouth something which comes out as: "Ciaran, you poke." and all I can do is stutter:

"What? . . . Ras? . . . Huh?"

For the moment there is nothing more to make of this. The sound of police in the corridor adds almost nothing to the dusty smoking stench of room K4 where to my mind not a single decent thing has ever happened in this time or any other and the only evidence of real life is a notice reading YOU HAVE YOUR RIGHTS.

I try and imagine the last time I felt this shattered, this bad, because the three bottles of Loose Camoos (?) I shared with Leesa last night have not only refused to go away but have doubled their effect into some kind of life consuming hangover, and I wonder if it would be better just to heave the whole lot up, heave up on the police room floor, drink maybe half a dozen Cokes and try and kill the thing that way. A moment passes before an officer pokes his head in through the door he's just opened.

"Oh," he says, "sorry boys. I didn't know the room was . . ."

A tall, big-browed man, he does not seem to be able to take his eyes off me and I can see in the background, as my hungover eyes slip slightly out of focus, a pair of uniforms that look remarkably like the deep blue uniforms of USP Security. Not quite being poke enough to say he remembers me from somewhere the officer does, however, introduce himself as:

"Petreath."

Figuring he is Helena's "Detective Penrith" my ears prick up. It's pretty obvious to me that his being here with USP Security has something to do with Karen. He hangs on to the door, raising and lowering those huge brows of his like a castle lifting and then placing its drawbridge.

"You know," he says finally, "you're sitting there, you two, like a couple of regular fellas."

The remark springs out but nothing, from me or Ras, springs back.

Moments later, we're walking down to the elevator which, when we have gone down two floors, opens to reveal a room about the size of school science lab, and looking kind of the same. An African American guy, maybe 6'2", maybe 6'6", maybe Nation of Islam, sits in the corner wearing a white coat and a police badge and reading a copy of Mixmag Update. He barely looks up on seeing Petraeth but, slapping Mixmag down, walks over to the door opposite and, taking several keys in a jangle from his pocket, unlocks it. Petreath nods. He points for us to go in. The African American guy says in a low, Barry White, voice:

"Enjoy."

I'm getting a feeling that I cannot accurately describe, though I'm confident it is not a good one. I think this deep hangover of mine might actually be a case of me coming down with something, a major case of claustrophobia or, perhaps more accurately, a terrifying dose of agoraphobia and I might not, after this, want to leave the terrace at all; but, instead, just stay there all day and night hoping the *Flashdance* revival is really happening and I can dance till I drop in front of our dresser mirror, waiting for Karen, wearing a sweatband and a great pair of cycle shorts.

"You boys from around here?" asks Petreath, ominously.

Ras says something incomprehensible. Then adds: "He doesn't live with me. I'm . . . going to Honduras." which does nothing to clarify the situation.

Petreath braces his left arm against the wall in which, I now register, are a considerable number of drawers, and grasps one of their handles. In fact, now that I have noticed them the drawers recede as far as I can make out, a whole shimmering desert of cabinet doors as big and as unforgiving as the State of Wyoming, sloping both right and in reverse toward a blank white wall on which there is a red fire alarm.

"Worst part of the job, this," says Petreath, who has the ability to be both your uncle and your worst nightmare of a high school teacher at the same time, a totally terrifying English Literature teacher type.

Clasping the handle, he pulls back hard and the drawer slides out and out comes a silver table top. On this table top, glimmering and stainless steel, lies Goody.

If only I could cut! Whip pan. Ripple dissolve. But one thing's for sure, I cannot take my eyes off him and the whirr of a motor somewhere and the beep of some kind of alarm is deafening there in sight of Goody's paleness, a paleness so extreme that it's translucent. I swear I can see right through him, as if I have x-ray vision, some kind of genuinely special effect that punches through his grey mealy flesh to the still and seething meat, intestines, organs, Alert!, that remains of him, and now I can't stop myself.

I haul off and heave up. Everything emerges, splattering and spraying in dull speckled brilliance over the steel trolley and the floor while somewhere close by Ras is whispering:

"Yes. Yes. It's him."

Petreath: the complete professional. "Too bad. Heart, huh? Too bad. You got family you can . . . call?" Stuff like that. Words that fall from him so elegantly that, were it really the movies here, I'd be confident of Oscars, of Best Newcomer or, who knows, nominations for Petraeth for art direction.

"Attack? Attack?" I'm thinking. Sometimes the most incredible things happen on film and are recorded forever as evidence of the flimsy state of actual lived lives, the ephemeral nature of human existence.

Behind the drawers along the corridor I think I can hear rising a rumble of deadly approving laughter, and now it comes, my sense of a camera flickering, slowing, dying, that awful invisible smell of ammonia.

14

Majors in Film, Literature and Popular Culture are required to take 12 semester hours of Upper Level Courses. These can include:

Comparative Studies 667: Culture and Everyday Life
Women's Studies: 255: Motherhood and Visual Culture in
    France
English: 511: Understanding the Verb in Postcolonial Literature
English: 533: The Literature of Embarrassment: Special Topics
Music: 321: Rap and Philosophical Reasoning
History of Art 203: Surrealism and Dada
Sociology 222: Coming to Terms with Dystopia
Sociology 213: Themes in Post-Human Educational Theory
German 301: Wim Wenders

Film Studies 287: Star Studies: 2007 to the Present
Film Studies 333: Cinema and War
Theatre 501: Censorship, Sexuality and the Stage
Music 256: The Russian Trans-Modernist Movement
Comparative Studies 296: Icons and Attitudes in Latin American
    Dance
English 543: Finding the Center in Contemporary Fiction
History of Art 217: Jazz and the Material Arts
Comm. 588: Mass Communication Uncovered
Russian 305: Understanding Stalinism
Psychology 339: The Psychology of Ambulatory Progress
Classics 222: Horror and Sex in the Ancient World
Comm. 640: Famous Cartoon Strips
English 598: Animals and Poetry: Case Studies in Theory

(Library Shelf: Browsing Collection. *University
of Southport Student Handbook,* 2009–2010)

15

In El Monkey, a guy who is the spitting image of John Travolta
has just gone completely ape shit and punched out Nic from Supa-
Video. I arrive to find the place in turmoil. There's some stress
over the video shop, something about how awful the pay is, how
Nic has been cheating everyone, USP students, a whole bunch of
Machin Community College pokes, everyone he's being employ-
ing.

The John Travolta guy turns out to be the elder brother of one
of Nic's former employees and none too happy and, for the briefest of moments, I have this vision of Nic as a member of the West
Coast Mafioso and Travolta as an employee of a rival conglom-
erate, and a whole wonderful, wheeling scenario about dealings
in cheap re-branded, fake-branded liquor, supposedly Lambrusco
Bianco, Vladivar Vodka, Royal London gin and so on, and maybe
military secrets. But the moment comes and goes and I just watch
as Nic starts to back out of the place, offering to give the guy a

year's free rentals, a copy of his catalogue included, if he can keep his teeth, and return to his store-room to open a whole bunch of new stuff from MGM, Warner and the like.

Cleaning up, waiters fly everywhere serving their animated customers with Kimbap, Kimchi and Kongkuk. Today they're doing a Korean lunch special which looks, dare I say, excellent.

I've just spent two hours being grilled, de-briefed, call it what you like, by Petreath about Goody's death. Being, along with Ras, "counseled." All this stuff about the ever-present, all-encompassing, inevitability of things, which didn't actually go down too badly with me—though Ras could only take so much of it.

"Great for you!" he kept yelling at Petreath, who was apparently an expert in the area.

After which, when Petreath was off getting coffee and biscuits (his idea), promising to come back with "some thoughts that you both can think about," Ras explained that Goody was "much more of a guy" than I had ever realized.

"Did you know, for example," he said, "that he was the first one on the whole West coast to screen *Pink Flamingoes?*"

I said I hadn't realized that.

That he was a great fan of Mizoguchi and Oshima. Hardly my thing. And that he once worked on a documentary about . . . sea lions.

No, didn't know.

"Sure," he said, just controlling it. "On sixteen mil, actually."

"That a fact?" I said.

Goody had known Krotow from when they were both "just out of school" and moved to Southport, to the university, not for the great atmosphere of the Halfmarket, not for the great places to eat or the sense of a place condensed which Southport always seems to me, all pulled up together below the escarpment like a great little draw-stringed city, a neatly drawn together set reflecting the exact dimensions and style of who knows how many other places just like it, but for the beach, the sea, the old natural harbor, the surf, the quiet place it was before the university college became its own fully fledged university and the seafront was part of a wooden hick port town, marked out for a certain kind of redevelopment scheme that happened in, Man!, What? the 1940s or something?

I listen to all this with as much interest as I can muster. About Goody and Krotow being the driving forces behind starting the film festival and Goody and his underwater filming (?), surf-town stuff, how it was them who worked out that what USP needed was a late screener, some decent film entertainment, something for the sun bunnies and poke' kids that had started to move here. I tried to envisage this and the old theatre that the Roxy once was being converted back in the early '70s into a seasonal cinema for the tourists who came around this time of year, and still do, to catch what is effectively a pre Easter flush of summer, the boost this gave to the people to create the Southport Arts Festival and how this finally incorporated the Festival of the Waters. But this is a sore point and I can't quite focus on how I feel about it.

Today a letter arrived for me at the terrace from USP saying that I have so far failed to register for my second term Learning to Approach Film research skills and methods class and must do so today or I "will not (nicely underlined) be entitled to the usual student benefits."

Meanwhile, Helena calls and says she has found where Karen is staying; but that Karen is not too happy about her revealing this information on account of my film, so before she even thinks about revealing another thing, she says, I have to bring the tapes.

"No problem," I say.

16

At first I imagined I would trace Karen through the clothes she was not wearing, find her in a shop somewhere on the Halfmarket, in NEXT, RAW, PEPE, BURRO, BLACKOUT, ETAM, FAITH, FIRETRAP, PROFESSOR HEAD, THE DISPENSARY, LA FUMA, HYSTERIC GLAMOUR, FUTORI or FLYING DUCK. Not buying, because of her money problems, but looking. Wandering, maybe, between herringbone prints and v-necked sweaters, feeling the fabrics, comparing the cost, say, of an unknown and unsure brand with a respected and well-recognized one. That I would find her there and, using some great shot, an off-centered, angled medium shot most likely, something with incredible contrast and depth, capture her at a moment when she was absolutely reacting to the influences of the world around her. To get that on film so that in the composition of shots, the framing of them, the connections made between one and the other, the combining of *mise-en-scene* with the technical qualities of light and sound, the resonance and color and sheer beauty—yes, I think I can use that word—the sheer beauty of film, I would find her.

I thought, through this method, I would come upon not just Karen's sense of purpose, the thing that had brought her to USP, but her sense of self. Something well beyond whether she felt more strongly about film, or about literature. Something unconnected largely with the things that we did or said, the off-hand conversations that seemed to dribble down the stairs of the terrace, dash themselves off against the checked marble foyer, its dim and musty smell from the coats and jackets we threw on what was once maybe a rich family's coat pegs, the mirror now greened and chipped; conversations we let shred into nothing in the bright flat light of the Halfmarket. Instead, a kind of inner reflection of Karen, her shimmering white core that only correct atmospheric effects, proper costuming, careful scripting, clever prop placement, considered use of camera could ever hope to find. Except that it became certain, almost immediately, that my plan was flawed.

For one thing, who's to say she would do the obvious thing and spend time in the Halfmarket at all? Who's to say she wouldn't head straight over to Helena's and had been staying there (denied by Helena, but nevertheless . . .) since the day she left the terrace? Karen at that white marine apartment window, tipped back on a chair just edging onto the balcony, overlooking the boat harbor with its white yachts all quietly jiggling together, just to escape those morons, the madness of our own terrace? Or that she might not just head out over the escarpment, through the grounds of USP itself with its sculptured gardens and playing fields, the research facilities in glass and steel, the cheap old redbricks where Administration and Information Services picked over who knows what, head right through this and emerge on the other, eastern side, down toward Roeford and the suburban spread.

If I did find her, and managed somehow to get the set-up I needed, braced perhaps against the old pavilion scaffolding that lined the ceiling of El Monkey, who's to say it would capture the vitality and poignancy of the moment? That there wouldn't be some other interruption, her parents for example, or the hours she might spend in the library reading about medieval martyrdom (?), the conduct of the Dauphin (?), Reims Cathedral, the siege of Orleans, the Burgundians (?) that wouldn't take her away again before I could capture that shimmering real self I was after.

Instead I resolved to go for the more direct, though certainly less impressive route, to gather the tapes from the locker in the sports center, where I had left them, call Helena, and meet her later at Candia.

17

When I step off the bus I'm stuck right in a middle of a mass of quite well-behaved but otherwise nondescript students.

They're making their way into the USP Main Building with its archways decorated with reliefs of Heaven and Hell and characters such as the Etruscan flute player whose name escapes me and the god Horus assuming the form of a falcon and blackbirds which represent poets and magicians and the shield of Zeus, Adyton, bearing the head of a Gorgon, and the four rivers of Eden, and Mithra the god of light and the golden calf. . . .

As I'm caught up in all this, tempted, but resisting the urge to call out into the crowd "Heyeveryone, is that Johnny Depp over there?" I'm thinking how like yet also so very unlike those around me I am. I am thinking that my commitment to film has made me aware that the making of a life, the kinds of things that make it up, each of its tiny elements that maybe the unfilmic don't notice, don't realize exist, the subtle attentive moves of a face, the shape of a shoulder, the angle of a jaw, things which a fleeting glimpse in a mirror even can't reveal, that this is what life today is.

It's these accumulative details, I want to tell them, which both bind us together and separate us in our world: because of the sheer possibility of how each little element might be pushed and urged into generative contact with another, something that maybe they personally haven't recognized yet. Or whatever. Maybe they haven't thought about. I suddenly have the strongest of urges to call out:

"So, are you awake yet?"

Yet, instead of saying this, something which would probably not make a lot of sense to any of them, I simply pick their faces as they pass, setting myself fast in the middle of the entrance, letting them jostle and push past me toward the sunlight which sallowly fills the inner quad.

Is it possible, holding back as I am, that I have just spotted Leesa Kennedy, sitting over by the statue of Horus with Ras's MS prize pups and that, although they are way over past the crowd waiting to enter the old raked USP lecture theatres on the left and right of the quad, that I can actually hear what she is saying to them? That she is telling them about the Festival of the Waters Film Festival and inviting them all to be her guests shortly on the opening night. There will be, she says, films ranging from contemporary Hollywood hard tickets, films like *Hearts in Atlantis* and *Evolution* to certified classics like *The Matrix, Reservoir Dogs, Raging Bull,* along with a substantial New and Innovative film series, which will highlight the sheer excitement of today's bright and upcoming directors? And is she, as they look through what appears to be the Festival program, simultaneously describing to them this great opportunity she's found for students to both make some money and get involved in film in some way (as she herself has discovered! My God!). Have they, for example, ever acted?

Do they feel comfortable with their bodies? Are they concerned by nudity in films? Are they familiar with the early work of Paul Verhoeven?

No, when I think on it, this is just something I have made up, some flashback, some mad idea which gradually, as the buzzer horns in through the arched sandstone colonnade dissipates fortunately into nothing.

four

Dark City
1998, 105m, Color
Sci-fi thriller, /15
Entertainment (U.S.)

I

I'm sure as I pass up the College of Arts and Sciences main stairs
that over by stainless steel sculpture of heavy bolts and polished
right angles donated by Donatti Constructions, an "abstract" I
guess, that is Colleen waving to me, and I wonder (because the
place is covered in posters for it) if she has anything to do with
SPACE AND TIME, the inaugural Southport Arts Festival exhibition of so-called "visionary art" which her supervisor, Heather
Rebane, is holding tomorrow in the USP gallery, and who is now
calling out:

"Ciaran! Ciaran!"

"Ciaran," she is calling. "Have you seen Karen?"

As I still cannot forget the picture of her and the Wurlitzer, in
fact can still horribly see Cole propping there in front of her, his
eyes scooting over every visible portion of her skin like some kind
of mad naked chef, and Kevin just behind with Grace and Alice
further behind them still either sobbing or . . . or laughing, I can't
be sure, and I have no intention of mentioning my call to Helena
or, in fact, of answering her at all, and leave the stairs at the first
floor without even acknowledging her.

There's an almost natural rhythmic movement, a sixth sense,
that I'm developing with situations like this, almost as if I have

absorbed the scoring of Master P featuring Sikk The Shocker who did much of the totally brilliant music for *Scream 2*. Dee-dah, dee-dee-dah, dee-dah-dah-dah. The whole determined movement music of the thing.

All the pokes are rushing past me to their classes in Pharaonic Culture, Crime and the Urbanscape, New Readings of German Expressionism, me just moving through them like I'm strolling casually into a long darkening, flame ridden tunnel, alert as Hell . . . past School of Art, History and Archaeology, Modern European Languages and, most ridiculously of all, Sociology (which does not belong in this building but, apparently, USP has grown much larger and now has an office space problem; the Physics Department being likewise recently housed beside Business Management and the University Office of Industrial . . . er, Industry).

When I reach the door to the Film Studies Office I arrange my breathing at a neat, steady pace and knock hard on the door.

I don't, needless to say, consider for one moment that I am about to be confronted with my own death, that there might be behind the door five pumped-up guys in ski-masks who will simply bundle me back down the corridor and take me away in a white super-stretch limo. No. Everything appears as straightforward and ordinary as a leafy suburban street, a guy out front of a white lattice windowed bungalow mowing his carpet of grass, a nice little picnic with my best girl and my collie dog, a flight with some newly airborne snow geese over a vast sub-Arctic pine forest. And, though I feel a slight pang of loss at this, this simplification of the possibilities, I can't say I mind entirely. There's an honesty about it, if nothing else.

Then the door opens and Professor Krotow steps out.

I catch my breath, and think about running. I feel my phone in my hands and start, however tentatively, to bring it up to my right eye. Meanwhile, he just stands there, intently reading something in his hands. So, my finger on the button, I shoot off half a minute of hard fast close up, his face colored all pink, all round behind that clipped white beard, his lips fleshy, a pair of thick-rimmed half glasses tipped forwards on his nose, as I stand there not knowing what to say or what else to do.

"Oh, Droste," he says, noticing me finally, "there you are." almost calling though I am no more than three feet away from him. "We have to talk."

I am, momentarily, unable to piece two decent lines of dialogue together. Whatever I reply goes entirely missing.

"I've been wanting to see you," he continues, still reading but reaching out a hand to guide me down the corridor toward his office, his arms full of papers of some sort or another. "Didn't you receive my notes? I've sent, I believe, three."

"No," I say. "No. . . . I mean, I don't recall."

"We've been wondering about you."

In his office he takes up the place behind his desk—the place, I might call it.

"Where have you been?" he asks.

I don't answer. I don't have an answer. To say I'm confused would be an understatement. What about Helena's story? His impending arrest? In the light through his office window his white hair is a kind of halo, his hands gigantically reaching outwards as he stretches and then dives down on the papers he's now deposited on his desk.

At which point, having found some reference to me in his papers, he starts talking rapidly about his role as Head of the Department, his "academic duties" matched, he says at laser speed, "with a strong pastoral responsibility," simultaneously setting about confronting his files which are piled so high as to cause a vertical problem with the composition of my now developing wide shot.

I would like to ask him about Karen, raising with him the question of her current problems, noting my personal commitment to seeing her reach her full potential, mentioning perhaps that I am not sure that her faith in her subject, his subject (if he doesn't mind) is entirely well-placed in light of the current state of the world beyond USP, of the national employment market and the things being said about "transferable skill training." But the fact that I know about Steve Milroy's film-making holds me back a moment and this fact, the dangerous truth of it in light of the position of his he's describing, the importance of his leadership and so forth, is too too obvious and I keep quiet and wait, hoping that in a moment things will settle back into their simple, forward-moving groove.

Not, of course, that he's waiting for me to speak. Not, actually, that he has paused for one second to hear what I have to say. He's just going through the motions of shifting one file from the pile on the desk to a growing pile on the floor, calling out now and then to a woman (unseen) in an outer room:

"Do you have a file, Maggy?"

"Maggy, do you have a file for . . . Droste . . . Ciaran Droste?"

He busily moves through the final few documents he has left on his desk, slapping one file down to the floor after another and, watching, unnerved by him being here at all, I realize I cannot meanwhile make out his shape which, in the half-light, through the lens, is hidden beneath his single-breasted black-white check blazer and, although I have a full shot of his head with the venetians are closed and the desk lamp is on, I can only speculate at whether he is complete at all beneath that blazer of his or just somehow an animated android, a very convincing biorobotic entity, a replicant, and I think I say outright to him:

"Excuse me, sir. Have you heard Goody Ansel died?"

"Well," he says, as if I haven't spoken, "you're planning for your graduate project to make a . . . a film?"

"Didn't you two, after all, move here to Southport," I say, or maybe think I say. "To join a . . . commune or something?"

". . . and to do a critical study of . . . How will you do this, this . . . film, you mention, of . . . of Karen Manson'?"

"When was that exactly? Sixty . . . nine, was it? Sixty . . . eight?"

But he does not seem to catch my drift. He simply won't let up. "Well you might do this . . . And then you might do that."

And so he continues, jabbering about Expressionism, Impressionism, New Wave, poetic realism, the rise of the screen star, what he calls, the fool!, the loss of identity in contemporary Hollywood film, the idiosyncrasies of directors . . ." And I shoot. Shoot. Shoot. Until he is fading. Until I can barely . . .

"I have every confidence that you are capable of . . ." he says

"And perhaps when you have mastered . . ." dah-dee-dah-dee-dah . . .

And, funny enough, just when he begins to disappear completely, when I am defocus dissolving him away to nothing, I think I hear him say:

"Yes. Yes, Ciaran, I tell you: there isn't much you can't do with a film camera these days."

Then I am standing, inexplicably, alone in the corridor as the last few pokes rush past me into their seminar rooms and the light rain which is falling outside now spattering on the dusty skylights above, and the echoic sound of someone walking away in the distance, and the dark, and my phone still filming away blankly at his closed door in what is, quite frankly, both a great shot and very, very frightening.

2

"Photography is commonly regarded as an instrument for knowing things. When Thoreau said, "You can't say more than you see," he took for granted that sight had pride of place among the senses. But when, several generations later, Thoreau's dictum is quoted by Paul Strand to praise photography, it resonates with a different meaning. Cameras did not simply make it possible to apprehend more by seeing (through microphotography and teledetection). They changed seeing itself, by fostering the idea of seeing for seeing sake. Thoreau still lived in a polysensual world, though one in which observation had already begun to acquire the stature of a moral duty. He was talking about seeing not cut off

*from other senses, and about seeing in context (the context he called
Nature), that is, a seeing linked to certain presuppositions about what
he thought was worth seeing."*

(Library Shelf: T055589, Susan Sontag, *On
Photography,* Farrar, Straus & Giroux 1977, 92)

So fab!

3

Ras has chosen, and left for me here at the terrace this afternoon,
the following DVDs: *The Killer Tongue; Scream Queen Hot Tub Party;
Blade Harvest III; Chopping Mall* and *Dollman vs. Demonic Toys;* but,
bizarrely, he has not turned up to watch them. So I am watching
the DVDs with a guy called Reinhold, who I met some months
ago at Supa-Video, in New Releases and who, apparently, works
for a DVD company himself in the area of marketing and distribution.

I have gathered from the Sports Center all the porn I took
from Steve Milroy's house and called Helena to say that as soon as
she can arrange it I will be waiting here to come down to Candia
as soon as she calls. Which is fine, she says, by her . . . and even
apologies for the fact that she has had to wait for Karen to return
"from getting some cigars at the Seven Plus" she says.

Reinhold's sitting across on the sofa currently watching *Blade
Harvest III* and is up to the part where the newly created zombies, who used to be a five piece touring band called The Country
Rebels until they picked up two skanky band birds and took them
back to the tour bus and subsequently were slaughtered with fire
axes by the two groupies who had themselves newly been turned
into zombies from Hell, are now beginning to play in a bar which
has hired them for the evening and a group of construction workers from a local rail bridge repair project (a fact which becomes
relevant later when a city express train loaded with blind teenag-
ers on a school outing comes hurtling towards it) comes in and
the girl behind the bar, possibly Maria Pitillo wearing a straight

black wig, tells them to take it easy but they have no intention of toning themselves down and then, taking up their beers, they turn on the band calling them "Piss-poor" and "Rubber-kneed" and "Firkin' busted man" because, of course, they don't know that once this very song is over, appropriately titled "I Got To Get A Girl Like You," the band is going to jump down off the stage and, producing flick blades, machetes, scalpels, cleavers, scythes, sawn-off shotguns, is going to slice the entire audience into tiny, bite-size pieces, except, of course, for Pitillo who crouches under the bar as glass rains down on her like, well, rain and calls 911.

I'm sensing I'm getting nowhere waiting here and lazily shoot Reinhold in close-up to try and bring him round, but that actually fails miserably. He's been saying that he has to travel long distances for this company he works for and, though it sounds like a great job, it isn't really (because he is paid both by retainer and percentage and therefore has to sell a whole heap of DVDs in whatever hick town he is forced to visit, and that this is not always possible because people fail to support some of his directors, which is a shame on account of the fact that some of them are real talents, and he mentions some names which mean nothing to me and I feel, at this point, about as depressed as I am ever likely to get, and he says he wants to get some sleep shortly, maybe change his job too, maybe become a DJ, which he knows a bit about because of his connection with electronics, or move into clothing, some Ben Sherman or some B.C. Ethnic or G.U.R.U wear or something, which is easier to sell).

"More of a cut for me," he says, and then lets out their huge barking guffaw.

I want to say I understand his joke, but I don't, actually, and I spend some time reviewing the rushes from this morning's stumble into Professor Krotow's office and I think about how Karen might have taken what I said as I sat there describing my film of her to him, the ways it had panned out so far, my disillusion with the whole idea of finishing it, the way I thought he might be right that attending the *Learning to Approach Film* research skills and methods class could be just what I need, that I feel kind of adrift from things at the moment and had hoped to screen an excerpt of Karen at the Film Festival but that this didn't seem to be turning out and that he said he thought:

"You shouldn't go changing your ideas this far down the track." And that I thought this was pretty good advice; actually very much on the money.

I feel like, whatever else the world is doing, however else it looks out there beyond the cased terrace window over yonder, whatever great experiences others are having, I'm stuck uncomfortably in here marking time.

Reinhold called his father about ten minutes ago, his father who works for GM apparently, in sales and distribution, and he is now going home for dinner this evening to his parents' place in some suburban monstrosity and is going to stay overnight. Maybe he'll go to Europe in summer, to Italy maybe, he says, where he might try and locate the Italian film-maker Dario Argento, whose films (*Suspiria, Bird with the Crystal Plumage, Four Flies on Grey Velvet* and so on) he really admires and the company he works for at the moment actually distributes.

He's smoked, to date, a full pouch load of some foul mule grass that he bought from a guy in some hick town on his route and is just staring at the screen, even though I'm sure he's seen this film at least five times before, and I try to tell him that I might just take the professor's advice and finish the film.

I tell him I have this great idea for the final sequence of Karen whereby Karen's friend Colleen goes missing and is found the next day flat-caked, slapped-down and fried-up into two dozen of Plexus's All-New Bean Burgers ("Taste them," I say. "Tell me it hasn't happened already!"), while maybe Al Pacino falls in love with Jamie Lee Curtis (poor ruined Al having split with his stunning ex just minutes before she was gunned down by Andy Garcia in a hit that went wrong) but Jamie is on the make with David Duchovny who has implicated her in a deal to--

"Supply imported pirate videos," I say, "at severely discounted prices."

But what seems at first just wild speculation suddenly changes when I suddenly imagine in this final sequence someone who could be Gwyneth Paltrow, or is Leesa Kennedy, one or the other, strolling down onto the Promenade. It is early evening, my phone pans to a sunset which is so crimson it's almost purple, a mariachi band is playing, seagulls are gathering on the breakwater over by the marina, fluffing up in the light breeze, sharing small white fish between them, there are late surfers in the sea just sort of peeling off along these long lines of glowing sea swell and the music starts, it's "You're Still The One" by Shania Twain, as the credits roll, and everyone,

"The whole audience," I say, "at that point, just begins softly to cry because it's just so incredibly brilliant?"

But Reinhold is too wasted and isn't listening. And so, finally, I leave him the key to the terrace, tell him that if Helena calls he should tell her to call my phone, go out into the Halfmarket and, when a bus almost immediately comes into view I stop it and head in the direction of USP.

4

The university's College Road is teeming with people with books and bags and a guy on a sleek looking motor mower trimming the grass edges and a bunch of porters trying to load one of those ancient moving-platen type photocopiers onto the back of a USP pick-up.

With a scene like this I can't help thinking of the *Night of the Living Dead* and how quickly I make this link makes me smile and I let the scene melt into itself and dream, for the briefest of moments, of being George Romero and changing the face of modern film-making with just one great movie.

The story goes that Romero was working in advertising in Pittsburgh and his job was, primarily, in advertising. Because it was the 1960s, I guess he was selling flowers and batik clothing or something; but, one day, his bosses have this flash of an idea that they want to take some of their money from advertising and, with it, make a feature film. It is a great idea but they have no vision of how they are going to do it until in walks young George Romero who been busy doing ads for surfboards and health drinks and Bob Dylan albums and cheesy pictures of guys in flares, and he convinces them, with not too much difficulty, to make a horror movie.

The rest is Film History.

They go out to Evans City, thirty miles from Pittsburgh, and they start shooting. Everyone who is involved in the film has to contribute some finance. So the film is truly generated by the needs, the imagination, the determination of its makers. They use an old farmhouse which, though it is scheduled for demolition, they still rent at $300 a week. Everyone acts. Everyone crews. The film was so successful it launched Romero's Zombie Trilogy, the second being *Dawn of the Dead* (1979) and the third, the haunting *Day of the Dead* (1985).

With these simple but definitive films Romero has changed the face of contemporary Hollywood.

5

The space behind the Maldon Building seems different in the light. The windows above are reflecting the clouds moving fast across what is essentially an otherwise clear sky. I don't know whether it is because I am still very affected by remembering the wonderful Romero story or whether the dilemma of not yet having heard from Karen has finally hit home, or whether I'm now reacting badly to my meeting with Professor Krotow, "his unpredictable return" if he ever left, as it were, but I begin to feel my eyes welling up and, although this makes no sense at all, I'm starting to feel my cheeks growing wet and I really would like to pause a while and take stock.

Only the determination I have to find Ras keeps me focused and the wind that is coming up manages to dry my cheeks and I make for the steps by the dumpsters opposite. Soon I am on my way down and, seeing the glasshouses lining up in front of me, feeling much better. The door of the first is open, and I step in.

It's a strange light inside, an unhelpfully opaque light, as if the air itself is glass too and for a moment this disorientates me, this glass air.

To steady myself, I take particular note of a sign near the door. It outlines the rules for using "The USP Green Center" and explains how this particular Science Center, "one of the most advanced on campus," is temperature controlled year round and therefore all persons entering it must make a particular effort to keep the door closed. Which, after reading these rules through carefully several times, I do.

There is a fast low hum in the place, and the way the big black vents in the glass walls are turning and the direction of the warm air that blows through them, explains that the noise I encountered last time I was here was the sound of a generator and that this generator circulates the air that is making the place almost sub-tropical and, as it strikes me that this same air could well fog a camera lens, even an expensive one like a Bolex or an Eclair, I'm just glad I'm not shooting any of this.

I'm thinking, mostly, of getting to Hell out of here when, suddenly, out ahead in the far bottom left of what would be "the frame" I spot someone among the big leaves. I prop and, regardless of my camera phone being off, consciously attempt to focus, realizing as I do that the figure is Ras.

Dressed in his usual black and khaki, he's also wearing some kind of red cap and, before I even think about it, I call out:

"Hey poke!"

The path toward him is half mud and half a pattern of dull pebbles and there's the constant trickle of greenish water somewhere and the route ducks between these plants, possibly prehistoric or something, arranged according to the size and shape of their leaves so that the closer I get the bigger and more heavy with their cheery green water they get, the massive flushes of fronds, the pendulous trumpet-shaped white flowers, the thick fibrous trunks, the bright, red, yellow, fruits:

"Ras, man," I call, into a full splayed hand of fronds and fibers, "it's like a jungle in here."

"You know Rheinhold?" I say, parting a shiny bowing double-trunk to step on through, still only a vaguely accurate sense of Ras ahead. "Rheinhold the DVD guy?"

"Well, he came round," I say, "but the guy is a bit of a poke and . . ."

Suddenly the leaves thin to almost nothing and I push through into the open. Ras is standing in a friendly pose by a huge banana plant. He looks, in his black and his red, not unlike some kind of rare spider, the kind of tropical bird-eater you'd find in a wilderness like this. At first I think he's alone and I wonder if I could maybe take the risk of turning my phone on and shooting him "in action" among the trees, "trimming a stamen" or "plucking a seed." There's something about the place with its dripping walls and glass ceiling which reminds me of . . . the womb maybe (?). Somewhere mysteriously fertile. Or a space craft that has gone off course and crashed on a remote and uncharted planet. Or an experimental bathoscope at the bottom of a monstrously deep trench in an equally monstrous Pacific sea. Or the shower scene in *Psycho*. Or a love story in which the guy is a quadriplegic, but brilliant, and the girl, a little vague but not unattractive, is a famous jewelry heiress and wants to escape the limitations placed on her by her wealth. . .

But Ras is not alone. Not a moment passes before the leaves part and one of the prize plums is standing silently next to him.

First one plum. Then two. Then a third. Then all the plums appear, covered in mud, their eyes are as big as beach balls. I notice now that all around the pathway I'm on is not, as I assumed, soil. Instead, there's water, lying long and low in black troughs, being fed by long snouts from who knows what nearby source and . . .

"Hydroponic gardening," says Ras, interrupting my tracking of the limp stream back to its mighty waterfall.

"O," I say, my phone feeling heavy again now on my cheek.

"Ciaran," chirps Plum One, but I ignore him.

"We grow plants in water," he says.

"I know that," I say. "I mean, I know what hydroponics is."

"It's our final degree project," says Plum Two.

"Really?" I say, the words making perfect, atrocious sense to me.

"We have this experiment . . ." Ras starts, surveys the water a moment, weirdly grasps his chin with his muddy right hand. Continues: "Before our Honduran field trip. Our trip to . . . Honduras."

"Oh," I say, now hoisting my phone and zooming in suddenly on the water which is flowing bizarrely all around us.

"Honduras," I say. "Right."

I think it would be safe to say that Ras at this point looks a lot like Russell Crowe in *Proof of Life*. Like that great scene in *Proof of Life* when Crowe hangs 70 "thrill-seeking," "stupendous" feet in the air from a helicopter without any form of safety line in order to try and save Meg Ryan's droll husband from death at the hands of guerillas working to unbalance world peace, and the scene is shot with an 85mm lens, a polarizing filter, a red tricolor filter, from a Elemack Spyder dolly and a Chapman crane with the lighting high key, rating f8 on the meter.

"Ciaran," says Ras, or Russell, or maybe, maybe what I mean is that he looks like Russell and Ras, I can't be sure, "can I introduce you to my parents."

Like two neat porcelain souvenirs the Bergendahls, Mr. and Mrs, suddenly pop up into the scene, all shiny and stiff. Him in a . . . suit, a blazer, her in a . . . dress, a cream two-piece, possibly woolen slim-line dress. And, to a tee, grin!

I wish I could get my phone to my eye but the moisture is too heavy and, just for the moment, I cannot see a thing.

6

Cinema

At the time the cinema first developed in the West, Japan was in the throes of the Meiji Restoration and was enthusiastically embracing everything associated with modernity. Motion pictures were first imported in 1896 and, in characteristic Japanese fashion, they were making their own in 1899. Until the advent of talkies, dialogue and general explanation was provided by the benshi, a live commentator. This was necessary for foreign films but the benshi quickly became as important as part of the cinematic experience of film itself.

(Library Shelf: Browsing Collection. Taylor. Chris, Robert Strauss and Tony Wheeler, *Japan: A Lonely Planet Survival Kit,* Lonely Planet: Oakland, 1994, 44)

7

It's now just after 5 pm and the shops are spilling out their spumes of sack-toting den mothers and Kris Kringle office dads carrying home marked down *South Park* toys and now discounted Jerry Springer campaign badges. Ras and "his folks" (his words) have gone to El Monkey for the early-evening "coffee specials." Figures. Pretty soon Helena will be arriving at Candia to pick up Milroy's porn and she has promised to bring Karen and to explain to her why I have been acting so weird, the fact that it is not outrageous to act a little intense when a director is so heavily involved in a project, that this doesn't diminish in any way my love for her, or our life, and that, as she probably knows by now, she was largely right about Milroy and did she think we should say anything to the rest of the terrace, although I get the feeling, as I always have, that Kevin was the reason they had done it, that he convinced the others, and whatever money they were paid was nowhere near enough, no matter how much they figure their identities will remain anonymous to others and, not to raise the question of STDs, well, not to raise it because they know each other and it is just something that, the Leesa thing in the back of my mind, I've been kind of thinking about. . . . But how, in fact, can they stand to look each other straight in the face after something like that?

I think there is an issue, of course, that a film like *Karen* must remain true to its material, the unrelenting to and fro of life in the terrace, the strange turns in Karen's life, the madness of USP and its swarm of free-thinking, fast-talking, totally desperate pokes, the modern movement of the Halfmarket and the lapping beach beyond, the great times and the low and, though I accept that Helena might well have got her story wrong, perhaps even that her employers were merely checking details of an otherwise ordinary yearly audit connected, no doubt, with the requirements of government funding and accountability to this and so on and so forth, yet the Krotow business remains largely unresolved and there are, needless to say, gaps and concoctions, strange turns which her clarification could assist and I could shoot these, perhaps, in a flashback sequence or as a dream of hers, something stormy, or as set of spoken conjectures made to an unidentified male friend in an equally unidentifiable narrow brimmed hat, from behind, in a booth at El Monkey. There are a number of possibilities.

I have not entirely given up the idea of screening some part of the film at the Roxy and during the Festival and, as Ras will be taking over from Goody temporarily, until the management find a replacement (which might, in fact, even be me) and then he leaves for Honduras, who's to say I couldn't convince him to find a gap, a late night slot for me some time—with or without the dubious approval of LK?

My ultimate aim, I'll tell Karen, will be to find *Karen* a major distributor, say Fox or First Independent. At the end of the spring, when the films markets open for the next year's season. Screen it perhaps at Sundance in January. At Rome in February. At Madrid in April. I'd maybe settle for Warner, but I'm not likely to go with Metrodome, even though Kevin Smith's work definitely has some enduring value.

I sit down in a booth by the door and call Kyle over to order a Reuben Sandwich and an espresso Guatamalan and I ask him, joking very, very casually, though with measured emphasis:

"I don't suppose you've seen Gwyneth today? Gwyneth Paltrow?"

"Seen her? Oh yeah," he says, passing me my cutlery neatly wrapped in a pink paper napkin, "her and Sean Penn. I hear they're an item. So Ben Affleck was saying. They certainly gave me that impression, right? But you know how it is with Ben, always the kidder? Now if you were looking for Mira Sorvino, say, well that would be a different matter. She's just out back making some *ensaladas*."

He calls: "Hey Mira, you there babe?"

I realize by this, and by the fact that he is now laughing OTT, like the baboon that he is, that Kyle has no idea whatsoever that I am dissing him and I sit back and enjoy the moment.

Has he ever felt, I wonder, the real honest feeling, the meteoric public interest in films like, say *Speed* and *Gladiator* and *Remember the Titans?*

Has he ever considered that this interest is so much more authentic than the art on the walls here, the Lichtenberger, whatever, and that in film terms it would be a simple matter at this point to cut to a picture of Soapy the Seal from the Central Park Zoo (balancing mackerel, no doubt, on his preternatural snout), or to superimpose several scenes from *The Thing*, the sequence, for example, where the guy's stomach bites off Richard Dysart's hands, the drooling tentacled snarling chicken-dog makes a break for it, and the decapitated head sprouts spider's legs and scuttles across the floor; or I could be restrained, cute, subliminal, and simply dissolve Kyle's whole ugly head into the leaves of a fine blue-grey calabrese.

"Well," I say, feeling satisfied with the possibilities and taking a long slow sip of my Guatamalan, which is unbelievably and suitably peppery, "I still must commend you on the great variety of the food you serve here, Kyle. You know: the almost worldwide distribution of the food you personally serve here."

Not catching my drift, he's still chuckling away as he returns to the kitchen but not before pointing out to the likes of Fynella, his girlfriend, who is sitting, discussing surgical procedure (I'm guessing), with someone who looks more like Albert Schweitzer than George Clooney, that the menu is largely a pile of dog shit and she'd be better off eating at Burger King where at least she'd get large fries at half price if she purchased the Spring Warmer meal deal.

I'm not waiting long before Helena walks in. She's dressed impeccably in tailored blackcurrant-colored pleated trousers and a blackcurrant single-buttoned jacket and a pair of blackcurrant Funk leather ankle boots. And she is not, I must add, alone.

There are bits of me that were prepared this. The Roger Corman in me, you might say (I'm talking *X: The Man with the X-Ray Eyes*). The Abel Ferrara in me. Always another twist. Another possibility. There are bits of me, heart-rendered, achingly honest bits which still think *Xena: Warrior Princess* is a great show and get misty-eyed when I miss *Hong Kong Phooey,* that actually asked for this further complication, fearing that my audience would at this point lose interest without it and trusting, as I must, that I could revive their interest so that with, well, something else, they would truly love my film.

So Helena enters Candia, strides, gallops up to my booth, accompanied by Steve Milroy.

8

"Well?" says Helena, heaving out smoke, not even ordering.

"I have them," I say, "here," reaching down to my duffle bag-backpack on the floor, my eyes avoiding but nevertheless recording Milroy.

"Where's Karen?" I say.

I wait but she fails to answer for what seems like ever, so I intimate ("Where was that big house, anyway?" . . ."Wurlitzer sure made great jukeboxes didn't they?" that kind of thing) that I know what I've seen, that I know he's part of it, that were it not for having a certain affection—yes, I actually use this word!—affection for Leesa, I would have just handed them over to a guy I know ("Mr. Petreath" I say, which I think makes my point), and let deal with the whole thing.

When I am finished Helena, smoking, pouts strangely, wrinkling that sharp rounded jaw of hers, both to herself and then, with something like curiosity, at Milroy who has been perusing a copy of The Times he is carrying with him. He, for his part, lights one of her cigarettes for himself, a low tar cigarette and, without a flicker of guilt in his hard brown eyes, draws back hard.

He reminds me at that moment of no one so much as that doyen of crime, that film star of back alleys, that crooked cop in the "adult" book shop, that prince of cheap-shit liquor stores, Harvey Keitel. Goddamn punk upbringing rings out all over the place. Dragged up from the filthy sewer of some backstreet Hoboken childhood casts its shadow onto the table.

"Have you seen Ras?" Helena asks suddenly, brightly. "Or . . . anyone? Kevin?"

"No," I say (So, I was right!), my left foot down firm on the duffle bag. "No, not for a few days. I think he's, like, laying low."

"Oh, sure," says Helena, and gestures (hand sweeping across the table in a neat smoky line) for Milroy to take a seat . . . which he does, Harveyly.

All sitting now Helena orders a Colombian, I go for a Tanzanian Kilimanjaro coarse grind dark roast Viennese and Milroy, obviously nobody's fool, looks up from his paper and settles finally for a fine grind Costa Rican, but insists on it being Turkish. As I wait, and Milroy reads, I imagine my phone drifting slowly between us as behind the sound of the coffee grinder rages away, Kyle whistling something that I believe, unbelievably, is "My All" by Mariah Carey, it is obvious that we three have been thrown somehow, drawn into each other's orbits by split-second decisions.

When, at last, Helena speaks it's in a voice so low I can barely hear her:

"We need to go somewhere," I think she says, not even touching her Colombian, "else."

"Right, Nell," says Milroy.

"What?" I say. "Why's that exactly?"

"And take a look at what you . . . have," says Milroy to Helena, more to Helena (that is: Nell) than to me.

"And . . . talk," he says (to me now).

"We're interested, Ciaran . . ." says Helena. "In finding a particular missing tape." For some reason, I can't stop repeating to myself: "it is so absolutely true, you can't go past working with professionals. I mean, it always, always pays off in the long run."

" . . . in what you've got," finishes Helena.

"Kid," says Milroy, placing his *Times* on the table and his left hand beneath it. "I'm a film-maker, you know?"

"I know that," I say, with what I can only call a "well-balanced" sense of irony.

If his left hand holds a gun, then the barrel of a gun is facing me from beneath his paper. If that were the case then no one else but Helena could see it. He would be pointing perhaps a .38 across the table at me.

His other hand, his right hand, points now toward the door. I get up slowly, both in the world of his right hand, and more ominous world of his left.

Outside, where the light rain has stopped and the sky is turning a kind of streaky bleeding henna, I move nervously along, through the groups of mallrats, cashiers and shop assistants who are all bizarrely, down to the very last one, wearing arctic-fleece zippered tops in lime, lemon or peach, passing RAW, FAITH, FIRETRAP, THE DISPENSARY, FUTORI and FLYING DUCK and past the glass doorway of what used to be Computline Communications, before the cell phone industry rationalized and they closed, toward the terrace.

There is an aloofness about Helena which would be disconcerting if not that I am blanking everything out except for my image of Karen, the delicate sadness she currently occupies, the light moments of adventure and struggle we've shared (our stacked trip on the train from Roeford to Southport, the play she did based on the life of that tragic film star River Phoenix, my first few moments of her film, as she bounced up to my phone all bright on the bed and delivered a monologue on . . . on her favorite brand of peanut butter), her laughable calls homes (that fat franchise-owning father of hers; her skittish Prague-loving mom, once edited an article for *New Idea* on "Your Daughter's Lovers: How to Talk to Them," apparently) and I have this conviction, momentarily at least, that we'll get to the terrace and Karen will be there waiting. So Helena's profile, which is nothing if not angular and horribly fixed, doesn't bother me too much.

We reach the terrace and I let them both in.

"It's okay," I say, a little nervously, "I'll show you all I have."

Helena tucks her short thin bob behind her ears as Milroy says: "Very sound."

The words fall heavily into the stairwell. I knock on the flat door, but unfortunately no Karen answers.

When I let them into the flat, they gather in close. There's stillness in the air and the slight smell of the mule grass which Rheinhold has left and which I am unable to do anything immediately about. But I guess, distractedly, pathetically, that he's on the road somewhere now, selling Val Kilmer pictures, something featuring Leonardo Di Caprio, a great new comedy starring Robin poking Williams!

Obviously I am, at this moment, losing my grip.

I suddenly have the uncontrollable urge to recommend to someone, anyone, the following filmsites:

http://www.seven.com
http://www.flatliners.com
http://www.mimic.com
http://www.wishmaster.com
http://www.payback.com
http://www.existenz.com
http://www.carrie2.com
http://www.faceoff.com
http://www.ninthgate.com
http://www.americanpsycho.com
http://www.bodypiercer.com
http://www.goosebumps.com

I put the first tape into the player and roll the film, explaining: "But this is not all"

Neither Helena nor Milroy seem to register this, though as the film starts I say it again and, for good measure, emphasize not.

Whatever is in Milroy's hand beneath the paper is relentlessly pointing in my direction and, speculating on it, I can't forget the day I found him in his office with his head in a bag and how disturbing that was, not just the sight of him naked and dying, but the mystery of it, I guess, the reasoning that brought him to it. And this unsticks me, makes it difficult to concentrate.

The first shot—Wox! in one of his films, in this particular sequence of one of his films!—is of the open door to the big beach house, the porn house. It's framed (I cannot avoid how nicely) by the windows which are darkened. The camera pans, smoothly, across the now slightly lit living room, revealing a two-seat mahogany-colored settee, upturned, a pine hi-fi cabinet, two uplighter lamps, in gold fleck, a Mathmos lava lamp, with green and blue lava. In the "big country kitchen," where we travel in a quick, natural movement, who knows how many packets of Nature's Natural, Crunchy, Couscous with Garlic and Herb, boxes of Provamel Soya Dream, jars of caperberries, Mixed Fruit, Green Tea. Then the actors enter.

The same basic scenario features in all of the films, though sometimes the location is different, sometimes it shifts to the university, to labs in the university, to one of those little rooms that hide up in the clock tower (great view of the graduate lawn, incidentally) and seem to contain "leather goods," to somewhere that looks like some kind of inner university council chamber, a long oaken table, pictures of "Provosts of the Ages."

"No," says Helena, beaking her face forward. "Not here."

Milroy is scratching his right temple with his thumbnail, grimacing because he's doing it quite hard to what?, tame a nerve probably, trying to find with his left hand (now visible, I know) his last cigarette in the packet in his coat pocket.

"What is it?" I ask.

"It's not here," he replies, but not to me. To Helena who then asks him for a cigarette, because she's right out, but he's only got one so they share the one he's finishing. He shakes something from his hairline, a hairline which is slightly receding, kind of '70s rock star receding I'd call it, not in downy way or anything or in that old folks combed over fashion, just kind of slinking back, hard-edged, edging away from the forehead like it's seen something it doesn't like and doesn't want to get close to.

Suddenly: "There's another tape!" he barks.

And then reels off a whole line to Helena about not having found anything in Krotow's apartment.

I'm not entirely following what he's saying; but I see he's frozen the last film in the video player at the point at which a white pickup is delivering Kevin and Cole and Colleen and Alice to the big white house, the camera zooming in and stopped now at extreme close-up, just the corner of the frame where someone who looks remarkably like Karen (?) seems to be standing.

"I need to get it back," he barks at me.

"Oh," I say, the vids in the duffle bag beside me seemingly no longer an issue.

"You see," he says, pacing, exhaling, "you must understand us here, Ciaran—none of this, the . . . err, fraud, the films, was

Nell's or my idea. It was her. Leesa. And I think she has taken a particular tape to Julian. To Professor Krotow. And said it is ours."

I watch the film flickering on the TV; it looks like an old movie, a silent movie perhaps, one of those first movies anyone ever made.

9

Another fabulous cocktail to share with friends:

Zulu Swizzle

3 msr dark rum
2 msr Kahlua
4 msr Cola
1 msr Bourbon
3 msr vodka
½ msr almond syrup.

Making Time: 2–4 minutes

Garnish with a melon ball and slice of lemon. Serve in a glass with ice, to taste.

10

I've stolen Ras's bike and I'm heading flat out down the Promenade, past the beach on one side and the stores on the other. I'm going so fast the air has turned into ice and is slicing the skin from my face, arms, hair from my head, searing away something from around me which is thick and scaly and growing by the minute. I pass the following well-known vehicles: Firebirds, Fieros, Cadillac CTS, Trans-Ams, Infiniti FX, Daytonas, Magnum SRT, Le Barons, Toyotas, Mazdas, more Toyotas, the sea on one side and the stores turned to a kind of white granite, slicing, carving through the beachfront with my phone out front recording it all and no desire to stop, go back to the terrace, slow down, looking for a deal, a sweet deal, a three picture take-up, a new life, a window, a view, places in my heart.

225

I am trying to digest what I have been told and can only just manage. How the real culprit was Leesa Kennedy, who stole from the Arts festival. That she would use students from USP as her stars, coerce them with all that talk about a free-thinking, creative environment, all that hippy crap she got from her mother. And that Goody Ansel, Helena pointed out, would screen them for her any time she wanted on account of something he'd had going with her mother in the '60s, something with '60s libertarian magazines like *Suck* and *The International Times*. Seems she's been doing it for a while now, with the last three cohorts of USP students, just building this great little industry of hers.

"If you see what I mean?" said Milroy.

I saw.

When Steve Milroy said he wanted nothing to do with it she offered to implicate him in things anyway. "It wouldn't take much. Just for her to take it to Julian. He is the Departmental Head." And for a while—"the suicide thing"—he lost the plot a little. He was, after all, the one known for his film-making, Festival of the Waters Special Award winner and all, and who was going to believe that it was the professor and not him?

"I got . . . scared," he said.

"Yes," I said. "I get that."

"The bitch," said Helena, or Nell. Both.

Only, as luck would, and so on . . . an audit was called because the Arts Festival had decided to hold their parade this year, do an event with international yachting stars, introduce a prize for local . . . err, potters, and so things were uncovered that would otherwise have gone unnoticed. At which point, Leesa decided to close the things down and just disappear. She had plans to start a new career "in the art world." Spend the rest of her life with her mother listening to Bob Dylan, I guess, doing Tai Chi, sniffing the flowers, silk-screening batik designs, visiting their personal chiropractor! She certainly had made enquiries about purchasing a gallery, apparently (estate agents have records to confirm), "original works and rare prints," in London, Whitehall, where she would probably have grown her hair long, taken to wearing men's loafers, faked an East European accent, dah-dee-dah-dee-dah, everything.

"Then you came along," said Milroy, stretching back on the old sofa in the terrace, "with your film."

"That's right," said Helena.

"It's about Karen," I pointed out.

11

The police arrived at 9.00 this morning. They have found, because I have led them to them, several videos stashed above a cistern in the College of Arts and Sciences staff toilets, "tapes" which Professor Krotow (as Head) denies he knows anything about but, because I have included in the stack some scenes of him talking to his students, including one long sequence in which he talks about "the beauty of the body," "the perverted scene of human discourse," "the sites of gender liberation and the sexual revolution" a whole load of nonsensical but incriminating crap, chances are he is wasting his breath. They are looking for more "tapes" and plan to search the entire College.

I know that this is falsifying the truth; but the comedy of the thing strikes me as worthwhile and when they eventually find that he knows nothing about film, nothing whatsoever about the cinema even though he sits on the Film Festival Committee, that he is in fact a professor of medieval literature they no doubt will let him go. But, in the meantime, what fun. What a grin! And to think he didn't even know until now that film has the power to transform his life.

With the "truth" out, dozens of parents have been calling USP, wanting to find their kids, check on their babies. All very touching. Kevin and Grace and Alice and Monika and Colleen and Cole are being counseled by some of the university's trained "crisis counselors" who work for Nightline, assisted I might add, by Lieutenant Petreath who actually made a special effort to visit me and thank me for pointing my friends in his direction. Above the university the news bird of KMTV is circling around like a giant seagull, a white and glistening . . . gull, filming us as Ras and I and some of the prize pups wave Hooch sweaters, furry trapper hats, several Tommy Hilfiger t-shirts, dancing around the graduate's lawn and out in front of the library where a guy—not known—sells discount CDs, including totally new singles by Usher, Savage Garden, Five, and several people are slipping the steps on skateboards. Finally, with all the activity, a girl from Psychology, Psychology or Philosophy I think, faints from all the rush. She looks, well, dead, and we gather around, but no one does anything.

The opening film of the Film Festival is showing tonight at the Roxy. Ras is projecting and I'm going. When Krotow is brought down the English Department steps he is screaming, ranting about his love of teaching, his commitment to his students, his innocence.

He spots me in the crowd and blanches, sideways, props even, but I simply laugh.

"Loser," I shout. "Man, what a loser."

12

Chocolate muffins with peanuts and hot orange sauce

(Serves 6) For that end of semester gathering, try these regular favourites
10 fl oz dark chocolate sauce
12 chocolate muffins
5 oranges
2lb peanuts
5 msr rum
1 msr cherry brandy
1 msr Southern Comfort
6 scoops vanilla ice cream
Mint

Cooking Time: 4–8 minutes

1. Warm the chocolate sauces in a pan, until it melts.
2. Microwave muffins for 2 minutes. Place on a plate.

3. Add to sauce: peanuts, rum, cherry brandy, Southern Comfort.
4. Pour sauce on muffins.
5. Serve with scoop of ice-cream and garnish with a sprig of mint.

13

As night falls I make my way out. Without Karen I can't stay in the terrace and I can't raise Ras so I figure he has already headed over to The Roxy. He's taken the additional news about Goody petty well, finds it hard to believe, actually thought Krotow was a good guy, knew nothing about Goody running private late night screenings, but kind of likes the idea of him having done it.

"It's real anti-studio stuff, you know," he says. And I have to partially agree.

He has not mentioned Honduras again, but I know he is going and we've made a deal that when I sort things out with Karen we'll both come and visit him and maybe eat . . . "some esquites together," I said, "some frijoles charros."

I feel like I'm starring in *Switchback, Copland, Retroactive,* man! *The Borrowers, Inventing the Abbotts!*

"Stallone is much better than people think," I keep saying to myself.

"Pierce Brosnan is by far the best James Bond."

"Who says Alicia Silverstone can't act?"

"Personally I have no time for Ben Affleck."

"Do you think Jude Law is, actually, the next Matt Damon?"

"Tea Leoni has a distinctive look."

"Vince Vaughn was great in *The Locusts*."

"Anybody know what ever happened to Richard Linklater?"

I'm passing the Griffith Building when I spot a crowd at the entrance, staff, professors, the board of governors, the whole *Ferris Bueller's Day Off* collection of them at the entrance to the USP gallery. Everyone in black dinner jackets and faux-fur coats. For reasons I can't immediately work out I can see Colleen amongst them and she sees me and calls out my name:

"What's going on?" I reply, not going over.

She is dressed in a white, call-it-a-frock, with a floral edge, possibly daisies, and something faux-fur around the collar, all of which does not do anything for her complexion which eeks out blotchy and red.

"It's Heather's show," she says.

"O," I say, moving away. "Groovy . . . I guess."

"Listen," she calls. "Where's Karen?"

I ignore this and head west, east, who knows, away from her.

"Bali." I call back, not admitting that I think, actually, she is back in Roeford at the moment with her parents. "Is that possible?"

When I arrive at Candia the place is too packed to get in. Kyle is on the door but says I should probably come back after ten. I say that actually he is probably what was left when the *Starship Troopers* got hold of Elizabeth Davidtz and fed her to the big bugs, though this never happened and the fact that he thinks it did is evidence enough of what an absolute muppet he is. At El Monkey the crowd is no better and I resolve just to head to The Roxy, though the screening won't start now for nearly an hour and I'm not paying good money to see the last matinee which is, believe it or not, *Six Days, Seven Nights.*

I am re-passing the university in the bus when I notice the crowd has still not moved so I get off and I wander over and, thinking this might be a neat way to end things, let my phone roll and dolly-in, keeping closely behind the oak trees which surround the car park so that I will not be seen again by Colleen.

The crowd is growing pretty restless and some of the women, perhaps the wives of Nobel Prize winners (you know, it is possible in places like USP after all), absolutely straight pharmacists, deep sea oceanographers, novelists, guys who think they can cure cancer, discover the secret language of gang warfare, prevent further global warming, unearth the Arc of the Covenant, Christ knows, are saying that they would like to go home now. So much for SPACE AND TIME they're saying. Then something starts happening behind the glass.

I slip up into the crowd and move, dolly, zoom, forward with it. The doors of the gallery are opening and it's possible to join the crowd streaming in, and remain largely unnoticed. Inside the light is so low, golden, downlit, unsuitable, that I think I might miss something. But I shoot wide and then stop-down and things are fine, good even. The crowd surges forward, and so do I. But then it stops. There's red lit now. Crimson. The lights change to golden and the music starts. Something classical, I think. Something by a classical musician. Like? Pick a name. Then someone, a woman toward the head of the crowd, starts screaming.

I push to the front, shooting, filming, framing and reframing, stopping down, down, focusing, and catch a glimpse of Heather Rebane as she comes down from a balcony which has been built to the rear of the gallery. She appears to be dressed in a . . . wetsuit? Is that a wetsuit? Striding down the staircase, marvelously marble look set, towards the crowd, she smiles like a goon or, hey, Julia Roberts! Then, as I pan, not a whip or anything like that, just slow, providing continuity of interest but changing the center of attention, and she points, left, right, lights focus on where she is pointing and, at what she is pointing at . . . in glass cases, on steel rods. There are, if I am not mistaken (and I'm not) animated sculptures of hands, legs, feet, detached, alone, colorless almost, faux hospital fodder, a brain on a pink carousel which turns and plays the Halleluiah Chorus, eyes (whose? I wonder) on toothpicks, like *hor d'oeurves,* looking everywhere, animated torsos slit from navel to rib-cage, green lit from inside, the partly scalped prosthetic skulls of old men, perfectly re-created, conduits of elastic intestine, scalps on the foam heads of mannequins, cunts, pricks, in cute gnomish garden displays, a cross-selection of rubber feet of varying size, prosthetic thigh bones, ears, piles of . . . what?

five

Groundhog Day
1993, 103m, Color
Comedy , PG
Columbia, (U.S.)

I

Faked stuff, I guess.

When I arrive at the Roxy Ras is already in the projection room. There's a crowd in the auditorium and Ras is kind of mildly nervous. In a minute a member of the Film Festival committee is going to welcome the crowd, and he's currently locking the tape of the opening film into the player attached to the video projector, and looking out for her signal. I look out through the projector window and can't believe my eyes when I find that the person introducing the film is, in fact, Leesa Kennedy.

She's dressed in a black stretch velvet evening dress and looks "the part." I feel nothing; though she does look, it's undeniable, an awful lot like Gwyneth Paltrow.

Interestingly, the film she is introducing is called *Jeanne D'Arc,* a new film from a local director apparently (?), which only makes me wish even more that Karen was here. But I am trying not to panic, trying to think this all through, trying to work out what Leesa is doing here, under the circumstances, I mean. But I can't quite grasp it.

Helena has apologized for ever having lied about knowing where Karen has gone but she couldn't be sure how much I knew, whether Steve had spoken to me and so forth about the pressure he has been under to keep all this quiet. Which is understandable.

Next week I'll head over to Roeford and see if I can find Karen and when I do, because I'm fairly confident I will (she's left behind, after all, a whole wardrobe of things), I'll explain how it has all panned out, the possibility of me working here in the Roxy, how Honduras is country which, apparently, has one of the highest rates of coronary heart disease in the world, but actually consumes more tomatoes, which are supposed to prevent heart disease, than ninety-five per cent of the Western world. Go figure.

"You know, Ras," I say, "Karen and I are going make it."

"I know that," he says, and grins like an idiot.

"That's from *Groundhog Day,* isn't it?," he asks and, barely able to hold myself back, I have to admit he's absolutely right.

"You poke!" he laughs, we laugh, as down on the stage LK signals the start of the show.

Ras lets projector run. The porn queen, all cute and buttoned in a suit that looks remarkably like the deep green one Gwyneth wore in *Moonlight and Valentino,* says a few words about the importance of film in the modern art world, about how film is the bridge between the world of fact and the world of fantasy, about how she learnt long ago that art must reflect the world around it and that film does this much better than any other medium, and welcomes those who have come from out of town to jolly Southport for the jovial festival, the local dignitaries, Mayor whoever, USP Provost, members of . . . some club, a local, what? war hero, a boat rescue crew, some life-saving stars, the ladies auxiliary, members of the Southport Society, the Watercolor Artists of Southport Annual Committee, a visiting Japanese businessman who wants to build a sleek new marine observatory (fish in their naturally watery habitat, that kind of thing), the Halfmarket mall management, USP's own Dolphins (a football team), the representatives of government agencies, members of "several PTAs," the Gang of Five (a well-known local "vocal group" apparently),

actors, directors, distinguished . . . screenwriters. And then raises her slender hand and Ras lets the film roll.

The first scene is interesting. It appears we're entering a considerable forest. A great loping pine forest. Possibly in the spring
because the ground is carpeted trunk to trunk with brown nee-
dles, a complete coat, and there's new tender growth sprouting
on the trees. The film shows this. There's lots of close-ups. The
shot's now a tracking shot and particularly excellent, smooth
as wind through the branches which we can't hear because the
soundtrack is provocatively mute at this point. In the distance, as
the depth of field alters to encourage us in, there's a vast expanse
of water. It looks like the sea. But the director's not interested in
this and soon brings the focus back to the forest. The soundtrack
now begins something rock-n-roll, perhaps a group like the Rolling Stones I think, or the Led Zeppelin maybe. Some '70s stuff
which sounds, frankly, just okay. . . . In the distance there's the
first hint of someone among the trees, and the line of sight shifts
abruptly so that suddenly we're rising up, up into the trees and
can make out what's a ahead more accurately.

In a clearing, or more accurately on a bright little mound,
just beyond the tree-line, a group is gathering in brown hood-
ed cloaks, kind monkish I guess, shuffling around, as we swoop
down toward them, through the pines, toward the center of the
clearing and the great bonfire they've built around a cross. And
now, in the top right of the frame, a pick-up truck, just rounding
a bend over yonder, bouncing and thumping over the rough track
into the even more wrought clearing.

The monks (?), priests, whatever, start to mill around, forming a ragged circle, as the pick-up arrives and its doors open and
two more of them get out and unload from the rear a writhing
sack, remarkably like a duvet as it happens.

They carry this writhing miraculous duvet toward the fire and
lay it down there while arguments seem to have broken out among
little groups of the monks, some wanting to carry on with what
they're doing and others wanting just to stop it. Take a monkish

break. One actually charges the camera and is restrained by three others. The effect of this is to drive the camera harder into the crowd and for a moment the rush of things seems to overtake it and the only things visible are the shadowy chins of the throng which appear now and then from out beneath the hoods of their uniformly brown cassocks.

Then the group parts, and Karen is standing there. This, of course, nearly knocks me down.

"Hey, great!" I cry (in a whisper); but Ras, who's keeping a close eye on the video projector, doesn't join in.

Three of monks take hold of her—off-camera they've pulled her out of what remained of her entanglement in the duvet—and they're dragging her toward the bonfire. She's terrific. Fantastic even. Frankly, beyond anything she's managed so far for me. They're explaining what they're going to do and she's shaking and screaming and the music is going along like "something something is a gas gas gas" and they're lifting her onto the bonfire and tying her by her ankles and wrists to the cross. One of the monks then steps forward to say a few words and the camera, angled now to shoot Karen from below, picks up the interior of this monk's hood and I swear it appears absolutely to be Leesa.

She says her piece. Then the camera zooms in. Karen, brilliantly, is a mess. She looks like she's about to pass out but, craning her head forward toward the camera screams at it for help, directly at the camera mind you, and the impact of this is such that some of the monks start to walk off, like they can't take it anymore. But Helena, whose face is visible now just inside her hood, it appears certainly can. She goes up to the bonfire and, taking the cigarette which is now in her mouth, reaches down and lights the fire. Which bursts into life (possibly previously fueled). At which point, Karen screaming silently is truly awesome and the soundtrack overpoweringly thumping away with "something something try some time, something get what you need" does nothing to diminish this. The smoke rises. She faints. The flames seem to reach her. She wakes for a moment, but only to sob out something indecipherable, perhaps (wonderfully!) a heart-felt pray. And then she's gone, the flames rising higher and higher until they . . . just . . . simply . . . engulf her.

CUT: I think I hear someone somewhere say: CUT.

The voice is familiar. Is it Joel Coen of the Coen Brothers (*The Big Lebowski, Barton Fink, Raising Arizona* and so forth)? The Coens are great. It could be David Cronenberg maybe. It could be who? . . . Wes Craven? No, it really does sound exactly like Steve Milroy.

Whoever. One thing for sure, it sure looks good and Karen is brilliant.

Only thing, Ras seems to have broken down in the corner and is jabbering something about how he never meant to get involved. How he never realized the three of them actually meant to do it for real. How truly sorry he is. What a joker (?).

I just love the cinema . . . because anything's possible.

acknowledgments

There are quite a number of contemporary film-makers I would like to thank, but if I mention some and not others those reading here might get the impression some film-makers have been most influential, while others have had little impact. In reality, the influence of film and film-makers on the writing of *Camera Phone* is much wider than, say, *CinemaScope*, and far deeper than the deepest Deep Focus, or Depth of Field, as it's called. I'd also like to thank the worldwide users of mobile telephony—in some parts of the world most often called "Cell" Phones, in other parts "Mobile" Phones. Those phoners in train carriages: thank you for your wonderful and varied lives, which you have freely and openly shared, and which have influenced so much here. Ciaran and I feel a genuine debt of gratitude to you. You'll find that debt in several chapters. Those in hallways and corridors, outside offices and inside restrooms, those in restaurants, cafes, seated in parks, walking along streets, somehow existing both *in* the street *and* somewhere else, *simultaneously*. What miraculous existences we all now have! Thank you sincerely for your many contributions. Thanks to friends and colleagues with whom I have regularly discussed film, and with whom I go on discussing it—especially its evolution in this new transportable world in which we live. To Kate Bouwens for excellent copyediting assistance. To Louise, and to Myles and Tyler, who know where all in here is coming from: much much love, always. And to Dave Blakesley, a publisher, editor extraordinaire! He knows where to get his apples, and his technologies too (no witchy reference intended). Sincerest thanks, Dave. Onward! "To Infinity and (Way) Beyond!" ;-)

about the author

Brooke Biaz (aka Graeme Harper) is a fiction writer, scriptwriter, and cultural critic. He is Editor-in-Chief of the international journal, *New Writing*. His awards include the National Book Council Award for New Fiction (Australia), among many others. He has been a Professor of Creative Writing at a number of universities, none of which are the University of Southport. His most recent works of fiction include *Moon Dance* (Parlor Press, 2008) and *Small Maps of the World* (Parlor Press, 2006).

www.ingramcontent.com/pod-product-compliance
Lightning Source LLC
Chambersburg PA
CBHW020831260626
47169CB00003B/934